DOWN ALL THE DAYS

Christy Brown's first book – an autobiography of his childhood in a Dublin slum – was published in 1954 and with part of the proceeds, he bought an electric typewriter. Seventeen years later, *Down All the Days* was published.

Born in Dublin thirty-eight years ago, one of twenty-two children, Christy Brown is an athethoid with no control over his body apart from his left foot, and his speech is gravely impaired. He has never been to school but was laboriously taught to write by his mother, using a piece of chalk on the linoleum floor. It took him several years learning to read, Dickens having been one of his favourite authors. Dr Robert Collis, a well-known paediatrician, had a big influence on Christy's life, teaching him remedial exercises and encouraging him to write and have published both his books. Christy Brown now lives with one of his sisters in Dublin and is working on his next book.

'Perhaps the most unique novel ever written' – *Saturday Review*

'Christy Brown is one of the most discerning and lively observers of Irish life' – *The Times Literary Supplement*

'Sometimes brutal, sometimes broadly comic ... the book is brilliant in its own right' – *Sunday Mirror*

'Amazing, breathtaking, outstanding' – *The Financial Times*

'Christy Brown can write and think and feel as superbly as any Irishman since O'Casey' – *American Publishers' W*

By the same author in Pan Books

THE CHILDHOOD STORY OF CHRISTY BROWN

CONDITIONS OF SALE

This book shall not, by way of trade or otherwise, be lent, re-sold, hired out or otherwise circulated without the publisher's prior consent in any form of binding or cover other than that in which it is published and without a similar condition including this condition being imposed on the subsequent purchaser. The book is published at a net price, and is supplied subject to the Publishers Association Standard Conditions of Sale registered under the Restrictive Trade Practices Act, 1956.

CHRISTY BROWN

DOWN ALL THE DAYS

UNABRIDGED

PAN BOOKS LTD : LONDON

First published 1970 by Martin Secker and Warburg Ltd.
This edition published 1971 by Pan Books Ltd,
33 Tothill Street, London, S.W.1

ISBN 0 330 02665 8

2nd Printing 1972

© Christy Brown 1970

Amapola (Lacalle)
© Edward B. Marks Music Corporation
Used by permission
© Edward B. Marks Corporation
Reproduced by permission of Campbell Connelly & Co Ltd.

Let The Great Big World Keep Turning
(Clifford Grey)
Reproduced by permission of B. Feldman & Co Ltd.

My Lhean Love (Joseph Campbell)
By permission of Simon Campbell

Printed by Cox & Wyman Ltd,
London, Reading and Fakenham

For Beth

*Who, with such gentle ferocity, finally
whipped me into finishing this book . . .*

1

He sat in the boxcar on the edge of the excited group of boys, wondering what all the fuss was about. They were all mustered around the three squat metal boxes that stood against the far side of the big canvas tent into which they had paid their pennies, and over the door of which hung a huge banner with big garish letters that read 'Picture Gallery'. He had never been to a carnival before, and it thrilled him; the noise, the dust, the barrel organs grinding out the gaudy music-hall tunes, the scarlet-ribboned monkeys clambering up the arms and shoulders of the tattered music-makers, squeaking madly and pelting the laughing audience with peanuts and banana skins; the brightly coloured tents with their Vanishing Lady and Madame Makura the fortune teller and the Smallest Man in the World; the huge catherine wheels and chairoplanes whirling high overhead; the shooting galleries and lottery tents and the gay young girls screaming on the bumper cars in a raucous din and den of noise, their wide-flared summer dresses flung high by the onrush of air, the boys and young men laughing and winking and making obscene signs with their fingers. He had sat entranced by it all, his brothers pushing him in through the crowd with lusty yells of 'Gangway!' and 'Let us pass, mister!' and then they had found this 'Picture Gallery' a good distance away from all the other tents, almost on the edge of the large field where the carnival was being held to help the local church building funds. The scruffy-looking fellow on the door had grinned at him and was about to make some sly remark, but then smiled weakly when he noticed that the boys were a tough-looking lot and some of them very tall for their age. They had pushed him into the dimness of the tent, and there he now sat, quite forgotten, as the boys swarmed excitedly around the queer-looking machine-like boxes from which emanated a strange luminous green glow. The machines had handles clamped on to the sides, which the boys turned slowly as they looked down into the opening at the top. Some of the boys were very quiet, very intent, absorbed in watching; others whistled, and howled, and slapped their thighs or the behinds of their mates, with ribald cries of 'Will yous look at that!' and 'Look at the dollies on that wan!' Presently his big brother came back, rubbing his eyes with his knuckles, and looked down at him thoughtfully, then grinned and pushed him in the boxcar up to one of the machines.

'Jasus, no!' cried his eldest brother Jem, rushing over in panic when he divined Tony's lewd intention, his honest fat face showing real horror. 'You can't show them dirty pictures to a cripple!' The others all laughed; Tony gave Jem a shove that sent him sprawling, then hoisted his crippled brother on to his shoulder. From his perch on that broad promontory, he could see inside the 'picture box' quite clearly, and he was amazed at what he saw. As Tony began to turn and manipulate the control lever on the side, a whole perfectly defined and delineated little world in miniature began to flicker and blur and hover finally into focus upon the small square oblong screen that was fixed to the luminous bottom of the box, the magic Pandora box so humbly and unexpectedly hidden and enclosed by four rusty metal sides. He was enchanted; everything drifted away from the fringes of his awareness and perception, and he was utterly absorbed in watching the marvellous fairy-tale microcosmic world opening up before him. It was like being in the local picture house on a Saturday afternoon – the famous 'Bower' as it was known locally, so typical of local humour, since there was not a flower or shrub or plant in sight; except here it was even better, more engrossing, for here the screen was so small, and everything so quiet, and the rowdy rude turmoil of the audience

8

so far away, that he alone was the spectator, the sole looker-on as the little luminous performance sprang into life on the little luminous screen, drawing his mind downwards and on to it like a magnet.

A woman was preparing for bed; that is to say, she was taking off her clothes one by one, quite slowly, quite daintily, holding each skimpy garment delicately by the tips of her fingers before dropping it out of sight, which he fancied was the way people in foreign countries went to bed. She was a buxom, jolly-looking young woman, who kept smiling and simpering to herself, as if thinking of something funny, enjoying a private joke. Her movements were dreamlike, unhurried, melodic, like a ballerina; every gesture she made seemed to flow, to ripple as she swayed and floated about the bedroom disrobing herself, peeling the black silky garments from her pearly body with a slightly unreal, self-conscious lassitude. Then to his annoyance the picture shook, blurred, went out of focus; the woman appeared too bunty, her head too large for the rest of her, a Picasso-like distortion of reality that would have amused him, only now he really wanted to see the woman as she really was, for something strange was happening in his mind, or in some far corner of his mind; a certain memory was floating to the top, to the surface of his thoughts, but before he could grasp it, identify it, it darted away, back into the subterranean cave where such things remain hidden most of the time. Tony, still hoisting him easily on his shoulder, stopped joking with his mates long enough to steady the control handle and the picture resumed its normal perspective and proportions, enabling him, watching avidly, again to behold everything quite clearly and without interference.

The woman was standing sideways; she was clad only in her black shift now, and her breasts thrust forward arrogantly. He started to sweat. Again, the memory hovered in his mind, tantalizing, tormenting; when, and where, and why had he felt like this before? The woman started to raise the silky sheath from her body, lifting it over her head; he

9

saw the dimpled hollow at the base of her spine, over the curved buttocks ... and he remembered.

There were six of them sleeping on the large straw mattress spread out on the floor in a corner of the back bedroom; his mother called it a 'paliass', which made him laugh. It sounded like a friendly donkey. As usual, he had made sure to get a good position, wedged comfortably between two warm bodies, and he had been snug enough, until he woke up with a rotten smell in his nostrils. Someone had let off, and he knew who the culprit was, so he grabbed a hunk of Pete's behind and squeezed vigorously with his big toe and second toe, until Pete grunted and cursed roundly in his sleep and squirmed away. Mother said that the reason why Pete farted so much was that he had the 'windy colic' and so she gave him more senna pods and 'opening medicine' than the others. Saturday night was always senna pod night; they were supposed to be very good for the bowels, a part of the anatomy he could never quite locate or understand very clearly, except that they were somewhere in the belly and caused pains when he couldn't pass his motion in the lavatory. Therefore, to his mind, bowels were somehow mixed up with lavatory pots and he was always horrified in case one day he would look down into the depths of the pot and see, underneath him, the entangled mass of his bowels scoured from him by the force of the senna pod leaves he had taken. On account of his gusty habits of exhaling posterior air, they nicknamed Pete 'Windy', which sent Pete into a rage for it was also the name that people called cowards, though his brother could never be called that, for he spoke more often and more forcefully with his fists than with his mouth.

Saturday night was also the night when his eldest brother Jem came in steaming with porter. Jem was only starting to drink, just an apprentice at it but very willing to learn, and was not as used to it as their father, who made it his second profession. Their father had been drinking since he was twelve, when a pint of stout cost only a penny and a 'half one' three-halfpence, so that he often got 'locked' on a shilling which he earned as a messenger boy. Their father used to say that, instead of blood, he had alcohol running in his veins; that seemed very strange, for he could fancy the whiskey and beer bubbling and hissing in his father's veins like red-hot lava, and he supposed it was this that made his father look and act so wild sometimes, his eyes bulging out as if they were on stalks and the lost wild look in them. But Jem was not quite eighteen yet, and drank secretly with his pals, in mortal dread of their father finding out, and so each Saturday night he stumbled and staggered up the stairs in his stockinged feet, maybe starting to hum a snatch of a song to himself before remembering their father in bed in the front bedroom, listening maybe, the heavy black belt on a chair by the bedside. This Saturday night was no exception; up came Jem, up the darkened stairs, holding his boots in one hand, feeling for the handrail with the other and puffing heavily with exertion and excess beer, hiccuping garrulously, excusing himself to himself, mumbling in a placating whispering soliloquy: 'I'm not jarred, Pop – true as God I'm not – wouldn't do a thing like that – just a few jars, that's all – but not jarred, Pop – true as God . . .' Jem made it, just made it, into the back room, before a sudden upheaval shook him and he barely got to the window in time before he emptied himself of all that black bileful porter – right on top of a prowling tomcat, damping that animal's amorous spirits. The cat fled squealing indignantly and shrilly. Jem fell back into the room and lay on his mouth and nose, in his good pressed suit, and mumbling and muttering something about taking the 'pledge' in the morning, and soon he was snoring and whistling down his nose.

There was one good bed in the room, pushed into the far corner, in which the three older girls slept; two of them were already asleep, having washed themselves in the pantry behind a locked door, plaited their hair and cleaned their teeth and scraped the dirt from behind their finger and toenails, for they were going to the altar in the morning to 'receive', and their mother was very strict on going to God

11

looking clean and neat and tidy. Lil, the very eldest, though only twenty or so, was 'going steady' so the others said, and was not yet in; though she often got belted for staying out late, she was seldom in early, and even on the nights when she did not go out, she would sit below in the kitchen reading her romance novels and love magazines until all hours, until their father would shout down at her to come up to bed and stop wasting the light. He had seen her reading a big thick book the night before called *Gone With the Wind* which their mother said would bring the curse of God on the house because it was supposed to be dirty. He would have tried to steal a peep at it, but it was so big somebody was bound to see him, and anyhow he was only supposed to read his catechism just now in preparation for his confirmation. He found the catechism very boring, but his mother said it would make him holy. He read and read it, but never felt very holy. But then he didn't really know what it felt like to be holy. It probably meant floating on air or something like that, and that did not appeal to him, for he was sure he'd fall down with a bang.

He could never go to sleep very easily, and would lie awake in the night while the others snored and snored, thinking of many things, things he felt rather than saw, for there was not much to see from within the four rough wooden sides of the old boxcar, and there was not much to be seen from the front window either, except other houses facing, and buses, and cars, and the kids playing and running out in the streets. Sometimes there would be a great roar in the sky, and looking up, he would see an aeroplane passing, and he would watch it until it was just a dark speck in the distance and then nothing, and he would dream about that for hours, thinking of the people it was carrying inside it, so far up above the world, and how it could float on air like that, and where it might be going. He wanted to be inside a plane one day; he could imagine what it would be like, high over the clouds even, with green bits of the earth opening up between, and the whole sky intensely blue and unbroken above. It would be like

12

flying very near to God, he fancied, and if there was a hole in the sky anywhere to be found, it might be possible to enter heaven just like that, like climbing in through an unclosed window or a crack in the roof. Maybe that was the only way most people ever got into heaven – as burglars.

This night sleep would not come; he lay between two of his brothers and wished himself to sleep, but it would not come. Through the frayed lace curtains on the window he could see the moon in the sky, shaped like a silver half-crown, going under a large soft cloud that was likewise frayed around its yellowish edges, moving under the cloud like a strange shaped fish under water, or a form seen through smoked glass, a pearly swan gliding elegantly in and out of cloudy reefs and lagoons. He loved to watch the moon; he would see the faint pencil markings on it, as if someone had begun to draw something on its glowing surface, then tired of the game and stopped. He would trace a sort of pattern of the markings and make pictures of his own; the moon reminded him of a big round frothy white bubble of milk swimming in a huge black-blue sea, and the stars were the lesser bubbles in that same sea. He discerned a very bright reddish star, quite close to the moon, and as always he held himself rigid and began to sweat, for it seemed only a matter of minutes before the two would collide and set the sky on fire with a terrible bang. Sooner than watch, he ducked his head quickly under the bed-clothes and shut his eyes tight; under there, all was pitch blackness, dense and thick, pushing in upon his eyes, pressing upon the pupils, making them ache, as if someone were rubbing their knuckles against them. He prayed by the time he came up for air the star would have passed the moon safely.

He slept; a deep, dreamless sleep, and when he awoke, hours or minutes later, his mind was quite clear, sharp, lucid, but quite empty of either thought or memory, without possessions, like a clear, bright, well-swept empty room. Into that clear emptiness hovered something soft and dark; as soft and dark and light as a leaf floating through the air,

13

falling into his mind gently but clearly, sharply defined, finely etched against the luminous night sky outside; a form at the window. She stood there, a perfect silhouette, her arms upraised, her hair falling darkly down her back, her bare shoulders creamy in the moonlight; she sighed, stirred, as if she had been standing a long time at the window, gazing out; her dark-burning-silk slip hissed as she raised it over her head and sat down on the edge of the bed shadowed in the recess corner. Unable to draw away his eyes, held by something he did not understand but which hammered hotly inside him, he saw her reach behind with her hand, humming softly to herself; then, his whole body suddenly flaming and a loud roaring in his temples, he saw her pale breasts appear over the dark satin cupolas; she bent a little forward, putting away the bra, and her young breasts shone, the lace pattern of the curtains swaying on her flesh, the nipples dark as berries in snow; it was beauty, and perfection, and terror for him who watched in all the muteness and turmoil of his nature. She still hummed softly, happily, to herself, but above her quiet joyfulness she caught the sound of his moan, as if from some deep pain, some animal distress; and moving swiftly, she came and knelt down on the floor beside where he lay, holding her dress up to her with one hand and feeling for his forehead with the other, stroking him gently, thinking he was having a bad dream. He did not dare look up; he could not swallow the spit that lay burning like a bile in his throat; he cursed her fiercely in his mind to go away and leave him alone. The next day, and for many days after that, he could not look at his sister, or meet the puzzled inquiry in her eyes, and he did not know why.

And so he remembered, as he looked at the woman undressing on the miniature screen inside the circus tent, where and when he had had those same painful, ecstatic, guilty feelings, and the remembrance burned in him, yet added a subtle zest, a delicious forbidden excitement; the woman was taking the last silk sheath from her body; a

14

haze of anguish and pleasure swam and danced before his eyes; the woman, now naked, was slowly, slowly turning around ... The screen went dead, blank; his brother stopped turning the controls and put him roughly down again into the boxcar. The other boys stood about, not knowing where to look, hands in pockets, whistling, trying to look as if they had noticed nothing; his brother stood above him, tall, resolute, strong-limbed and straight, and he hated his brother just then, hated all those other so knowing and so capable fools who had just witnessed his shame and guilt, for they had made him conscious of these emotions for the first time ever, and he felt soiled, muddled. He wanted to lash out blindly and in rage; he felt betrayed, felt the dagger thrust of that betrayal knife through him, and his hatred was the only clean thing left in him now, the only clear, articulate thing left in him, a white tide of violence roaring and soaring and flaring to livid life.

Blue-veined pillars of marble rose steeply to the huge dome; in the arrowhead rays of sunlight that streamed downwards from the stained-glass windows, innumerable motes and dust specks danced and gleamed like fireflies; footfalls echoed weirdly in all the hushed spaces; each echo lingered and trembled away into infinity; the wheels of his good chair, his 'Sunday chariot', sounded loud and harsh to his ears as his mother wheeled him down the great centre nave of the church; it was early afternoon, few people were present, so he was glad nobody else minded his squeaking wheels, though in the immense stillness they sounded awful. He liked looking at the statues; they stood on their pedestals, bigger than life, some with uplifted swords in their hands as if ready to hurl every potential little Lucifer from heaven in one almighty flash, faces frozen in wrath, muscles bulging like corded snakes on their arms and legs; others were more kindly, especially the female saints, with faint sad smiles on their delicate faces, hands outspread in gentle supplication, looking like somebody's favourite sister or aunt, reproving, yet patient and tender. He took a

15

harsher view of the little fat angels who flew around the laurelled craniums of their more illustrious companions, holding bows and arrows and simpering painfully, little fat dumplings of creatures who looked as if they were bored with the whole angelic business and just wanted to play hide-and-seek or leapfrog like other children. It must be very tiresome to be a minor angel. Sometimes the organ would be playing up in the gallery at the back; the music would stream and flow out through the spaces, great waves of deep throbbing sound rippling above in the hushed air sending mighty echoes sweeping and soaring to the vaulted dome. A priest would sometimes stride past, cassock rustling, bearded face oblivious in prayer, sandals slapping upon marble.

Sometimes, if they lingered in the short days, the figure upon the huge cross over the centre altar would be half-veiled in shadow as the evening lengthened through the windows; the twisted face was so melancholy, the twisted limbs so eloquent of agony and betrayal and loneliness, that often he could not bear to look at it and looked down quickly to the diamond-patterned floor, trying to think of something pleasant; but always he felt that face following him even when they left the church. He had often seen it before, in books and in the catechism, but seeing it hung up there before the high altar, so huge and lonely, suspended in space, made him full of an inexpressible sadness. The green glare of day blinded him as his mother wheeled him down the broad steps and out into the gardens and grounds of the church. This was the pleasantest part of the whole Sunday; the avenues and paths between the huge old trees were splashed and mottled with big blobs and splotches of sunshine thick and yellow as butter; sparrows and thrushes and lithe-winged linnets would swoop low in their path, twittering crazily and joyfully before darting away into the deep-shadowed woods; moist fingers and fronds of moss twined around the gnarled barks of ancient trees; flowers swayed and nodded bejewelled heads glistening with dew and raindrops; leaves floated in the little stream that ran

16

under the wooden bridge around the island of Calvary; against the linen-white clouds of autumn the church spire glinted reddish in the sunset, sharp and slender as a pared pencil.

On occasions they would go into the graveyard behind the church, and there, safely out of earshot, his mother would read out the inscriptions to him on the sunken headstones. Some of them were funny. 'Here lies the mortal remains of Mary Jane Doubleday, who had ten children within holy wedlock and died joyously praising God ...': 'Pray for the soul of good Martin Merriman, pious begetter of twelve children, who passed his time on earth in good works and fortitude ...' His mother would laugh and hoped God had a sense of humour, too.

On the way home the houses of the rich blinked complacently in the sun, flower-bordered gardens and trim lawns, the occupants sitting out in striped deckchairs with handkerchiefs or newspapers spread over their faces and heads to protect them from the heat, their pedigree dogs lolling at their feet, too polite to bark, too lazy to scratch themselves. To live in one of these fine houses would be rather like living in a china cabinet; constantly on display, afraid to move too vigorously or sneeze too loudly for fear of breaking something. There would be no wild games down here; no yelling horde of Apaches or murderous posse of cowboys brandishing handles of sweeping brushes or broken legs of chairs; no attaching yards of string to door knockers, then hiding in gardens across the street and pulling on the strings, making the people open their hall doors to invisible callers again and again; no fishing for pinkeens down in the Poddle river and cramming the squirming tiny little eel-like creatures into water-filled jamjars to be carried home on boyish shoulders, more richly prized than any pearl-bellied oyster; no roasting horse-chestnuts on sticks, or lying in their pelts on the big flat boat-shaped slab of rock in the middle of the river, toasting in the sun. He wondered what the children of the rich did instead of all these things, which to him seemed the blood, flesh and bone of childhood. Probably played the piano and learned to say 'they' instead of 'them'.

'Did you bring him down for the Relic, ma'am?' the women would sometimes ask his mother, ill-met on the way home, stopping to smile kindly down at him in the wheel-chair, seeing him laid out already in the brown habit, clicking and clucking their tongues like not very wise old hens, nodding their shawled heads knowingly. 'Ah, the poor little angel! But never mind, ma'am; the Relic will do him a power of good, so it will. Now take that Mrs Mulholland up the road a bit from you in number seventy-six, that has the poor simple boy . . .' And the weeping women of this other little Jerusalem would go on, with obvious relish, to relate the remarkable instances of progress and enlighten-ment that had taken place in the condition of poor simple Joey since his ma had started taking him down regular-like every week for the Relic; no longer did Joey eat the grass and weeds in the back garden, to which he had previously been partial, or hurl milk bottles and beer bottles out of the front window at passers-by, a favourite pastime of his up to now. 'The oul faggots!' his mother would mutter darkly under her breath, very turkey-cock red in the face, and push past the commiserating comforters and homewards.

It was quite late when they got home; the house was empty, except for his father, who seemed in a sour mood and lifted him roughly out of the wheelchair on to the sofa; he caught the whiskey smell of his father's breath as he was lifted. He heard them arguing in the pantry, his father's voice loud and thick, spiced with curses, his mother speak-ing low, softly, trying to placate him. His father swept through the kitchen, his face all thunder and went upstairs, banging doors all the way; after a while his mother came in, wiping her reddened eyes on her apron. She said the heat and the pushing and the long walk home had tired her out and she was going to take a little nap, and that he should do the same. So she made him comfortable on the big horse-hair sofa under the window, putting a cushion under his head and an old topcoat over his shoulders.

He heard her go slowly, heavily up the stairs and cross the room towards the big double bed in the corner; he heard their voices; presently all was quiet in the house, save for an odd creaking sound somewhere above him; he slept fitfully, hot and troubled, and had a dream in which the Virgin Mary kept coming and going all in her gown of Reckitt's blue.

2

HE WONDERED what was going on behind the wall, but nobody would tell him; the lads kept going behind it at regular intervals, and on coming back they would either look jubilant, cocky, and heroic, or else they would come back drooping somehow, wilting, looking sheepish, and furtive, sending anxious glances up and down the street for signs of approaching adults. This patch of waste ground was where they pitched their tent and, sage and serious as any generals, drew up plans for attacks on rival street gangs from other and less civilized parts of the district. It was a raised acre or so of ground, high above the main street, and so excellent for observation, but the boys never took risks and always had a lad posted whose awesome duty was to 'keep nix'. This evening this boy seemed especially active and his eyes never once wavered from the unsplendid vista of the street stretching away between rows of houses and shops and public houses and pillar-boxes into the smoky traffic-loud distance. It was a high stone wall behind which all the mystery was taking place; it formed the boundary between the local bakery, from which always there came wafted on the garbage-tainted air the delicious smell of fresh loaves, and beyond it the innumerable backyards of corporation dwellings, an iron-clad heritage of broken bedsteads, rusty bicycle frames, crumbling sheds, rotten mattresses, lines of washed clothes gathering up the soot and grime of smoking chimneys – and occasional green rows of cabbages and mad improbable blazes of geraniums and dahlias flowering like manna in a desert.

The last boy to come out from behind the wall spat long and squarely at a fluffy, watery dandelion and said with disgust that it wasn't worth the tanner he'd spent on it. 'But did it hurt?' asked a small, wizened, bespectacled boy crouching on his hunkers beside the smouldering fire they had lit with old rags and discarded cardboard cartons from the bakery, who had pretended to be engrossed in his comic, but who kept watching the comings and goings from behind the wall, icicle drops forming, dropping off, and reforming on the pinched blue tip of his nose.

'What do you want to know for, Four Eyes?' said the disdainful one, spitting again into the fire, a thin tobacco-brown jet that squirted from the corner of his sideward-moving mouth. 'You wouldn't know where to put yours, so shut up!'

Poor Four Eyes fell silent under this rebuff and went back to reading the comic adventures of Lord Snooty and his merry gang.

'Still and all,' said another, a bit of a philosopher; 'it's better than toffee apples any day of the week!'

They went on talking in this way, analysing, comparing, criticizing, taking no notice of him in the boxcar a little away from them, until one of them looked over at him and grinned as an idea came to him. This boy was named Charley and was a member of the intelligence corps of the gang, noted for his alert and original methods of breaking the heads of the enemy.

'Hey fellas!' said Charley now, his face aglow with the inner radiance of his sudden thought; 'what about *him*?' he said, nodding towards the boxcar. 'Maybe she'd do it to him for choice! Yeah, maybe she would! On account of him being a . . .'

Charley never finished what he was going to say, for at that moment Pete jumped up and lashed out with a most beautifully delivered uppercut, straight on the prettily dimpled point of Charley's chin, and over went the great original thinker, right into the fire. The others jumped up in panic and disorder as Charley writhed and squealed like a roasting pig, and squirmed agonizingly about on the burning heap of rags until someone had the foresight to tear the trousers off him, and off ran Charley down the slope, clutching his blackened, smouldering buttocks and running like one gone berserk down the street, until he dived head-long into a garden with high bushes, while neighbours rushed out to their front gates, men in shirtsleeves and women in aprons, and yelled blasphemies and shook their fists and called down the wrath of God on 'that bloody gang' again.

They all waited up on the hill and hid in the long rank field-mice haunted grass until things quietened down in the street below; then he heard a girl's voice from behind:

'What's up, fellas?'

'Charley Norton just got his arse toasted, that's all!' someone politely informed her, lighting up the battered and bruised fag-end he had fished out of his trouser pocket.

She laughed, a clear and gay tinkle in the cool air of evening, and he watched her, fascinated, as she strode from the direction of the wall and flopped down on to her belly, wriggling up to them in the grass. Her ripening young form bloomed out of the thin inadequate dress; her face was thin, pinched, dirty, yet graceful and delicate, her mouth wide and mobile, her hair falling in two thick-braided coils, the brown of it slashed by a wide white innocent-looking ribbon. She wriggled in between the lads; one of them put his rough black-nailed hand on her raised rump under the dress; she slapped it away slowly, lazily, turning her face aside, staring up at him huddled in the boxcar against the evening sky.

'Lay off, Larry!' she said in a friendly way, but her eyes were on him above her in his squat wooden tumbril, and

21

they glowed with green fire, like the eyes of a cat in the dusk.
He heard one of the boys calling her Jenny.

3

THE SUN slipped down without anger behind the old blind
pensioned-off houses on the other side of the Grand Canal,
turning the faded grey-brick walls to burnt umber and
trailing orange ribbons in the muddy weed-choked waters.
In the distance the angelus bell rang out for six. The spires
and domes and rooftops of the city rose against the haze of
the summer sky, the tall useless monuments to dead heroes
starkly out of place and unhappy in the emergent chrome-
and-steel metropolis surrounding them, big green buses
rumbled past like lugubrious elephants with 'Guinness Is
Good For You' emblazoned on them in garish lettering,
jam-packed and sardine-tight with suburban families returning tired and fretful yet suntanned from the beaches and
strands of Dollymount or Killiney or a ferryboat excursion
to Ireland's Eye, carrying home plastic bags full of penny
winkles and cockleshells and crabs and fish bought cheap
off the traders on the pier at Dun Laoghaire or Howth.
Gulls hung almost motionless in the sultry, jaded air,
sweeping slowly now and then in desultory search of food
scraps, wings barely seeming to move, floating like figures
on a skating rink.
   The grass shot up tall and cool and sweet-smelling,
enclosing him in a bamboo world. Down near the roots the
earth was dark-brown and smelt of summer; insects buzzed
and hummed in and out, friendly denizens leaving him
undisturbed. From the river below came the low deep
throb of a barge chugging past, laden with turf neatly
stacked in brown pyramids, fuel for the factories and

foundries of the city. This boat had a bright blue hull and its funnel was painted in red circles; it even had a little flag fluttering from its stern. Sometimes the men who sailed these barges would stand on deck, waving and shouting greetings to them, sturdy and strong in thick wool Aran sweaters, cloth caps and brown leather leggings that reached to the thigh. They might sometimes sing out snatches of songs and old country ballads in strong country voices; he wondered about these men, where they came from, sailing their terrier-like little boats through all the wide green land, laughing and singing and feeding the swans, and smoking their clay pipes, and maybe thinking of their women under the stars.

Under his closed lids he could see, with the same thrill and wonder, the intricate lacework of tiny veins dark against the luminous day outside; the noise of traffic and people receded from him, filtered now by the wavering walls of grass enclosing him; his limbs were no longer tense and twitching and ceaselessly unstill, but lay peaceful in a strange lassitude; and, entrenched in a waving, tremulous, diaphanous world of green grass and blue sky and the river murmuring below, he dreamt and slumbered in a bamboo dream.

They walked slowly home, jeering the girls and taking pot shots at the pears and apples that drooped over the garden walls of the swanky houses along the way. Jem was wailing that they'd get belted when they got home for being late, and he elected to push the boxcar himself, but the others would not let him run fast and kept standing in his way and making monkey faces at him. Jem, his round moon face red and perspiring with both exertion and rage, battled grimly on. Tony kept taunting him, calling him coward; he was all set for dallying behind with a brown-faced little wench called Nancy, for already her breasts were beginning to show under the blouse. Jem puffed and panted and cursed all bloody women, and wildly charged at the im-peding mob with the boxcar. They all laughed and scattered and thumbed their noses at Jem and called him terrible names. Jem toiled and staggered, for the way home was mostly uphill, and Tony finally took over the rôle of horse, abandoning the nubile Nancy reluctantly but promising to meet her later up the lane that ran beside the bakery.

The tension was electric in the air when they reached home. The other kids were sitting on chairs, mute and not daring to move. Lil was leaning against the wall, her eyes dark and large and tragic, holding up a pair of tattered nylon stockings between her red-tipped fingers and saying to herself over and over in a hushed sort of voice: 'He slashed them on me, he slashed them on me with a knife, he did . . .' Her blouse was ripped down the front, her eyes were smudged with tears and ruined mascara, her red mouth quivered with silent sobs. He stared at her fingers, the nails curved and pointed and varnished and the torn shreds of nylon running over them. He felt the familiar fluttering inside him, the hard sharp constriction of his bowels melting in fear, the fiercer twitching of his limbs. Jem sat down weakly and tried to tell funny jokes; nobody heeded him. Tony stood very upright, fists knotted, a muscle in his jaw jerking, his eyes very blue, very cold and hard. 'What's up here?' he asked Lil, not keeping his voice down.

She seemed not to have heard; she just swayed against the wall, holding up her butchered nylons in her hands, and saying over and over: 'He slashed them on me, he slashed them with a knife, he did . . .' She spoke not with anger or with grief, but tiredly; her voice was suddenly that of a tired woman, instead of a young girl going to meet her young man on a Sunday evening in summer.

Sounds came from the pantry. A struggle seemed to be taking place, delft breaking, chairs being overturned, a dull thudding sound, a soft moan. Tony, pale and rigid, strode towards the closed pantry door. His movements seemed to bring Lil back to the reality of the moment; she sprang forward in front of him and stood with her back against the pantry door.

'Take your tea, Tony,' she said in a quiet voice, but her eyes were pleading and desperate.

The rest of them came alive, too, and crowded around

24

Tony, the younger ones clinging to his arms and legs, holding him back. He remembered a passage in a book called *Gulliver's Travels*, where the pygmies had all swarmed over the giant-like man, pinning him down, like the hull of a ship encrusted with tiny barnacles. Lil's forehead glistened with sweat; she looked small, fragile, ineffectual. The sounds from inside the pantry increased; he heard his father's drunken snarl; more crashing delft; feet slipping, scuffling; his mother's voice, gasping, out of breath, yet desperately firm and urgent:

'Don't ... no, don't hit me there ... there's a child in me ...' Lil swayed and put her hands up to her mouth, as if to stop herself from screaming. Tony broke away from the net of small clinging hands and broke into the pantry, as the smallest child began to yell and bang its tin mug on the table for its bread and milk.

4

THE PRIEST arrived, leaving his bicycle leaning against the wall outside, a young man fresh from the country with a blue, closely-shaven chin and thick, dark eyebrows; he entered, unfolding the purple scapula and laying it around his broad shoulders, dipping his fingertips in the little glass of holy water on the improvised altar in the spick-and-span kitchen, and began intoning prayers in the strange-sounding language that was so beautiful to hear. He listened to the voice of the priest, lulled by the soft cadences; the words meant nothing to him, but the sounds fell into his mind as soft rain falling on a pond. The prayers finished; the priest made the sign of the cross and stooped over him; the moment had come. He opened his mouth; no words came. He swallowed, tried to speak, to say something, even make an

25

intelligent sound just to show he understood what was expected of him. Nothing happened; several little eternities seemed to pass. He felt pain, the salty taste of blood as his strong teeth bit convulsively into his lip. He sweated profusely; the priest's face was a gentle moon above him through the haze that clouded his eyes, full of compassion and patience.

'Take your time, my son,' said the priest, laying both hands upon his head as if anointing, which only made him worse, more agitated; his fingers twitched and clicked like knitting needles. 'Think, my son,' the priest said; 'think of the last time you committed sin.'

That made it easier; things slipped into their proper places in his mind. He nodded and grunted readily as the priest in a gently assuring voice made helpful suggestions as to the sort of sins he might have committed; but when it came, as it always did, to the big sin he stopped in confusion, feeling hot and dismayed and unwilling to look the priest in the face. The priest repeated the question and he could do nothing but nod, acknowledging his guilt. 'Alone, my son?' the priest inquired, as always, 'with yourself? Not with anyone else?'

He shook his head, puzzled. What did it mean, 'with anyone else'? It was always when he was alone, when nobody could see, upstairs on the bed, maybe, or in the lavatory. Always when nobody was there, this feeling would come, sweeping over him in warm waves, tossing his thoughts up and down, lighting fires in his body. He did not know why it came, or why he succumbed to it. Vaguely whenever it came he thought of many things all jumbled together; the night the dread came to him, the deep dread and unknown pleasure, watching his sister in the moon-washed darkness; the muddy-faced girl in the thin short dress lying on her belly in the grass gazing up at him. Often he would get this same feeling seeing a pair of high-heeled shoes under the table, or nylons drying on the clothes line in the pantry, or . . . so many things, all jumbled together, lighting small fires in him, shipwrecking his thoughts, everything fading away,

26

receding, melting in a warm mist before he knew what was happening; the feeling, at first, as of climbing to a dizzy height, where it was hot and alive and pulsating; then the other feeling, the anti-feeling, as of falling, descending, tumbling down to where everything was dark, and chill, and familiar. He felt the same way then as in the carnival tent the day he looked at the naked woman; the same crushing feeling of guilt, and shame, and the struggle to look people in the face.

So with mumbled grunts and semi-said words, but mostly with his eyes, he told the waiting priest of his great black sin that was always sinned in solitary dark communion with himself, and the good young priest nodded gravely and told him to think of the Holy Virgin whenever such bad thoughts entered his head and gave him for his penance ten Hail Marys and six Our Fathers; and when the awful moment of blessed communion came the priest raised his voice slightly as a signal for his mother to come in from her vigil in the pantry and assist. And in his mother came, swollen with child, the unfamiliar face cream she had liberally used that morning not quite concealing the black marks of bruised blood under her eyes. She knelt and held the cloth under his chin, steadying the jerky movements of his jaw as the priest approached with the holy bread held delicately between thumb and forefinger. He tensed, screwed himself up into a ball, and flung open his mouth desperately; he got the faint sweet taste of the wafer on his tongue, and he swallowed quickly as his mother put the tumbler of water to his lips. The priest prayed silently a little longer, then smiled and blessed him and his mother and went out, pulling on his bicycle clips. He always expected to feel different after receiving communion, for he knew it was Christ who had entered into him, the catechism said so; he waited to feel different, waited to feel the newness and wonder and happiness creep into him turning his blood to wine and his body to a glowing tabernacle where only goodness dwelt. But he never did feel any change; he merely felt exhausted from the ordeal, and hungry from the fasting, and hung in a

sort of inward suspension, wondering how long he could stay
away from the big black sin.

5

HE WATCHED them carrying his mother down the narrow
stairs on a stretcher, two men in dark-blue uniforms and
peaked helmets. A crowd of neighbours and curious passers-
by were gathered around the big cream and blue ambulance
outside. Some of his younger brothers and sisters were
sobbing, and the kind portly women gathered them into
their shawls and aprons, petting them and patting their
heads, saying: 'God love her, and she with a houseful of
them already!' He did not cry; he looked on with a strange
detachment as his mother was carted away, the rising bulge
of her belly under the grey woollen blanket, like a swollen
wineskin, her closed eyes sunken in the puffy flesh of her face
that glistened queerly, as if there was water underneath.
The ambulance drove off, the crowds dispersed; the woman
next door came in and got dinner ready for them and spread
their slices of bread with fat dripping from the remains of the
roast in the big pan. His father came in that evening from
work with a face like that of a man condemned to death; he
hardly noticed any of the kids, and did not eat the dinner
that Lil had knocked off early from work to cook for him.
Lil was working in a factory now, making sausages. She cried
silently into her hankie when nobody was looking. Jem had
bilious attacks and kept vomiting up green bile. Tony and
Pete and Paddy tried to play cards for buttons and the
pictures from cigarette packages, but nobody cared who
won. The little battalions of the younger kids did not know
what was going on and bawled and bellowed and murdered
each other about on the floor as usual, but Father did not

even shout at them to stop, or use his belt. When they went to bed that night they were subdued; no horseplay, no secret games of 'ponner' or gin rummy by the light of a gutted candle, no randy reminiscences by the boys; not as much as a curse. Instead, they all prayed; he pretended to, but he was really watching and wondering why they were all praying so fiercely all of a sudden. Very late he imagined he heard Lil weeping in bed, and his father coughed so often in the front room across the landing that he knew he must be awake and smoking.

He awoke in the middle of the night, hot with terror from a well-known nightmare, being smothered by someone, or some thing, huge, moist, and hairy; opening his eyes in the dead greyness, he could still see, horrified, the vague outlines of the terrible form before his eyes, in the room with him; as he stared, it faded slowly, into the familiar lines of the bed in the far corner, the old debauched dressing-table under the window, the slightly swaying shredded lace curtains, leaving him half sitting up on the mattress, shivering but reaching out frantically with his returning mind for the rapidly vanishing thread of the dream, the grotesque vision; there was something vaguely known and recognized about the terror-figure with the soft, furry, animal skin and flabby moist mouth, lying on him with its full soft weight; a faint, familiar odour of disgust, the hint of sniggering laughter once heard echoing down some dark, evil-smelling alley; a presence he knew, and loathed.

'Nancy, Nancy!' said Tony in his sleep, turning over on to his belly; across the landing once more came the harsh, metallic cough of his father; the last baby began to cry and Lil spoke to it drowsily and rocked it in its groaning cradle at her bedside. The hot sweat that had covered him had now turned cold, and he shivered, afraid to go back to sleep, afraid of meeting once more the dreaded unnameable thing that lurked and threatened in the awful dark beyond wakefulness; he waited for the first faint bells to ring out for six o'clock Mass in the morning.

Their father scrubbed them in the big enamel bath in the

29

pantry with a rough hairbrush and in scalding water until their slapped and chafed and pummelled immersed limbs ached and glowed, while Lil got ready a breakfast of 'coddle'; fat back-end rashers and plump sausages and black-and-white pudding all swimming in hot gravy into which they dipped thick cuts of dry bread and the hard 'heels' off loaves which were also called 'catskins'. They all dressed and filed out to Mass, and he sat outside on the top front step feeling the sun on his face.

He thought about his mother lying somewhere out there beyond the familiar streets and rooftops, in a hospital ward crammed maybe with other sick women all with swollen bellies. He knew about babies; they came somehow from inside the woman; that was why when women were having babies they swelled out front and waddled like penguins when they walked: the man somehow put the baby inside the woman; this was something he did not understand; it was vague and a bit awful, yet it excited him to think about it; it made his heart beat faster and he remembered again the young blue-chinned country priest nodding gravely and telling him to pray to the Virgin Mary whenever such thoughts came into his mind. He deliberately pushed both the priest and the Virgin out of his mind now, basking in the sun and letting his thoughts fly about like leaves in windy weather. He knew that this whole business of baby-making started when the man and woman went to bed; what made it happen he did not know; it was something they did, together, that somehow caused the baby to start growing inside the woman. He had never believed in the story that babies could be bought; his parents were too poor. He knew that Jem and Tony knew, and maybe Lil; yes, she must know, for she was very old and over twenty, but he did not know, and he was sure that neither Paddy nor Pete knew either, or not very well, despite their grown-up talk out of the sides of their mouths. If the people who smiled in at him on their way to Mass could know what he was thinking as he sat there cross-legged in the sun, their faces would drop and they would stare at him as they would at a horrible hunch-

30

back with a gigantic eye in the middle of his forehead. He ought to be praying for his mother to come home soon; instead he kept thinking about babies coming out of women. Something flashed up at him; a bit of broken glass flaming in the hard sun, deep blue with greeny flecks in it, chipped at the edges like a broken diamond, flaming wickedly up at him, burning into his eyes; he felt positively sure that if he touched it the glass would burn a hole in his flesh; like the glittering eye of a serpent it blazed balefully up at him, frizzling his thoughts.

'Hello,' somebody said.

A shadow fell upon the smoking glass, putting it out, making it look dull and ordinary again; he jerked his head up, snarling; she was standing tall and slim in front of him, smiling like an ordinary girl, the long pigtailed coils of hair falling about her face. Her big toe peeped through a gap in her white runner; her knees showed bony and scrawny under the short pleated skirt, and there were scratches on her shins.

'I brought you some comics,' she said, throwing a bundle down on the ground between them; she squatted down on her heels, knees apart, displaying the dark triangle of her knickers, the half-moon shape of her buttocks outlined against the gauzy backdrop of her skirt; she watched calmly the storm in his face, faintly smiling. 'Is your ma going to die?'

The street had gone suddenly quiet; a bus glided by without noise; people went by like moving figures on a silent screen; even the sparrows hopping about in the garden looking for breadcrumbs were suddenly frozen in mid-air.

'She's in having another one, isn't she?' she asked, edging closer, not drawing her knees together; her face was suddenly old and ugly, wrinkled and creased like an old woman's. 'Your da must have a whopper!' she almost cackled, her voice hoarse, rasping. She leaned forward slightly, and hunched her shoulders in such a way that her blouse flexed further away from her, showing the snowy tops of her breasts; she was so near he could see the wet pinkness

31

under her upturned eyes; she put her hand on his knee, her fingers inching up the leg of his short corduroy trousers, pinching his flesh. 'I'm not afraid of you!' she breathed almost into his face, her eyes glittering as he had seen them on that hill in the dusk, her lips curling back from her pink gums. 'I'm not!' She laughed, and springing to her feet she raced down the path, vaulted over the wall, and ran off down the Sunday morning street, bumping into people, her pigtails flying behind, her arms flung wide.

That night his father came home with two men who worked with him; they all carried parcels of porter and had half bottles of whiskey in their hip pockets. The two men gave the children shillings and dandled the little ones on their broad pinstriped knees, singing silly nursery songs. One of them was as old as his father and looked kind and jolly, but the second was younger and broad-shouldered, with hard eyes and thick calloused hands, and he kept sweeping his eyes over Lil as she got the smaller kids ready for bed. They pulled corks and drank the porter straight from the bottles, wiping their frothy mouths with the back of their hands. 'It's hard about the missus, Paddy,' the older man said to his father, munching a sandwich; he wore heavy brown boots and blue woollen combinations that showed at his trouser ends.

'Ah sure, she's dying all her life!' said his father sourly. He drank from the bottle, his windpipe jerking up and down; he cursed and boxed one of the kids soundly on the ear for bumping against him and spilling the porter. 'All her bloody life she's dying, since the day I married her!'

'Still and all, for the sake of the chisellers, I mean,' said the brown-booted kindly man, rubbing a small curly head and letting the child play with his watch chain from his waistcoat pocket. The young fellow was drinking silently and following Lil with his eyes as she went about preparing the kids for bed. The man with the watch chain sang a song called 'When Other Lips' and the sweat shone out upon his face as he sang. Father sat with his elbows on his knees in the armchair, staring down at the floor, a dark-green porter bottle between his feet. Lil took the children upstairs and her eye-follower finished his drink and uncorked another and said: 'You've a grand girl there, Paddy!' They all began to drink the whiskey. The younger one sang something about a naked woman jumping over a stile and the older man told him to 'cut it out' and the other fellow grinned and made a dirty reply; the beer began to be spilled on the floor, and when Lil came back she started to clean it up with the floorcloth. 'I'll help you, love,' the younger one said, rising heavily and following Lil into the pantry even though she told him it was all right.

'Dying all her life!' his father growled into the corned-beef sandwich he was munching, standing at the table, swaying; the other man was singing again with his eyes closed. 'All her crucifying life!' his father was muttering, drowning the beef with porter.

There came a sort of scream from inside the pantry and next moment Lil flew out with large frightened eyes, her fingers clutching the front of her blouse, her hair all wild.

'Da!' she said, in a choked voice, running over.

'It was nothing, Paddy,' said the younger man easily, coming back from the pantry, laughing quite pleasantly. 'Nothing at all!'

The man made a movement as if to brush back his hair from his forehead; the white blur of Father's fist whizzed through the air; the man sagged downwards along the wall, groaning, then began to pitch forward, as if in slow motion, but before he reached the floor he was jack-knifed backwards as Father's boot thudded solidly against the man's jutting chin; the sound of his head hitting the wall sounded dully through the kitchen.

Lil screamed; the older man struggled with Father, holding him back, grappling with him, trying to wrench the bread knife from his hand. A thin trickle of blood seeped from the mouth of the fallen man, down his chin and over his white starched collar.

6

MOTHER DID NOT die; weeks later she came home, thin and hollow-cheeked, walking slowly about the house, still smiling but with an effort; her legs were like matchsticks and she sometimes had to grab and hold on to the table or a chair to save herself from falling. She seemed changed, drained, bereft of something vital and alive in her, some central spark. Her eyes were dead, like windows with no light shining in them; the veins showed under the taut skin of her hands.

The new baby did not look new at all, but old and wrinkled and creased and quite hairless, a crabby old man's face on it; its belly-button stood out on its distended abdomen like a knot of wool as Mother washed and powdered it and rubbed Vaseline on its little red-raw behind. The same young priest with the bicycle clips and blue chin came and blessed Mother to give her strength and jokingly asked him if he had committed any new sins; he had not, because he had not thought of any new ones and just went on with the ones he was used to. The nuns came too, clasping their rose-and-silver rosary beads in their long dry fingers, pressing ten-shilling notes and food vouchers upon Mother, admonishing the elder girls not to use make-up or wear nylon stockings and high heels and to care for the younger children for their poor martyred mother. He wondered about nuns; he was more afraid of them than of the priests; he wondered how they could be called 'brides of Christ' because he knew most brides ended up as mothers, and if Christ had so many brides then heaven must be almost as noisy a household as their own.

One day a neighbour sat in the kitchen talking with Mother about births, and babies, navel cords, stitches, blood swabs. He kept imagining the blood dripping from the operating table on to the marble floor of the theatre,

34

smearing the rubber gloves and gowns of the doctors and nurses, and the moans of the opened up patient rising above the slow thump-thump-pumping of the transfusion machine and the rise and fall of the ether. The woman's daughter was also there in the kitchen, just married a year or so, a plump, fair girl with a round rather cowlike face; she cradled her own brand-new baby in her arms, rocking and crooning gently as she listened to the veteran talk of the two older women. Then without saying a word or making a single comment or excuse, she opened her blouse, took out one enormous breast, and began to suckle her infant; the almost lipless little mouth searched frantically for the fat nipple, and when it found it began to draw forth the milk avidly, its eyes puckered up in ecstasy, while the dreamy young mother held one hand under her heavy-hanging breast, lids drooping over her pale blue eyes, a faint simpering smile on her rice-pudding countenance.

Mother flushed and nudged her neighbour urgently, who did not seem to notice what was going on, and when she did see, she just smiled over at her breast-feeding daughter with mild reproach but mostly with pride.

'Now, now, Sarah!' said the mother jokingly; 'be a good girl and put that away. Don't you know the boy's there?'

Sarah fixed on him a long placid dreamy gaze from under her thick-lidded eyes and simpered some more. 'Ah sure where's the harm? He wouldn't know this from me right elbow!' she said, shaking her breast playfully as if it were some toy, making it wobble.

'Don't be too sure now,' said Sarah's mother sagely, eyeing him, 'he's looking at you awful bloody hard!'

'Ah, g'wan with yeh, Mammy!' giggled Sarah, and went on giving her child her breast until it hiccuped and spewed up some milk.

The lads went picking cinders every day after school on the huge tiphead at the end of the main road; they sold sacks of it at one-and-sixpence and two shillings, giving their regular customers the 'nuggets' or good stuff, but sticking everyone else with slack covered over by a layer of 'nuggets' at the top. With the money, which most of their parents knew nothing about, they went to see Tom Mix, Ken Maynard, Johnny MacBrown or Richard Dix at the picture houses. Some of the bigger boys were more ambitious and bought fags at two a penny or dirty photos in town which they hid under their mattress at home; others bought real slings, better than the ones they made themselves, to pelt at chimney-perched sparrows or take potshots at the green glasshouses in the rich gardens in the suburbs. Fights were always breaking out on the tiphead over who owned the best cinder-picking areas, and sometimes a free-for-all would erupt between rival gangs brandishing pick handles, legs off armchairs and a specially effective weapon which consisted of bits of torn-up sheets filled with stones which would be swung round and round in a circle in the air and then let fly, to break many a head and permanently dent many a nose. The air would be thick then with whirling cinders and other assorted missiles, the war cries and the agony cries of the gangs crouched in dugouts and trenches facing each other across the churned-up, hole-pitted, scraggy No Man's Land between, until tired of caution and foaming with the eagerness of battle, they would swarm over the barricades and rush headlong and fists flaying into each other, hand-to-hand and foot-to-foot warfare while curses crackled and wounds opened and blood mingled richly with cinder dust; until the tide of battle slowly changed and the vanquished would disperse in wild disorder, their bruised and bloodied comrades hobbling and crawling in their wake, yelling obscenities, crying for help, some to be captured and held hostage in the underground pits and huts of the other camp until a ransom of several sacks of the best cinders had been handed over in exchange.

Once in the thick of one such encounter, as his boxcar careered wildly at the head of the charging yelling mob in the heroic style of the Light Brigade which was then showing down at the 'Bower', he had been caught in the crossfire and concussed by being hit by a jagged stone on the head;

he not only saw stars, but a whole gold-spangled glittering constellation whirling in blackness; in the sudden inner stillness that descended on him he heard his brothers cry out in unison: 'The dirty lousy bastards – hitting a cripple! Geronimo!...' And off they all flew in maddened pursuit of the ungentlemanly enemy, leaving him upended on the ground, the sky and rooftops spinning crazily overhead and the warm sticky blood oozing into his eyes.

He crawled back into the boxcar, his head feeling huge and leaden and a dull ache starting up somewhere inside his skull. He was wheeled home in triumph, the boxcar his chariot, his throne, the most spectacular and successful casualty their gang had ever had and a perfectly valid excuse for long afterwards for making murderous surprise raids and ambushes on the foe. The folks at home did not seem fully aware of the significance of the gaping wound in his head, however, for Mother took one look and fainted, and Father took one look and loosened his leather belt ... He was put to bed with a hot bread-and-water poultice around his head; the others were put to bed with just bread-and-water and heavily larruped posteriors. He lay that night poised painfully between wakefulness and nightmare, seeing the fat, simpering girl with a knitting needle stuck through her huge bare breast and drops of blood oozing out of it instead of milk.

7

HE WAS crawling down a long, dark tunnel of pain; the walls seemed about to collapse, to fold in upon him; everything seemed to be breaking up, dissolving, disintegrating; he seemed to be stuck, submerged in a sort of gum mucilage; sharp brittle points of light flashed before his eyes; into the loud confusion of his mind things swam – forceps, scissors, syringes; clouds of nausea descended on him, stifling him, but he kept doggedly crawling towards a distant light, the remote yet glowing mouth of the tunnel, crawling through sluggish slime with agony at every inch; a queer boiling and seething began to rise in him drowning his brain, beating at it, bruising it; suddenly a great gaping hole opened before him; the ground swung, tethered, plunged; he was falling in wave upon wave of sickness, falling ... When he awoke it was still dark, but a different sort of darkness now, permeated by a dim unlocated effulgence; a circle of light shone remotely through a green bamboo screen; voices from behind it, subdued: 'Some difficulty with urine,' a man's voice said; 'You know what to do, sister.'

He tried to turn on to his side, but could not; a gust of pain swept through him, leaving him breathless: slowly one pain inside him began to overwhelm all the others; it felt like a weight that slid and rolled from side to side as he moved, swelling and growing inside him. He started to sweat, the drops clinging to his eyelashes, glistening like dim stars seen through a haze. This particular pain then grew and grew, mounting to an agony until he was ready to scream. Then the green curtains shook; a great blob of light came through, widening, dazzling; a shadow stood against the light; it was all dimness again, the metallic tinkle of instruments on a tray.

'I won't hurt you, dear,' said the nurse in a whisper, drawing back the bedclothes, sudden coolness on his hot wet skin. 'Just relax, like a good boy.'

He watched, filled with terror and awe, every muscle and nerve coiled taut as a spring, as she went about her task, inserting the soft rubber tube down his delicate passage, moving quietly, competently, as if it were an ordinary thing like knitting or stringing beads; he felt defenceless, outraged, ashamed, and conscious of a quick yet muffled pain as the tube sank deeper into him, but the relief when it came was so enormous that he forgot everything – the shame, the humiliation, the slight unfamiliar hurt; he felt himself being drained, emptied, and it was ecstatic.

When he had filled the basin, the nurse covered it with a towel, tucked in the sides of the blankets, smiled down at him and left; the pain was still there, but duller now, and it was a sort of lulling accompaniment to his dazed thoughts as the night sounds outside slowly grew faint and he slept.

Everything looked a strange greenish-brown as the morning light filtered through the cretonne curtains; he seemed to be in a room on his own; there was one high, narrow window; the walls were cream; he smelt Jeyes fluid everywhere, the same smell as when his mother used it in the lavatory; on the window ledge there was a small dark-green bottle with a white label. A bell chimed out somewhere; out in the corridors there came sounds of hurrying feet, swish of stiff skirts, trolleys being pushed past, remote thud of doors; nurses calling to one another, voices fading as they swept down on the hallways: 'Did you feed little Margaret yet, Joan?' 'Poor little Kevin's ulcers are bleeding again ...' 'That new boy in the den ... isn't he odd!'

A nurse came in and began to feed him with hot milk from a long-snouted jug; it was not the same one who had performed such a strange service for him last night, and he was glad, for he could not have met her eyes. He sipped the milk meekly and the nurse wiped his mouth and fixed his pillows; when she left he tried to think back; the slow pain-ridden journey through the darkened streets, being carried in a blanket up the stone steps, the luminous globe of light above the wide doors haloed in fog ... now he lay in a strange room, in a cool bed, marooned; and suddenly the sheets securely roped in under the mattress became his chains, soft linen chains holding him down. He remembered a sparrow lying writhing in the front garden, maimed by a shot from his brother's catapult, its wing shattered, squawking wildly; at first he had laughed with the rest, seeing it hobbling about with frantic futility, trying to fly, to regain its own element again, its own small dignity; then he had felt slightly sick and was glad when someone got a stone and put the wrecked, crippled thing out of its misery.

A dark-skinned man in a white coat with a sad-looking narrow face came in, sat on the side of the bed and began to examine him; then, drawing aside the sheets, this man began to touch and massage that part of him which was associated in his mind with two things – the lavatory pot, and the big black unnameable sin of which the priest spoke in such mournful tones. The coloured man, smiling kindly but with melancholy down at him, went on doing this strange and frightening thing, the strong, cool fingers massaging and pressing upon the lower extremities of him, saying softly from time to time: 'I'm not hurting you, boy?' He was not being hurt too much, but his face felt like a roaring furnace, for he was being touched and known in such a way and on such a part as never before, and he wanted to cry, or shout, or kick out in rage, anything that would save him from this awful indignity and stop this complete stranger from using his body and limbs in this frightful way; but the man seemed rather remote and absorbed as he pressed and kneaded the testicles slowly and dreamily, inquiring softly in between the firm, rhythmic movements of his hands if it hurt. There was some pain, but slowly it dulled down to a sort of sluggish ease, and then to a turgid, unexpected sort of pleasure that was unwanted but insistent; it kept rising in him, this glad guilty feeling, and he was dimly, fearfully aware somewhere of a certain muscular hardening ... Quite abruptly the man stopped and stared at him for some moments, a sort of sad surprise in his large liquid eyes; then he covered him up again, stood up, wrote something into a notebook, smiled vacantly at him and left, the tails of his white coat swishing.

Through the window when the blinds had been drawn wide, he saw the upper storeys of the genteel old houses on the other side of the street, their ancient brick faces glowing in the setting sun, like gaunt old ladies blushing at the indelicate manners and ways of the new times and at all the frantic turmoil and rush of the sprawling, rapacious, seething city sprouting its new modern marvels like mushrooms, brash young buildings outraging the slippered ease and gentility of these gracious dwellings. In one window of a house almost facing, he sometimes saw figures move, and later he watched a young girl standing there looking down at the busy street below; it seemed so odd and so wrong somehow for such a young person to be remotely connected with such an old house. He could even see a gay white ribbon in her hair, and she wore a yellow dress with fluffy cuffs at the wrists, but there was something infinitely and ineffably sad in her stillness as she stood at that gaunt window gazing down at the life passing heedlessly below; he thought of a princess in a lonely tower, and he wanted to wave to her, attract her attention, for he too was shut up and chained down in this sterilized silence. When she disappeared and did not come again to the window, he hated looking out then and seeing nothing but the blind eyes of decaying houses.

Two nurses came in, one a stout dour girl who waddled like a penguin and had a plump spotty face; the other was thin, sharp-nosed, mousy, with dark brittle eyes and a permanent leer on her face. The round one stuck a cold glass needle under his armpit – 'I had orders from sister not to put it in his mouth' – while the thin one put fresh linen on his bed; they were talking among themselves as they worked, but on taking away the last sheet the alert eyes of the wiry girl fell upon his nakedness and she leered up at her companion.

'I thought this was supposed to be a children's hospital, Eileen?' she said.

'So it is, silly!' said her companion, shaking the thermometer and squinting at it intently.

'Well, he's no child . . .'

They both looked and giggled and after fixing his bed they went out still giggling and whispering together.

8

'I'LL BREAK your bloody gob O'Shea, if you don't quit shoving . . .' 'Ah, g'wan and stuff your granny!'

The long beehive, serpentine rows of lumber-suited, short-trousered, butt-smoking boys wound sinuously up the narrow sideyard of the picture house from the derelict launderette to the steel-bolted side entrance, a surging, elbow-digging throng of barracking boys whistling, cat-calling, jostling, sly-pinching the hemmed-in behinds of boys immediately in front of them, flailing with gritty fists the would-be queue jumpers, lashing out at the unprotected shins of the offenders with toe-peeping boots, belting the bobbing, jerking napes of those fortunate youngsters ahead in the queue with hard rolled-up balls of paper catapulted from pieces of elastic held between the teeth. Big boys swapped lewd jokes and spoke with feigned masculine scorn about Betty Grable and her famous legs; small boys floated about like flotsam in this unfriendly sea of elders, clasping their threepenny bits grimly in their sweaty palms, whimper-ing in distress as they were pushed and shoved, some having queued for so long that, helpless to stop themselves, the urine ran down their bare cold legs into their mucky runners; mongrel dogs of a uniform dirty yellowish hue ran up and down yapping and yipping madly, snapping gleefully at shins and ankles at the hoarse encouragement of their owners; a churning torrent of brown boots, white mud-spattered sandals and just bare feet moving relentlessly towards the as yet unopened entrance with just one intent – to behold the corpulent Andy Devine push crooks and badmen about with a mighty thrust of his almighty belly.

The little peacock of a man in uniform on duty at the door stood smugly rocking on his springy heels, hands clasped behind back, a latter-day Emperor Jones, the sparse blond hair pasted rigidly back upon the narrow skull, his mean jackal face bland and imperious in the weak afternoon sun that peeped timidly and wanly over the heavy bank of dull copperish rainclouds in the east; this usher was a much-hated figure with the local juvenile population, with his sly ear-boxing ways and the thong of leather coiled in his hand, swishing it at those who got out of line, keeping the queue in order, as if herding cattle into pens, hated as much as any Gestapo zealot, deriving warped pleasure from flicking with his lariat the wind-whipped legs and reddened ears of smaller boys with an expert, metallic twist of his wrist, grinning at their howls of pain and protest and as often as not refusing them admission when they got to the box-office on the pretext that they were 'rowdy', sending them trudging miserably home in the pelting rain.

'He wasn't *born*,' the boys would mutter; 'he was invented—'

'By the bloke who invented Frankenstein!' another would add, not so much with malice as with a genuine air of conviction.

On this Saturday afternoon the scene and setting were the same; boys pushed, fell, scrambled over the fallen, cursed with incredible expertise, sang snatches of murky songs picked up from outside public houses on Saturday nights and behaved authentically as boys.

The rain started to fall, first as a cold drizzle, then more thickly until it was falling in long, lashing veils, sweeping the glistening pavements and seeping under the collar of his heavy lumber jacket, tickling his skin like cold fingers. He dug his heels deeper into Paddy's heaving ribs and clung tightly to his brother's broad shoulders, crouched up there like Sabu's monkey, his skinny arms twisted with convulsive strength as he held on grimly to his human stallion in that forward-thrusting, milling crowd of clamouring humanity waiting with tight-fisted threepenny bits to see another unfolding saga of the Wild West and feel for a time in the darkened cavern hall of the cinema the vicarious ecstasy of noonday violence and sudden death.

They had come early, leaving the boxcar as always at the end of the lane behind the abandoned launderette, and were now moving ever closer to the head of the queue. Through the rain sheets obscuring the broad fields and grounds of the old church in the distance, the huge gothic timepiece high in the belfry pointed almost to three o'clock; it would soon be time for the side doors to open and engulf the hundreds of rain-drenched but undaunted cowboy worshippers, to sit enthralled on the seemingly unending rows and terraces of 'woodeners', slapping, clapping, whistling and applauding the antics and adventures of their favourite celluloid heroes, the fierce yells of encouragement and glee when there was shooting, the loud boos and catcalls when there was kissing, which was considered a very un-cowboy-like activity. Rival shouts would fill the dim building: 'Watch out behind you, Buck!' 'There's that snakey Hawkeye creeping up behind, Hopalong!' 'Ah, don't be so bloody sloppy with that mot, Roy!' Then as the screen flickered and blanked out momentarily – 'Show the bloody picture or give us our money back!' The participants on the screen were less absorbed in the drama than the participants in the audience.

'Get back there, Brown!' ordered the ubiquitous usher, now as foul-tempered as the weather, pushing Paddy back. 'Take your place with the rest of the bleeding buggers!'

'But mister—' Paddy tried to say, balancing desperately.

'Get the hell back, you—!' snarled the uniformed warden, giving Paddy a shove that made him lose his balance, his sandals slipping and slithering on the rainy concrete surface . . .

In the bookmaker's shop adjacent to the picture house his father stood gloomily at the counter looking at the runners and riders on the race sheets for the next race, his face dark, bushy eyebrows twitching ominously, a sure sign of trouble, bitterly aware of the emptiness of his pockets, peaked hat slouched down over one eye; every horse he had backed had shown a distinct preference for remaining at the heel of the field; he had tried single bets, cross-doubles, each-way

44

trebles, accumulators – with not a morsel of luck. More and more as the day lengthened he saw his pint-hopes and whiskey-expectations dwindle rapidly; it became increasingly easier to jingle the few remaining coins in his hip pocket; the weekend stretched ahead of him like a desert as his wrath grew, thundering inside his head like the hooves of the horses galloping away with his pocket money.

He looked around as there came a bit of a commotion in the shop; he thought some lucky so-and-so had come up with an accumulator; then he saw the ragged boy standing in the doorway, the rain dripping off him, gathering in small puddles at his bare black-nailed feet; it was a boy off the street and his long lashed eyes searched frantically through the smoky mist of gambling men until he saw the man he wanted.

'Mr Brown!' the boy yelled hoarsely; 'come quick – they're after knocking down your Paddy and him with the lad on his back!' The hooves were now thundering loudly, setting up a black cloud before his father's eyes as he rushed from the shop . . .

He squatted on the drenched ground, looking with a curious detachment at the blood as it ran from an ugly gash on Paddy's knee; he was quite unhurt himself; but the hurt inside grew as swarms of gawking, gangling boys stood around open-mouthed as he lay helpless on the ground furiously trying to get himself sitting up in a more normal position and writhing all the more with his efforts; then he became aware of the silence; nobody spoke; there came only the shuffle of feet as the crowd swarmed nearer to get a closer view of the little drama; he could even hear the rain beating on the concrete, dripping into the gutter that ran along the wall, the incongruous lowing of an out-of-bounds cow from the grounds of the chapel beyond the boundary wall; he saw his father sweep round the corner, hat off, fists doubled up, and he seemed very tall and terrifying against the glowering sky.

'I can explain, sir,' the usher said nervously, stepping unwillingly forward, smiling sickly. 'You see, we must have some sort of order here, and your boy—'

There was a roar, like that of an enraged lion, and he saw it all take place then as if in slow motion; his father stepped back a pace, in a pose like John L. Sullivan, drawing his arm back quite methodically as far as it could go, and standing perfectly balanced on the balls of both feet he swung his fist swiftly through the air and exploded it on the scraggy, tilted point of the hypnotized usher's chin, sending the man flying backwards off the ground and crashing heavily into the locked doors, with such impact that they flew open with a terrific clap against the walls on either side. There was still the uncanny silence until a quick-witted lad saw the significance of the situation and shouted: 'Last in is a sissy!' Quickly his father scooped him up as there was a stampede of charging boys jumping or side-stepping or merely trampling over the supine form of the fallen usher, a pulverized pulp under the mass of feet swarming and streaming over him through the swinging doors of their drab and flea-bitten but enchanted palace absolutely free of charge; countless scores managed to seize the glittering opportunity of scot-free entertainment before the other ushers rushed down and restored some semblance of order and hoisted their bruised and battered colleague into the office for repairs, by which time both the damage and the justice had been done.

For many a Saturday afterwards the gang kept urging Paddy to let himself be felled again with his rider on his back; they even showed him how to fall without being hurt like the rodeo-wise cowboys on the screen, and Paddy was quite willing, but the usher was wiser now and became a martyr to their taunts and jibes, much to their disgust.

He never had to pay into the pictures after that.

'And I shall hear, though soft you tread above me,
    and all my grave shall warmer, sweeter be;
  for you will bend and tell me that you love me,
    and I shall sleep in peace until you come to me . . .'

46

In the long drawn-out peace of a summer evening he listened to the young voice of his mother singing around the for-once quiet house, her arms white with flour to her dimpled elbows, cooking stewed apple scones and brown wheaten bread, the brood of children having fled like birds finding the master gone and the cage door open, but he remaining behind, for his cage was a wide and airy place then with his thrush of a Mother singing about the captain-less house and the baking bread smelling sweet from the steamy little pantry, a brief but bell-like peacefulness abroad and she smiling with a gay woman-alive spirit shining out of her eyes though the songs she sang were sad. In the sweet-flowing stream of that voice his thoughts bobbed gently in the silver currents, light as leaves twirling and swirling gently to a hushed lorelei so that almost he could lose himself in unremembrance of himself, in a world of soft-vowelled whispers and immense calm; about the fire-bright house she went now, like a young wife holding the world in all the four rooms of her new-pin domain, with maybe a ribbon in her hair slashing the rippling dark of it and blue slippers on her feet and all the while her plump fingers kneading and pummelling the soft moist mound of milk-drenched flour on the table; and she would gather him warmly into her smile, taking the chains from him; it was always the morning of his life at times like this alone with her singing, happy in the simplicity of her ways.

He sat at the window; dusk had fallen; the lamplight outside had a little foggy halo around it; around the bottom of the post some boys played cards, not making much noise except for an occasional shout of disgust or glee as the tide of the game swung back and forth; on the grassy circle a group of girls played with a skipping rope, calling out street rhymes and skipping to the rhythm, now and then screaming abuse at some unseen boy pelting them with pebbles from a pile of sand left by workmen smoothing the surface of the road; lighted buses went down the main street lit up like hollowed-out pumpkins stuffed with burning candles; the ice-cream man rumbled down the street blowing his banshee horn, the tired old pony drooping between the shafts, and the kids clustered around the little yellow boxlike cart thrusting their pennies forward, and the man handed them down their cornets and wafers, a big red carbuncle embossed on the back of his hand like an apple sliced in half. A black tomcat stood silently on the back wall of a house, hump-backed against the huge misty-yellow moon that had come up from nowhere and now seemed to be rising visibly into the still-pale sky; the intricate pattern of the lace curtains was reflected on the rosy wallpaper behind him by the lamp-light, the shadowy, filigree flower-shapes moving strangely and seeming strangely alive in the slight breeze from the unshut top window.

Two men came staggering up the street with fast-linked arms, singing 'We'll Keep the Red Flag Flying High' and hanging on to each other like comrades or brothers long-lost across sundering seas; they halted outside the front gate arguing about Jem Larkin and the trade unions, slapping each other lustily on the back and shaking hands vigorously over and over again, laughing and throwing back their heads, throats bronzed and gleaming in the falling lamp-light; one of them at last roared the ultimate goodnight and the other fumbled with the latch on the front gate.

The big plate of cabbage and potatoes and pigs' feet stood steaming on the kitchen table, a heat haze shimmering over it. Father sat crooked on a chair, squinting at it, his lower lip lolling wetly over his chin, a thick vein jumping and jerking in his sandy temple; Mother sat by the fire patching the elbows of one of the kids' jerseys.

'Jem Larkin was crucified,' said Father in a slurred, porter-thick voice, his eyes heavy-lidded and mournful. 'Did you know that?' A coal fell from the fire and lay spluttering on the hearthstone, sending up a thin spume of black, acrid smoke; the water tap was dripping in the pantry, splashing monotonously on to a plate. Mother pushed an empty bottle up the sleeve to help her sew better.

'I said Jem Larkin was crucified,' Father repeated; the baby started to wail in its cot in the corner next to the fire.

'Can't you shut the bastard up?' Father growled, swivelling round on the chair and glaring balefully at the cot.

Mother dropped the jersey and stooped over the baby, giving it its soother and shushing it back to sleep; her hair tumbled into her eyes and she brushed it back with her hand.

'He was crucified, I tell you!' Father suddenly shouted, banging the table, making the plate of dinner hop.

'Who?' Mother shot out, startled as the baby screamed with fright. 'You've woke the baby—'

'Christ!' roared Father, slapping the table again. 'Is that all you can think about – babies? What about Jem Larkin?'

'Well, what about him?' asked Mother, anxiously rocking the cot and peering in at the baby.

'Amn't I after telling you a dozen times?' roared Father. 'Is it bothered as well as stupid you are? The poor man was crucified! Hung high on the cross of betrayal and crucified!'

'Ah then, he has plenty of company,' said Mother wearily.

'What do you mean?'

'What I say, mister,' said Mother, getting the baby quiet and going back to her sewing. 'There's more than Jem Larkin crucified.'

'Weeping Jasus!' said Father in disgust. 'You're not comparing yourself with that great fighting saint of a man, are you?'

'Can't you eat your dinner before it gets cold?' said Mother.

'I'm talking about one of the greatest Irishmen that ever lived,' said Father with heavy rancour, his clenched hand working on his knee, 'and all you can say is: "You woke the baby! Eat your dinner." Where's your patriotism, woman? Is it a bloody loyalist that I married? I'm speaking to you!'

'You know I'm as Irish as you are,' said Mother quietly, knowing it would be worse if she stayed silent. 'And that's more than Larkin could say, for he was English.'

'English-born, woman,' said Father jubilantly. 'English-born, but Irish in spirit! They all try to drag him down because he was born in that kip across the sea, that hoor-house across the water! It was the priests killed him,' Father announced with sudden solemnity, nodding his head in affirmation with himself. 'Them country dogs with their collars back to front – they killed him!'

'God bless and save us,' said Mother, blessing herself. 'You've drink on you or you wouldn't be talking like that about the holy anointed.'

'They killed him stone dead, I tell you!' insisted Father, wiping the saliva running from his mouth with an angry hand. 'Your holy assassins with their altar wine and silver collections killed the best friend the working man in this country ever had! What do you think of that?'

'Well,' said Mother placidly, re-threading her needle, 'wasn't he a communist?'

'Suffering Jasus!' exploded Father, the vein in his head jumping more violently. 'Is it sawdust you have instead of brains? Is every man a communist that tries to better the lot of his fellow working man? And what if he is?'

'Oh, eat your dinner, man!' said Mother with a sigh.

'I won't eat me bollacking dinner!' said Father, roaring again. 'I won't sit and hear Jem Larkin insulted in me own house by a so-so woman that knows nothing about anything but bloody babies!'

'Well, I've one up on Jem Larkin in that respect,' said Mother. 'He wasn't crucified having children anyhow.'

'He was crucified making this a better country for your little God-forbids!' bellowed back Father. 'Where were you and the likes of you when the fighting was going on in nineteen-nineteen?' he wanted to know, thrusting his head forward arrogantly to get her answer.

'Well, I can't answer for the likes of me,' said Mother, taking down the bottle from the sleeve of the jersey and examining the results of her sewing; 'but I was up in the Rotunda having your son.'

'That's a bloody lame excuse!' said Father in disgust, throwing his shoulders back against the chair and stretching out his legs, head on one side, canine fashion, squinting over at her sourly. 'How do I know it was for me?'

'One thing you can be sure of, mister,' said Mother, starting on another damaged sleeve; 'it wasn't for Jem Larkin.'

'You cow's melt!' growled Father viciously, beaten at last.

Mother bent over her sewing, pushing the still-smouldering coal under the fender with her foot.

'Where's me curse-of-God dinner, woman?' asked Father, jerking out of a momentary slumber and struggling upright on the chair.

'It's in front of you, sure,' Mother told him.

Father looked at it with a sort of bilious leer. '*This?*' he said, poking at it with a rigid index finger. 'This freezing mess? You call this a dinner? Get off your arse and get me a proper meal and me after slaving all day for you and your shower of shitty orphans!'

Mother, sensing the increasing ugliness of his mood, put aside her sewing and stood up uncertainly. 'But it's what you like,' she said, fingers toying nervously with a button of her blouse. 'It's what you always ask for on a Thursday – cabbage and potatoes and a pig's cheek and a few feet—'

Father pulled himself up, holding on to the table and glaring at her with sudden hate. 'And you know what I want, don't you?' he said, the spittle seeping out of the corners of his mouth. 'You always knew what I wanted, didn't you?' he said, lumbering towards her, taut-fingered hands groping at her blouse, yanking buttons off. 'This – and this – and this!' he muttered, pushing her into the corner.

'Don't ... the boy!' cried Mother in fright, her fingers gripping her torn blouse as she crouched against the wall.

'Let him see!' roared Father, staggering on his feet, raising his voice higher as the baby began to wail once more. 'Let them all see how you saddled me with your litter of bastards! There's probably another one in the bag as it is! You didn't crack till you had me tied hand and foot with a dozen shitty little effers!'

'They were all born decent,' said Mother, struggling to elude him. 'They were all born proper in the sight of God!'

51

'In the sight of my bleeding cock, you mean!' Father roared, flinging out a hand to save himself from falling, holding on to her with the other, shaking her up and down. 'Think yourself a martyr, don't you? Think you're bearing it all for the glory of God! You wouldn't know what it felt like to enjoy it, would you?'

'For God's sake – the boy!' gasped Mother, clutching the dresser for support as he shook her with his loose casual strength.

'You married beneath yourself, remember!' rasped Father, quivering with a sort of helpless rage. 'I wasn't good enough for you! Dorset Street wasn't good enough for the barons of Smithfield! You had to go without all your finery when you married me – your lace shifts and petticoats and hand-embroidered drawers!'

'Take your dinner – please,' Mother pleaded, worn out, struggling free and stumbling away from him, wiping the specks of blood from her lip with the back of her hand. 'Take your dinner in peace, like any Christian man.'

'This is what I think of your slop!' Father shouted, zigzagging back to the table.

The plate of cabbage and potatoes came flying through the air, just missing Mother's head as she ducked instinctively, crashing against the wall behind her, the vegetables clinging to the wallpaper, leaving great greenish stains. The table was upended and went over with a deafening bang; the baby squealed in terror as the clock fell and smashed on to the hearthstone. Father slipped and slithered crazily over the floor littered with meat and steaming globs of cabbage; he fell on to his knees, cursing, then started to vomit up without warning, the slimy bileful contents of his drink-sodden stomach spewing in a brown murky jet over Mother's slippered feet.

9

'Now Lord Norbury was a hanging judge
and from the rope he would not budge;
he did his job and did it well
and now he's roasting down in hell . . .'

SITTING ROUND the healthy fire on a winter's night their
mother would be coaxed into telling them tales about
McGinty's House, where they lived before moving from the
city out into their corporation house, and how it was
supposed to be haunted by Lord Norbury himself and some
of the wretched people he had sentenced to be hanged;
stories of cold unseen hands reaching out of dark corners
frightening the heart out of the women; strange sobbing
sounds and bitter moans in the heart-still dead of night
echoing up from the well of sunken cellars; young couples
courting on the stairs on warm midsummer evenings feeling
a presence behind as of a chill wind passing over them, and
strange, ironic laughter vanishing down the dim hallway . . .
A house once elegant where men had lived elegant lives,
frock-coated gentlemen with powdered wigs and aristocratic
noses dancing minuets fingertip to fingertip with ringleted
ladies in flowing satin and sweeping bustles, a dandified
group of musicians playing oboe, flute and harpsichord on
the raised miniature platform. Here, too, men had died
violent deaths at the hands of patriotic assassins in the great
upsurge of national identity and pride that heralded the
dawn of freedom in the land; some had been found in bed
with slit throats, others hanging from one of the ornamental
beams with protruding eyes and lolling, swollen tongue,
slogans of freedom and defiance scrawled in their own spilled
blood upon the cream-and-roseate walls.

The old house was thick with echoes of that period, so

53

genteel and exquisite for some, so brutally impoverished and unbearable for the vast majority of others, when priests had to go underground to celebrate Mass, and young men of spirit were hung, drawn and quartered for daring to raise their own flag; it was said both the tormented spirits of the inhuman judges and the vengeful ghosts of the wrongfully condemned roamed the halls and corridors. Nobody ever quite knew who the mysterious McGinty was that had given his name to the house, but as a landlord he certainly did a lucrative trade in ghosts.

They would listen enthralled, glancing at one another, then over their shoulders into the dimness beyond, and they would huddle closer to the warmth and glow and their mother's knee, looking up at her trustfully, quite unafraid of unearthly guests as long as she was there. It was usually Tony who got Mother going, and he would ask serious questions about such happenings and laugh often while the rest of them just listened and rolled their eyes, edging nearer together; still, they enjoyed listening, enjoyed the shiver and thrill that crept up their spines, and when they went at last to bed they would all snuggle down deep under the clothes and whisper for hours about the existence of ghosts; Jem would say – but not very convincingly – 'There's no ghost but the Holy Ghost!' and they would all want to agree with him except Tony, who would be silent for a minute, then point with his finger across the darkened room and ask breathlessly – 'What's that moving behind the curtain, Jem?' and Jem, who always slept on the inside close to the wall, would feel safe and say – 'Ah g'wan and get a Mass said for yourself!' and there would be silence, until Tony made a sound like that of a cat meowing softly into the dozing Jem's ear, who would scream and leap out on to the floor yelling – 'Ma, ma, there's a ghost in the bed!' This always brought Father in charging from the front room swinging the leather belt and they would all get it then, and afterwards they would all gang up on Jem and pinch him all over for being such a bloody mollycoddle.

'Tell us a story, Ma!' suggested Tony one night in

November; it was the night of All Souls, and they were sitting cross-legged around the hearth; it was said that if bread and water was left out before bedtime it would be gone the next morning, for the poor souls had to go without food in Purgatory and they would put in a good word for whoever left them a bite to eat and a sup to drink on the one night of the year when they were let return to earth; heaven was probably guaranteed for those who left out currant cake and hot buttermilk, though that was really a form of bribery not indulged in by believing people, so it was usually just bread and water on the ghostly menu.

Mother started telling a story about two young men she knew in her young days in the city who were coming home in the early hours of the morning from an all-night hooley well stacked with whiskey and porter and singing, when they saw this beautiful young woman sitting on the kerb under a lamp post on the other side of the street. The remarkable thing about her was that, at that unearthly hour, she was combing out her long gleaming hair with a silver brush and singing to herself – not really singing, but a lost, melancholy sort of keening that sounded more like a moan. She was wearing a long green cloak and had no shoes or slippers on her feet, and her hair shone like gold under the lamplight. The young men were amused and courageous with porter, and they called out to her across the dark, deserted street, but she paid no heed to their ribald male remarks and went on combing out her long, lovely coils of hair and keeping up her queer, mournful lament. They dared each other to go over and find out who she was, and finally one of them accepted the challenge and crossed the street; he had just time to say – 'Are you all right, missus?' when the woman looked up and let an unmerciful scream out of her and flung her comb at him; it flashed through the air like a flaming arrow and just missed him, and next moment off he flew like a redshank with his mate panting behind him and the mad, furious wail of the woman trailing after them.

'Well,' said Mother, giving the new baby its soother, 'the

man was sitting here this night!' and she blessed herself.

Hell was a place they often discussed, much more than they talked about heaven, for while one was supposedly full of the same sort of crowd and dense with holy monotony, the other place was a sort of melting pot in every sense of the word, where kings and emperors and high priestesses rubbed burning shoulder with dissipated butchers, debauched politicians and gold-hearted little street girls who had relentlessly pursued a lifelong policy of no surrender; so of the two hell offered the more fruitful ground for fierce argufying back and forth; it was somehow more of a thrill to talk about being damned than being eternally saved, which sounded boring, like being locked up inside a chapel forever with a bag of liquorice allsorts.

Once upon a tall-yarn-spinning night when they were all 'confined to barracks' because Father was in one of his midweek bad tempers on account of drought and would not let any of them out to play, they all sat round the small fire in the front upstairs room; Mother lay in the huge bed in the corner nursing the now not-so-new baby, for already her stomach was rising again, and the subject of hell came up; it was the abode of hardcase sinners who would burn down there 'forevermore' as Jem judiciously pointed out. 'How could you burn forever?' a smaller listener wanted to know. 'Try burning yourself and see how long you stick it!' said Tony, 'You'd be screaming like a madman in a flash!' 'I suppose *you* would!' said Jem, spitting into the fire, 'You're just a big mouth!' Tony looked at Jem squarely. 'D'you want a belt in the gob, you big heap of manure?' asked Tony, flexing his supple fingers; Jem sat back on his hunkers and said that was all Tony was good for – belting people in the gob; then his face brightened and he leaned forward. 'I bet you won't put your finger in the fire, hardchaw!' he said triumphantly to Tony. 'What's the dare?' asked Tony, scraping the dirt out of his nails with a chewed-up matchstick.

'Three lead marbles and me best conker!' crowed Jem, fishing his wares from his pocket and laying them out on the hearthstone, the big knobbly dark-brown chestnut gleaming red in the flames.

'What's going on there?' asked Mother drowsily, hushing the peevish baby against her shoulder, an old ravelled plaid shawl draping her shoulders, eyes shut in tiredness.

'Oh, nothing, Ma,' said Tony, flinging away his nail-probing matchstick, not taking his eyes from Jem. 'Nothing at all!' He spat once on his index finger, rubbed it against his trousers, held it up solemnly for them all to see – then laid it deliberately down upon one of the glowing bars of the firegrate. A second, two, three, four . . . there came a slight sizzling sound and the thick smell of burning flesh; the finger stayed as if glued to the red-hot bar; Tony's face was white, blank, his eyes glittering darkly as he stared across at Jem, who sat with his mouth hanging open, terror leaping out of his chalky face. Six seconds, seven, eight . . . somebody jumped up and got sick on the floor; when Tony pulled his finger away bits of shrivelled-up flesh stuck and clung to the bar; Jem was struck dumb; Mother scrambled out of the bed and screamed when she saw the burnt, blackened finger being pointed starkly up at her; the scream brought Father running up from the kitchen, and seeing everyone else almost in a state of hysteria except Tony, who sat stock-still staring intently and with quizzical interest at his own blighted finger, the leather belt came whistling through the air on its errand of chastisement . . .

So the back bedroom became Tony's prison cell for weeks to follow; at least that was the paternal intention, but every evening after tea Tony would open the window, shin down the water spout and clamber over neighbouring backyards, leaving Mother all thumbs and trembling lest Father chance to go upstairs and discover the jailbreak. 'There'll be quare jigs on the green if he does!' she would whisper, drawing on her shawl and going out on the front step to search for the fugitive while Father sat reading the newspaper in the lavatory. Then one evening there were shouts of 'Re-leevi-oo!' and 'Pussy-four-corners!' and shadowy figures of pursuing boys and pursued girls streaking past in the dusk but no trace of Tony, until somebody gave a wild whoop of the gang's battlecry outside the gate and yelled Tony's name out loudly.

'I thought that bugger was beyant?' said Father, coming in, buckling his belt, striding towards the stairs.

'So he is, so he is!' Mother said, trying to stop him.

'Out of me way, woman!' Father growled, pushing past her and taking the stairs two at a time.

Rushing in, he peered around in the dim room until he saw the relaxed and trouserless figure on the bed reading a comic in the faint light that came in from the window. 'Can I have a drink of water, Father?' inquired Tony blithely.

'Humph!' said Father, 'I know the drink I'll give you!' and he turned and tramped down the stairs muttering under his breath, his heavy boots loud with anger and disappointment.

Tony laughed, threw the cosmic adventures of 'Flash' Gordon to one side, took a crumpled sheet of jotting paper from his shoe, spread it out, lit a stolen match – companion of a stolen fag-end – and read over again with grunts of male pleasure the scrawled blue-marker-written note from the nubile Nancy and did several somersaults on the mattress in anticipation, for he had just rendered ineffective with a well-aimed shot of his sling the one obstacle to joy inexpressible . . . the light at the end of the lane.

10

IT FELT so queer to be dead.

He had never died before, or if he had, he didn't remember, but he knew he must be dead now, because everything was so queer, and he felt nothing but the intense cold and the terrible cold darkness pressing in on him, just squeezing everything out of him, leaving him empty. He seemed to be sitting on some street, and it was dark and endless, with not a friendly lighted window on it at all. He had never been here before; he was alone at first, but then he noticed the men walking sombrely up and down on each side of the strange dead street wearing black suits and black tophats, walking like undertakers up and down, looking at him as if sizing him up, guessing at his measurements, running an invisible inch tape over him with their piercing black eyes. He saw someone come up the street towards him, all in black and with a heavy black embroidered veil half hiding her face, but he knew who it was just the same. Why did you have to die with sin on your soul, son? Mother was asking him in a sorrowful voice. Why did you go and die with all that heavy sin on your soul like thick sour grease, scumming your lovely white soul? I can't help you now, son!

The street was getting darker, as if night was coming on fast, but along the edges of the unseen horizon a red glow appeared. Then he heard a voice close behind him.

Cold enough for the time of the year? the voice said.

He looked around and saw it was a very queer creature indeed that was speaking to him, a little crooked naked man with burnt-up skin and a fine pair of black shiny horns rearing up out of his forehead. He was holding a big black book in his hands and reading the black pages, nodding his top-heavy head from time to time and scratching at his red blistered lips with a nail-less raw finger.

In fact, said the stranger with a sigh, it's cold enough to blow the balls off a brass monkey.

Suddenly he knew it was the voice of one of his brothers, but the man was quite unlike anyone he had ever known.

The little man-devil tried to grin at him in a friendly way, but it came out as a sick hideous leer. By the way, said the stranger holding up the book, this is the book of your sins while you were alive. There's one particular sin here you kept on doing . . .

A sort of noise was coming up the street, sweeping up it like a gust of wind, crowding the dark air. He looked around

59

him and saw the glowing bars of a cage closing in on him; everywhere he looked now he saw fire, the red verbosity of flames licking up through crevices in the cracking, crackling paving stones of the street, but he felt nothing but cold, the freezing cold seeping into him; there seemed to be ice flowing in his veins.

You made a bad confession the last time! someone whispered in his ear. You didn't tell the priest the real bad ones!

He couldn't. It was too bad, too black to tell that nice clean-shaven young priest with the innocent child's face on him and the holy smell of incense about him. Besides, he couldn't get the words out, he could only grunt and make twisted ugly faces. He was sure the priest would never understand either the sin or the words.

You're right about that! said the female devil coming out of the swirling red-lightened darkness towards him, throwing away the gutted end of a cigarette. I could never understand one bloody word you said.

He knew who it was at once and his heart began thumping in that familiar way it always did when he saw her. She was wearing the same tattered frock and the broken sandals with her toes peeping out of them and a red ribbon in her hair. She carried a bundle of old comics under her arm. They were sitting in the hall at home.

Can't you talk? she said impatiently, throwing back a dark wing of her hair from her eyes. Can't you bloody well say something just once instead of grunting that way, like a pig?

He tried to talk, he tried to say something, anything, even one word, any word, as long as it was clear and easy to understand, but nothing came except the usual grunts, until he thought of one word he knew very well, and this word came without any bother at all. When she heard it, she threw back her head and laughed until she doubled up. Do you know what that means now? she asked when she could stop laughing and be serious, giving him a long wise-old-owl look from under her trim long eyelashes. Are you sure your Ma is not in?

She opened the door and peeped into the kitchen to make sure, but there was only the baby in the cot and the dog snoozing on the hearthstone. She came back and sat facing him, the little pink flame tip of her tongue curling along her lower lip, her green eyes kindling.

Do you want to see the hair? she said in a sandpaper whisper, drawing up her frock.

He tried not to look, he tried to look away, he tried to think about the Blessed Virgin, Mother of God, like the priest told him every time he was tempted into sinning, but in a blissful burning melting of will and a roaring waterfall rush of sin he looked straight at her and saw the flaming arrowhead of soft down between her scrawny thighs curling downwards like a little goat's beard. He just looked and looked while she stroked it.

Look at that while your tea is drawing! she said, sticking out her tongue at him. You won't see that in the Beano!

She crawled on her knees towards him, sticking out her belly and her hips, but he cowered away as if from fire. This seemed to enrage her, and she grabbed hold of his hand and tried to push it up against her where she was bare, but he hung rigidly back and kicked out at her and hit her in the chest; she keeled right over. She jumped up, eyes glittering, then she burst out laughing, lifted her frock, turned her bare buttocks to him, and yelled joyfully. Six pounds of fat bacon for you! she said, mincing away down the front path. Six pounds of prime fat bacon for you, mister! She went jinxing and jingling down the path, swirling her frock and showing him her bare behind until she went out of the front gate. Then she shook her hair demurely and walked down the street.

People were looking through the bars, peeping in at him as if he was some sort of queer new animal in the city zoo. Some waved in at him, while others sang lustily, making a funnel with their hands around their mouths:

'Look at him -- ah, what a farce
with a red-hot poker up his arse!'

The little devil-man at his elbow with his brother's voice kept reading out loud the sins he had committed that were all written down in scarlet letters on the black pages of the big black book, and when he read out the more grievous ones the crowd outside the bars clapped and cheered, whistled and catcalled, and threw bits of stones and other things in at him, but when they hit him he didn't feel a thing except always the biting, bitter cold locking his joints together stiffly. Other glowing little devil-figures appeared out of the flames and began to dance around him like red Indians doing a war dance, thrusting their burning spears at him and shouting out the names of his sins with increasing fury and momentum.

How many times did you listen at night to the sounds from the bedroom of your parents?

How many times did you lie on the bed and do it to yourself?

How many times did you look up the girls' clothes while they swung around on the lamp post or played hopscotch?

How many times, how many times, how many times . . .

He grew dizzy and tried to shut his eyes, but he couldn't; his eyelids wouldn't go down but stayed open, as if they were held up by matchsticks or pins. The devils were dancing around him, their bodies writhing grotesquely, their private parts hanging and swaying lasciviously and hideously, swollen outrageously and tipped with bright scarlet and orange. Then he looked down, and saw a great glowing hole opening up below him, the opened doors of a furnace with burning coals heaped inside and little devils leaping over them in a mad game of leap frog.

Welcome, brother! they called out to him, rushing up to him, their faces split with wide gangrenous grins. Come and play with us! He had a terrible raging thirst on him. His lips became parched and cracked like leather when he tried to ask for a drink of water, but nobody knew what he was saying. They began dragging him towards the furnace by his arms and legs and hair, and he tried to scream for help, but he only made grunting noises and they all laughed at him and asked him to make more funny noises, and prodded him with their spears, though he felt nothing, not even the heat of the furnace as he was dragged closer and closer to its great flaming mouth. And suddenly the demons became the lads he knew and played with on the streets – Charley, Andy, Tommy, Specky-Four-Eyes, all the boys he knew, who pushed him around in the boxcar. He cried out in relief, sure that they would recognize him and help him to get out of this awful place. But they didn't seem to know him and went on jabbering and jeering and jabbing him with their spears, spitting at him like cats, all the while dragging him nearer to the waiting furnace. Be sorry for your sins! they kept chanting. Say you're sorry now and you'll be saved.

No more peeping up skirts!

No more soft silent sinning on the bed with yourself!

No more listening in the night as your poor parents strive to bring children into the world!

He was so close to the furnace now that he could see the glowing walls shimmering with heat, and the terrible ice-jacket into which he seemed caked began to crack ominously, and he began at last to feel the intense heat. He wished fiercely to be sorry; he wanted to, but the awful thing, the worst thing of all, was that he wasn't sorry. He just wasn't sorry . . .

It was all just blackness and there were no fires. He felt as if he was nowhere. He wondered if being dead was really so awful. He wondered about it and shivered.

He heard the floorboards creak and wished morning would come.

11

THE HOUSES stood like squat, disgruntled cocker spaniels along the snow-mantled streets, wearing thick woollen snow-white shawls puckered by the black-ribbed line of gutters running along the sides of the rooftops, the serrated slates showing thinly in thawing patches. Where the main traffic ran a long mushy path of dirty-brown slush had been churned up; kids were already making slides down the road, using for toboggans frames of prams long outgrown by the babies who had used them, the lids off ashbins and sheets of tin uprooted from backyard railings. At first the snow had fallen in heavy, slanting veils, obscuring everything between ground and sky, mounting thickly on pavements and the golden-privet hedges of the little square front gardens, blocking the front paths until the men had to come out with jackets buttoned up to the neck and heavy Russian boots to shovel a passage through the encrusted snow for their womenfolk to get to and from the shops; then slowly it had thinned out and rare bits of sky broke the uniform dullness of the wintry scene, and a weak sun appeared, as timid and weak as a convalescent after a long time in bed.

From the window of the back-bedroom backyards lay spread out like a checkerboard, cut up into black-circled squares heaped with snow; mongrels prowled for food, moving like dark asterisks on the frozen earth, noses to the ground, snarling and snapping viciously at each other, bony with hunger; the cats walked with a more dignified gait, sliding gently under hedges and bushes, whiskers quivering like antennae, lean backs arched sinuously over bins and buckets of waste pigfeed, crouching under trees, almost hidden, merging with the shadows, ecstatic and intent with watchfulness, until at last a foolhardy but famished little sparrow would hop down from a branch in a forlorn search for nourishment; there would be a dark exultant streak through the air, and maybe a thin squawk of terror and agony from the doomed bird, then silence again as the cat loped away with its mangled prey between its teeth to devour it in the safety of a bush or outshed.

Up on the broad bleak wastes of the tiphead stretching away to the horizon, a snow-covered desert broken by ugly black warts where it had started to thaw, the noise of the traffic in the streets below was dulled and filtered, blanketed by the thick presence of snow that hung heavy in the air before it began to fall. Like rabbits the lads burrowed down into the snug huts and billets they had dug out and built underground, going down as far as ten feet or more; rough, hewn-out steps led down into the cellars, and the entrances above were camouflaged with planks of timber or corrugated metal spread over with earth and bales of straw swiped off the carts of the gypsies and tinkers. Deep down the earthen walls were firm and solid; the main 'room' would be cut in a rectangular shape, big enough to hold half a dozen grown boys, the floor covered with old rags and coats, and branching off this might be two or more adjacent corridors, so low-roofed that they could only be entered belly-flat.

It was freezing up on the hill, where they had parked him. They never let him go underground with them. He sat in the boxcar just above the slope, and could see all over the snowy wastes to the ivy-dappled walls of the church. He grew colder and more impatient; they had vaulted over into the church grounds to get fallen branches, but had not reappeared yet; it would be dark soon, and at home the kitchen fire would be bright and Mother would be baking griddle cake and the delicious smell from the scullery would make his belly roar and rumble with the hunger. He wanted to be there now, instead of sitting crouched in the boxcar in this bitter weather with chattering teeth and bare knees puce with cold. The church bell rang out for the angelus, the echoes lingering in the laden air after each stroke reminding him of ripples in a pond slowly widening and fading away.

A figure was moving across the white fields; it was a man wearing a red beret and rubber boots that reached above the knee. He stood underneath the row of elm trees close to the church wall, smoking; the little red tip of his cigarette glowed in the dusk, like a bright holly berry; he held his hands in his trouser pockets, moving them up and down against his thighs; he kept shifting his weight from one foot to the other. He seemed to be waiting for someone; he would smoke for a while, then step out and look swiftly in both directions; suddenly another figure appeared, coming towards him over a hill; a girl in a yellow mackintosh.

He caught her hands and drew her underneath the trees, throwing away his cigarette with an impatient fling. It fell like a tiny meteor, flaring briefly in the wind. They stood close together, his hand moving up and down her back like a black shadow on a wall. He bent her backwards, curving her like a bridge, until he slipped, lost balance and toppled over and lay on her, their bodies forming a black trembling line in the snow. When at last they got up and moved away, he watched as they merged into the shadow of the trees, still seeing the man's red beret and her yellow coat.

He thought about what he had seen as he lay between his brothers that night; it was his secret, and he would not tell anyone. And next day when they went back to their camp he waited for the others to be busy below ground, then pushed himself carefully down the slope and over the fields in the boxcar, pushing his heels against the ground until he reached the spot where they had lain; the shape of their bodies was still imprinted in the hardened snow, the dull yellow patch of the man's cigarette where it had melted; he nudged it with his foot and the soggy paper flaked and fell apart, the wet brown strands of tobacco staining the snow. He thought of it red and glowing in the man's mouth in the dusk the evening before.

12

'MY GOD,' said Mother, whispering, holding the single thin sheet of the letter, her hand shaking a little; 'My God . . .' She wiped her eyes quickly on her apron, put the letter under the clock on the mantelpiece, and went back to peeling the potatoes for the evening meal.

It had been a few months since the terrible night Lil had left; she had thrown all her things into one small string bag, hugged Mother fiercely, then run out into the fog and rain. Mother had stood still in the middle of the room, not crying, not saying anything, just staring at the kitchen door through which her eldest child had just fled. Lil was barely twenty, slight and fragile like a Dresden doll, her hair dark and falling over her shoulders, her eyes the biggest part of her. She had gripped the handle of her bag convulsively, a garish streak of lipstick on her mouth, that queer little hat perched sideways on her head that made her look a bit like Marlene Dietrich. Anybody might easily have picked her up with one arm; her high heels had clacked as she ran down the front path, the side of her face gleaming for a moment in the falling lamplight outside, before the fog swallowed her up. Her absence had left a gap in the fabric of the household, a hole through which cold air swept, as if one of the walls were missing. Father had called her, in his milder moments, a little bloody spitfire, for though he dwarfed her, she stood up to him like Joan of Arc, offering herself as sacrifice when he got into one of his fist-flailing moods, mostly on Saturday nights when he came in well nourished and the slightest word or look would be sufficient to trigger him off just like a keg of dynamite with the fuse always smouldering.

'Where's that bloody little guttersnipe, missus?' he would ask Mother, who would make up some excuse. 'Where's that daughter of yours till this hour?' he would repeat, though it might only be eleven. 'Out fornicating with that corner boy! I'll break her two legs when she does come in!'

Lil, who would probably be just outside the gate with her boy, would hear Father's voice and hurry in, knowing he would vent his rage on Mother, and almost as soon as she entered the kitchen she would be greeted with a fist or a lifted boot, and soon her rouge and mascara would be mingled with tears and blood as she wilted under a cascade of senseless violence, not knowing why she was being beaten, knowing only the blows and curses and enraged bellowings raining down on her. She often missed Mass the next morning, and would make up some excuse for not seeing her boy, for no amount of cream or powder could quite conceal the bruises under the eyes.

When she ran away, they all expected her to come back soon; Father said: 'She'll come whining back when her belly gets empty!' and went on reading the newspaper, but when she did not return he began going back and forward furtively to the window, pulling aside the curtain and peering out; he did this little performance night after night, and though he walked up and down in his shirtsleeves muttering furiously 'that bloody bitch!' there was a thick arrow of worry between his bushy brows and he began looking over at Mother with an almost scared expression on his face, as if mutely asking her for comfort and assurance, though he could barely bring himself to look at her or meet her eyes.

He came in that cold evening from work and sat down at the fire, spreading his gravelled hands out towards the heat, the sick look still on his face.

'The bombs are falling on London,' Mother said, lifting up his dinner and placing it on the red-checkered kitchen table. 'It was on the news today.'

'Aren't they falling all over Europe, sure?' answered Father impatiently. 'There's a war on, you know.'

'That's where she is,' said Mother, taking out the envelope and smoothing it out on the table. 'That's where Lil is. I got word from her this morning.'

'What do I want to read it for?' said Father, first looking at the envelope hungrily, then thrusting it away. 'If she's living in that haunt for hoors and hoormasters she deserves to be bombed! Hitler's doing a service to humanity by blowing it to bits!'

'And what about our daughter?' asked Mother quietly, laying her hands on the table and looking at him.

'*Your* daughter, ma'am,' replied Father, biting savagely into a fat sausage. 'Your bloody daughter! No daughter of mine would go and live in that Godless pagan place, where all they think about is one thing, and it isn't the price of bread.'

'You drove her to it,' said Mother in a tired voice, brushing back the greying hair from her forehead. 'You drove her away.'

Father stared, convulsed. 'Oh – so *I'm* to blame for that, am I?' he asked in an outraged tone. 'So I'm to blame for the natural badness and sinfulness that's in her, for the way you brought her up as you brought them all up – pampered and mollycoddled and never lifting a finger to them—'

'You make up for that.'

Father threw down his fork. 'Well, amn't I their bloody Father?' he said, trumpeting like a wounded elephant. 'Somebody has to beat the fear of God into the little buggers, and if you won't then it's my God-given duty to do it! Do you want me to give them rose leaves to wipe their arses with, or what?'

'What about Lil? All them bombs falling . . .'

'To hell with her!' Father said in disgust, getting up. 'You've spoiled my appetite.'

After that nobody ever mentioned Lil out loud before Father; instead they would gather in whispers and wonder where she was and if she would ever come back except maybe in a wooden box, with all those black-swastika planes flying in a thick locust cloud over that city, dropping their terrible bombs, the red-flamed dust rising, the splintered human bodies underneath all the burning rubble, the mangled and dying moaning and crying out for a priest,

69

maybe, the whole sky looking like some mad artist had thrown a huge pot of red paint at it. Poor little Lil, they thought with a sort of ecstatic fear, crushed beneath tons and tons of falling stone and timber, her queer little pancake hat down over one eye and her red-taloned fingers clutching the cheap cross and chain around her throat . . . Then, months later, came her second letter, and Mother had been so thrilled to see the familiar handwriting she had torn the envelope apart, then gone all pale and silent as she stared at the brief scrawl inside. When Father came in from work that night she placed the envelope beside his plate.

'What's this?' asked Father, jovial for once, pulling out a chair and sitting down. 'A love letter – or another solicitor's letter from some curse-of-God Jewman?'

'It's from Lil,' said Mother.

'The dead arose and appeared to many!' said Father. 'Take it away.'

'You'd better read it, mister,' said Mother.

'Why – she's not killed, is she?' Father said with a grin, munching. 'I suppose Mister Hitler told his best pilots – get her, or else!'

'She's married.'

The forkful of cabbage, halfway to its destination, was frozen in mid-air; slowly the fingers that held it slackened and it spilled over with a clatter on to the table as Father stared at Mother, his face almost comic with shock and disbelief; the same lively vein, like a barometer recording his moods, began jerking once more in his temple.

'She's . . . she's what?' he said faintly.

'She's married.'

He sat still on the chair, nothing about him moving except that furious vein; a sort of curtain had come dropping down over his eyes, over his whole face; a yellow-tipped stub of a pencil stuck up out of the top pocket of his cement-grey overalls; his hard-as-nails hands on his knees were limp and relaxed, the fingers strong and square-shaped; his neck seemed suddenly very thin and scrawny, wrinkled and creased like brown paper. A fly buzzed overhead and flew

70

against the electric bulb; it seemed somehow to break the numbed silence around the table. Father got up slowly, moving like someone with arthritis, and went to the window, mechanically pulling aside the curtain and looking out into the darkness; his hand tightened on the curtain, then dropped.

'She had to get married, didn't she?' he said, his voice strangely calm and detached, not really asking a question but speaking to himself, turning back. 'I always knew she'd end up like that,' he said as Mother sat speechless, looking helplessly at him. 'All that paint and lipstick – that devil's camouflage – all that shit on her face—'

'Mister,' said Mother when he paused; 'it wasn't like that at all—'

'I knew it,' Father went on, not heeding her, slowly pacing up and down, hands clasped behind his back. 'That's why she scarpered to that kip – a registry-office job – couldn't face a priest . . .' He seemed to become aware of Mother all of a sudden, and swung round, half stooping down, thrusting his face close to hers, almost spitting at her. 'She's your daughter all right . . . oh, without a doubt she's a daughter of yours . . . couldn't keep her legs shut!'

'God forgive you,' whispered Mother.

'And you – and you, Goddamn you!' roared Father, lashing out and striking her a glancing blow on the side of the head, dazing her as the children began to whimper. 'You and your hoor of a daughter! Married now are yeh! Seven-and-six for a licence and you're married over there, free to fornicate with any cat, dog or divil! She's gone up the Swanee now for sure . . . I'll find her, and drown her like a sick mangey cat – her and that hoormaster she's living with!'

'They're married lawful!' Mother gasped, gathering the children around her, hushing them. 'She's a good girl, a decent girl—'

'She'll bring in no bastard under my roof!' Father shouted. 'Decent – and she letting that creeping Judas have his way with her up some dirty smelly alleyway!'

71

'It's your own bad rotten mind!' said Mother, facing him now, her face flushed and eyes flashing. 'Kill me if you like, but I won't let you say that about any child of mine, not while there's a drop of blood left in me body!'

'Go to her then!' he bellowed, throwing another punch at her. 'Go to your little prostitute! She won't darken my door while I'm alive!'

He threw himself into his topcoat and planked on his hat, then he emptied Mother's handbag out upon the table, scattering its contents, scooping up whatever money he could find, and swept out like a tornado, banging the hall door so hard that a pane of glass cracked in the window.

A bare minute or two later two young men came in, wearing the green uniform of the Irish army. Mother stared up at them from over the shambles of the table, and blessed herself.

The soldiers were Jem and Tony.

'We had to join up, Ma,' said Tony, twisting his peaked green soldier's cap nervously in his hands. 'It was our duty as men—'

'Men!' said Mother.

'The freedom of small nations, Ma,' chorused Jem, sticking out his chest, rubbing his brass buttons with the cuff of his jacket. 'Poor little Belgium and all—'

'That was the *other* war, you bloody fool!' hissed Tony out of the corner of his mouth, jabbing an elbow into Jem's ribs.

'Then who are we fighting for now?' Jem wanted to know.

'Ourselves,' whispered Tony when Mother turned to one of the crying babies. 'Did you get a gander at what's in the quartermaster's stores?'

Tony strutted in his splendour, tall and lean-hipped, as if hewn from solid teak; it was difficult to believe he was not quite sixteen, and had bluffed his way into the army, using the name of an elder cousin, all of which came eventually to light after many agonizing months had passed as they played at being defenders of their country, mostly inside the

72

'glasshouse'. Jem looked as green around the gills as his uniform, a bit sickly, as if he had swallowed a bottle of medicine mistaking it for wine; he looked like a bloated drummer boy, a character out of a school pantomime a little overdressed for the part; he kept looking down and feeling his uniform, as if trying to think how he had ever got into it; it clung to him like the skin of an over-stuffed sausage, moulding his corpulent thighs and behind in a way that was painful even to look at, and which probably explained all the anguished puffing and blowing and redness of cheeks that accompanied almost his every movement.

'Sit down or you'll burst,' ordered Mother when she had grasped the situation and recovered from the shock. 'God, you'd look grand on a Christmas tree.'

With her two brand-new soldier-sons seated at the table and declaring war on the spuds and steaming bacon ribs, Tony at ease and looking every inch a budding Eisenhower, but Jem with his tunic wide open and his blistered feet reposing in a basinful of warm water under the table, looking like a rather debauched Bonaparte, Mother stood over them and surveyed them both critically.

'I don't know what your Da is going to say,' she told them. 'He will have a fit.'

'Ah, he was a soldier himself once, Ma,' said Tony with a grandiose wave of a picked-clean rib bone. 'He'll cry and be terrible proud of us when we get killed—'

Jem's sick look turned sicker. 'Shut up!' he mumbled morosely, his eyes wandering with mournful longing to the calendar on the wall opposite that showed a peaceful home scene with a large sleepy dog sprawled out on the hearth and a little grey-haired old lady knitting by the cheerful fireside in an armchair. 'Ma!' said Jem impulsively, turning to her with moist eyes; 'Ma! – the stirabout they give us in the mornings does be freezing cold!'

'Serves you right!' Mother said, heaping more spuds on to his plate. 'You can't join the sodality, never mind the army!'

They did not want to face the withering eye of Father

just yet, and tried to get out of the house before he came in from work, but he was early home that day, and just stood looking at them, one eye half closed, scrutinizing them.

'Mick Collins would turn in his grave,' said Father, walking around the two green figures who stood rigidly to attention. 'And is this the army of today? We'd might as well all commit suicide, for if you heard a shot you'd shit green!'

One night when they came in Tony told Mother that they did not have to report back for duty at the barracks, so they all bunked at home, three of them this time, for they had brought their friend Mutser, a big skulking under-aged giant of dense black looks, who was an orphan and living with his married sister and her twelve kids, so Mother took pity on him and fixed him up. When several nights went by and they still showed no sign of returning to barracks, Father got suspicious and said he would kick them all the way back, but Mother persuaded him to accept Tony's word that there was a temporary lull in the war overseas and the government were easing up a bit on the defence forces at home, allowing them more freedom. They never ventured out until after dark, and if they went out in the daytime they wore their 'civvies'; Tony insisted this was standard behaviour for soldiers in wartime, for there were spies everywhere, and the less they knew about how many men were in the army the better for the country.

The three very-much-at-ease soldiers were playing gin-rummy around the table one evening when there was the screeching of brakes and slamming of doors outside, then heavy boots coming up the path. Mother was going to the front door when Tony stopped her with a finger to his lips for silence, then dropped to his hands and knees and crept over to the window, peering out through a chink in the curtains.

'It's them!' he whispered hoarsely.

'Jesus Christ – they'll shoot us on the spot!' said Jem, diving under the table.

'Holy Virgin – who is it?' asked Mother, frightened.

'They won't take me alive!' muttered Mutser dourly,

74

wielding the poker. 'Right, lads – all for one and one for all—'

'Shut your bloody gob, you!' snarled Jem in a tearful rage from under the table. 'I'm no bloody musketeer! We're not on the pictures!'

There was a loud tattoo on the hall door. Tony slid like a shadow out into the hall and up the unlighted staircase.

'Take over, Ma!' he whispered, beckoning for the others to follow. 'You haven't seen a bit of us for weeks . . .'

When they had safely vanished into the gloom of the upper landing, in their stockinged feet, Mother opened the door calmly. Three soldiers stood there, the vivid red badges gleaming on their caps.

'Military police, ma'am,' announced the sergeant, stepping forward. 'I believe you have two sons in the Emergency Forces—'

Mother swayed against the door and clutched her bosom. 'They're not after being killed on me, sir, are they?' she gasped.

'Killed, is it?' said the sergeant gruffly. 'Sure we haven't moved out of Portobello barracks yet.'

'I warned them, sir,' cried Mother, her voice breaking. 'I warned them not to join up – only green lads themselves they were, sir, barely out of the Christian Brothers . . .'

'Bring the poor woman into the kitchen,' ordered the sergeant. 'Give her a sup of water before she faints on us.'

They took her solicitously by the arm and led her to a chair, filling a tumbler of water and making her sip it.

'There's a divil a bit wrong with them, ma'am,' the sergeant told her. 'Fact is, ma'am, the young gets have scarpered – did a bunk—' he coughed and cleared his throat. 'Deserted, ma'am. That's a serious thing to do ma'am, with our backs to the wall, like, and we not knowing the day or the hour when we'll be invaded. It's not playing the game, ma'am.'

Mother turned up her wide-open eyes at him. 'There must be some mistake sir,' she said, drawing herself up. 'I never reared a turncoat!'

'I'm not saying that, ma'am,' explained the bull-necked sergeant hastily, giving Mother odd questioning looks, as if trying to remember where he had seen her before. 'Sure they're only wild boys, most of them, with no better notion of being soldiers than they have of being altar boys. But I must search the house, ma'am,' he sighed regretfully. 'Orders is orders.'

'Oh, search away by all means,' said Mother calmly, 'but you'll find nothing but babies' nappies!'

The sergeant was about to signal his men to begin the search when he saw a large old-fashioned framed photograph on the dresser; he went over to have a closer look, then laughed and pushed the cap back on his head.

'Wonders will never cease!' he exclaimed, hands on hips, grinning. 'D'you not know me, Bridie?' he asked, using Mother's pet name.

She looked startled and stared hard at him. 'It's not—?' she said, 'it couldn't be—?'

'The Bull McCormack!' roared the sergeant, slapping his revolver holster. 'I was with himself during The Troubles!' he said, nodding down at the wedding photograph. 'You were only a slip of a girl then, and begob, you haven't changed a bit!' He kept pumping Mother's hand up and down, his little pudgy piglike eyes merry with surprise.

'Ah, g'wan with you!' said Mother, giving him her deadliest smile, suffering his bruising handshake. 'You and himself were great pals. Wait till I tell him you were here—'

'I was in Boland's Mills afterwards, you know,' said The Bull with pride. 'Aye, with the Chief himself, bedad, and all the boys, and I stopped a bit of Black-and-Tan lead, too!' he went on, drawing up the leg of his uniform and displaying a scarred indented shin. 'A British bullet was stuck in that leg for months, but it would take more than that to finish off men like meself and himself, eh Bridie?' said The Bull, swelling out, preening like a peacock on parade.

'Will we be making the search now, sir?' asked one of his men tentatively, looking at the clock.

'Search?' roared The Bull indignantly. 'Who said anything about a search?'

'But I thought, sir—'

'This lady is a friend of mine,' said The Bull, flexing his muscles and towering over his subordinate. 'Her husband and meself were comrades in a *real* war, and you wouldn't be doubting the word of a lady, would you now, O'Toole?'

'Oh, indeed I wouldn't, sir,' stammered O'Toole, smiling wanly. 'Any friend of yours, sir—'

'Then shut up and keep your place!' The Bull commanded, shifting his loaded holster more firmly into position.

'I've the kettle on,' said Mother.

'Ah, them were great days, Bridie!' The Bull reminisced afterwards as they sat at the table drinking mugs of hot tea, Mother hovering discreetly between them and the kitchen door, for the stairs had started to creak alarmingly. 'Great stirring days, to be sure, for we had soldiers then that would make you look like simpletons let out for the day,' he said, turning to his two subordinates with a sneer. 'You never knew when you were going to get it – in the back or the belly. Do you remember Gansey Finnegan?' he asked, turning back to Mother, his corrugated face moist and misty with scalding tea and vainglorious memories.

'Is it the fella with the patch over his eye, you mean,' asked Mother, 'that always called after the factory girls?'

'The very man! Poor oul Gansey – d'you remember what the girls used to call him?' asked The Bull, licking his lips with relish as he waited for Mother to answer.

'I – I can't recall,' said Mother unwillingly, her face telling him that she remembered quite well. 'After all them years—'

The Bull laughed and slapped his thigh again. 'Emptyfork!' he said between gulps of inward laughter, his face going purple. 'That's what they used to call him – poor oul Empty-fork! D'you know is he alive or dead?'

'He's married, with a houseful.'

The Bull whipped around furiously as his two mates

77

started to titter. 'What the hell are yous sniggering for like two oul wans?' he demanded.

'Ah, don't be hard on the poor men,' Mother interceded. 'They're just enjoying our chat.'

The Bull grunted, but soon got back into good humour when one of the kids crept between his knees and showed a fascinated interest in the black shiny revolver the sergeant had strapped to his hip; this delighted The Bull so much that he scooped the youngster up and took out the gun, saying that the kid was every bar of its Da.

'That's a real dangerous thing to be throwing around,' said Mother, standing near the kitchen door now and hearing stealthy noises in the hall.

'Safe as a house, Bridie,' said The Bull heartily, waving it aloft. 'Sure the safety catch is on—'

At that moment there was a sharp banging noise that sounded shattering in the small room; chairs were over-turned as the soldiers jumped to their feet, then the kitchen door was flung wide and in ran Jem with his hands lifted high over his head and his eyes wild with fear as Tony and Mutser tried desperately to pull him with them out through the open hall door.

'Ah Jasus, mister, don't shoot me Mother!' screamed Jem, falling down on his knees. 'Take me back to the clink, but don't shoot me Mother,' he cried as everyone stood around stupefied.

The three of them were rounded up and escorted out to the waiting van; The Bull said he would do his best to get them off easy for old time's sake, but they could look forward to a good long rest in the 'glasshouse' anyway.

'But what caused that terrible bang?' Mother managed to ask the bucolic sergeant before the van moved off.

The Bull suddenly started laughing. 'A bit of coal in the fire!' he said, shouting back at her. 'Me gun wasn't loaded...'

13

'WELL, ME DARLING MATT,' said Red Magso looking up at her newly dead husband's framed picture over the dresser, the full naggin bottle of whiskey in her large rough hand; 'you won't be troubling me tonight, for it's the worms you'll be having for company . . .'

There was no hint of grief in the new widow's voice, only a grim astonishment that after over thirty years of marriage she was now suddenly free, that all the bruising, battering, black-and-blue days were over and she could from now on come home from those furtive visits to the women's snug down the street without having to suck liquorice allsorts to kill the whiskey smell.

'Still and all,' sighed old Essie, pulling her faded snuff-scented skirt down over her skeleton knees, 'he made a lovely corpse.'

'He'll get more peace where he is,' commented the widow, 'than ever I got while he was in it. I even tried sleeping in separate beds, but he said only Protestants did that.'

'It's a suit of armour you'd want in bed, sure,' said Essie, 'and it's them that had the tin opener to let the draught in. How did you manage at all, Bid, and you with an army of them?' old Essie asked, turning to Mother.

'Sure what's the use of joining the army if you don't soldier?' Mother countered. 'Wouldn't you like a bit of something, Magso?' Mother suggested as the widow un-screwed the cork of the bottle. 'You mustn't take that stuff on an empty stomach.'

'There's a few ribs in the pot,' said Red Magso, taking a hearty swig, her roaring-red face getting more inflamed as she gulped down the whiskey. 'Bejasus, girls, there'll be no holding me from now on!'

'Sure isn't it a bit late in the day for you, Magso?' said

old Essie, enviously eyeing the naggin bottle.

Red Magso got redder, her red-lashed beady blue eyes blazed. 'Amn't I in me prime, woman?' she said, slapping herself on the chest, thrusting out her large bosom that swelled out in the blouse like the full-blown sails of a schooner. 'Take a look at *them*!' she cried proudly; 'you won't buy the like of *them* in Woolworth's!'

Old Essie placidly patted her own shrunken frontage. 'Sure they only get you into trouble, woman dear,' she said, shaking her head. 'Showing them off to a man is like waving a red cloth at a bull. The more bones you show the better.'

'Men is brutes, d'you know that?' said Red Magso, taking out her false teeth and wrapping them in a hankie. 'All men is bloody brutes.'

'You never said a truer word, Magso,' old Essie agreed, following with her eyes the erratic journey of the whiskey bottle to and from the puckered mouth of the widow.

'Show me the man that doesn't want his bit,' said Red Magso, wavering in her chair, 'and I'd go down on me knees and kiss his feet.'

'Except the clergy, of course,' said Essie piously.

'Oh, be all means except the holy clergy,' said Magso with a loud hiccup. 'I'm a Catholic meself, though a poor one.' Then she turned and asked, as if just suddenly realizing what Essie had said: 'Of course you mean the Catholic clergy, don't you?'

'Sure what other clergy is there?' asked Essie, squinting her eyes and measuring the contents of the bottle in the other's hand.

'Well, there's the Protestants,' answered Magso with another moist swig, bringing her hand across her mouth; 'God love them.'

'But they're not *priests*!' said old Essie, a bit scandalized.

'There's some as good and better than priests,' said Red Magso, wiping the mouth of the bottle with her palm. 'And they don't make as many bones about extending the blessed hand of charity as some of our own fellas!'

'I don't like arguing about religion,' said Mother, appearing from the pantry with a plate of steaming rib bones, 'for it's a sure sign of bad luck.'

'You'll spill the bloody stuff!' cried old Essie in alarm, unable to contain herself any longer as the widow nearly let the bottle slip in trying to guide it in the general direction of her mouth.

'I was wondering why you were looking at me so hard!' said Magso, proffering the bottle grudgingly.

'Ah, that would warm a corpse, so it would!' chortled old Essie, smacking her lips after a longish sip; 'Meaning no disrespect to the poor man that's gone,' she added conscientiously.

'Bejasus, you nearly forgot to stop!' Red Magso said in an aggrieved tone, holding up the bottle for inspection. 'I thought you said you didn't like whiskey?'

'I don't – it takes me breath away—'

'Then it doesn't take it away far enough,' said Magso, putting the cork back and shoving the bottle inside her blouse. 'It's safe now anyway, between the two best suckers in Dublin.'

'All the same,' pursued old Essie, bold with whiskey but annoyed that it had been put out of sight, 'I never took charity from a Protestant minister, not on me poorest day.'

'And who took any charity from any so-so minister, will you tell me?' cried Magso. 'I'm no bloody swaddler!'

'Essie didn't mean it that way, Magso,' said Mother, handing around more ribs. 'Sure aren't we all Christians?'

'Some people will take alms from any cat, dog or divil,' Essie said, two little spots of fire appearing surprisingly in her own pallid cheeks. 'Not a morsel of pride have they!'

'Well,' said Red Magso, sitting straight up in her chair and again fixing her eyes upon the picture of her dearly departed spouse; 'you can say what you like about the man we buried today – and he was an oul bastard in his time – *but*,' she went on, nodding her head emphatically, '*but* – he never let the nuns feed his wife and family!'

'Sure the poor sisters are only there to help us all,' said Mother, 'doing God's work—'

'Aye – but they're not there to feed them that won't

81

work!' Magso said, slapping her knee vigorously.

'My man was never a day idle in his life,' cried Essie, 'till he caught pneumonia out in the rain working at half-pay for the priests!'

'Work, she calls it!' echoed Magso, making the sign of the cross. 'Work, God bless the mark! Sitting on his arse all night long before a roaring fire in a hut minding oul oil drums on the road! Oh Matt me darling!' Red Magso cried up at the picture, 'you that did more work in bed than that frostbitten oul crow next door ever did in a month of Sundays!'

'God's curse on you, you red-headed oul hoor!' Essie yelled, jumping up. 'You that was sucked out of the Vincent de Paul!'

'Remember the poor soul that's gone to heaven today,' said Mother, stepping between them.

'I give her a seat in the front car – the *front* car, mind you!' said Magso, her great bosom heaving; 'I pour the drink into her, and she turns around and insults me in me own house, and me still in me widow's weeds!' Red Magso suddenly began to cry, her face like a big moist red balloon. 'Oh Matt me fine man!' she sobbed, fishing out her hankie and blowing her nose in it, not bothering to remove her false teeth still wrapped in it. 'Why were you taken so quick? You was full of fire that night making me feel young again, and in the morning there you lay beside me with your eyes and mouth open and you as cold as yesterday's mutton!'

'Isn't that the lustful oul bitch for you!' old Essie said in disgust. 'Sure it's a wonder the poor man wasn't in his grave long ago with trying to please the likes of her!'

'Ah, didn't you feel soft like that yourself once?' Mother said, reproving old Essie and trying to get the sobbing widow to sit down in the armchair.

'I remember me wedding night as if it was yesterday,' said Essie, pushing back her long grey coils of hair. 'And it's something I won't forget, for what with the heat off him, and the weight of him, and the smell of stale porter that came from him, I was happy when the sun was coming up!'

'And he took it with him and all,' Red Magso was wailing up at the picture, her rage now overcoming her sorrow. 'He took it with him and all!'

'You didn't expect him to leave it behind, did you now?' leered old Essie.

'You oul bastard!' raged Red Magso in a very red rage, shaking her doubled fist up at her framed spouse. 'You took even that with you! You took the only bit of comfort left to me!'

'He took what with him, ma'am,' inquired Mother, much puzzled.

'What d'you think?' panted Magso. 'What d'you think? His bloody army pension!'

'Bejasus, I was wondering what she was whining after!' said old Essie. 'I'm glad to see you're yourself again anyway, Magso. Let's drink to that.'

'I will, with a heart and a half, Essie jewel and darling,' said Magso, her tears suddenly drying up as she felt inside her blouse for the bottle; 'if I can find the bloody bastarding bottle!' The bottle had slipped further down inside her blouse and was now firmly lodged somewhere in her corset; they began prodding and probing all over with their hands, and the widow started to shake and waddle as if doing a somewhat frenzied tango, but all her gyrations were to no avail, so there was nothing to do but peel off the black mourning dress and unstring her bone stays. As she stood in the middle of the room in her slip, her heavy breasts overhanging the bony ridges of her corset, the bottle fell to the floor; then – a car pulled up outside and on looking out old Essie suddenly shrieked and exclaimed:

'It's the Jewman!'

Before they could get Red Magso back into her dress, there was a loud knock on the hall door; as usual, the money-lender turned the key, gave a gentle little tap on the kitchen door, and walked in.

'Well, Missus Reilly,' he said jovially, a little fat oily man with kid gloves and a fur-collared overcoat, clapping his hands together; 'I'm a bit late today—'

83

He stopped as if struck by lightning, for the massive widow was standing there only in her slip, her huge muscular legs planted squarely apart and her face screwed up in fake lascivious complacency; without saying a word she started doing a jig around the table, clasping her hands to the tune of 'Napper Tandy'.

'Well, me sowl Isaac,' sang Magso, waddling her voluminous behind at him as she jigged around the table, lifting the slip up over her fat dimpled knees; 'I have you where I want you now . . . assault and battery, indecent advances, insulting behaviour, attempted rape . . . you won't show your nose again here in a hurry!'

'Please, Missus Reilly,' quavered the moneylender, backing towards the door as Red Magso jinxed up to him, 'please, my good woman – we will forget the small sum you owe me – we will forget everything – no, please ma'am – you are not yourself – I understand quite – but please – I am a happily married man – I am a gentleman and I know you are a lady – look, here is a little something for yourself – there is my good name – Missus Reilly I protest . . .'

Then Magso started to scream: 'You dirty oul disgust! Take your hands off me! Trying to take advantage of a poor widow and me only after burying me good man! Neighbours, neighbours!' The moneylender fled stumbling down the front steps with Magso at the hall door yelling furiously and throwing clumps of dirt after him from her front garden; as doors opened along the street and housewives rushed out instantly on the side of the bereaved widow and loomed ominously towards the all-too-familiar car, the moneylender scrambled panic-stricken into the driver's seat and just got off in time as the horde of outraged and over-charged customers yelled maledictions and banged on the windows as the car gathered speed and shot away. Though nobody for a moment believed Red Magso's lurid story, they all declared she was a very brave woman.

'D'you think it was right to do that to the poor man?' Mother asked, when the commotion had died down and they had got Red Magso back into her clothes again. 'He was as pale as a sheet.'

'Don't be soft!' snorted Magso, puffing as she settled back into her stays and patted her breasts back into position. 'That oul bee would rob his own mother.'

'All the same, girls,' said old Essie with a wary glance up at the large picture of the Sacred Heart on the wall facing, 'I think it's time we said a little prayer.'

'I've a pain in me jaw praying all morning,' said Magso querulously, taking up the retrieved whiskey bottle. 'I've done my bounden duty by him, now the oul demon will just have to take whatever's coming to him.'

They soothed her into joining them in a decade of the Rosary, sitting at the table like people at a seance, with closed eyes and clasped hands, but in the middle of the fifth Ave the sonorous Magso suddenly broke into 'Just a Song at Twilight' and after a brief uncertainty old Essie joined in, the tears once more starting to stream as the widow gazed soulfully up at the faded roaring-twenties photogravure of her dead husband complete with dickie-bow, hard collar and stiff brushed-back hair; until the remembrance of all she had endured from him again swept back and overwhelmed her.

'Why am I crying over you?' she screamed, jumping up, saliva running down her chin. 'You persecuted me while you was in it and took me youth away!'

She swiped up her false teeth where they lay on the table, and flung them at the picture; there was a crash of glass as they hit the picture, knocking it sideways.

'Crooked in death as he was in life!' Red Magso shouted up at the wrecked picture swinging haphazardly on its nail.

She slumped down at the table and went on singing with her head in her hands as the other two women crept out to get their husbands' dinner ready.

14

FATHER WAS leaning crookedly against the table in his smart weekend suit, trilby pushed back cockily on his head and shoes shiny and tip-tapping, drinking bottles of dark brown stout from the open porter parcels on the table, humming an old-time music hall G. H. Elliot number about wanting to go to Idaho, when suddenly the couple stood there in the doorway.

'This is me husband, Da,' said Lil.

Silence as the mythical charms of Idaho faded from Father's lips and the quick-rising froth of the stout bubbled and flowed over the mouth of the rigidly held bottle; somebody switched off the radio; the thick blond eyebrows jutted out in a terrible forked omen of thunder.

'A bloody registry office!' breathed Father at last.

'This is me husband, Da,' said Lil again, clutching her small bundle of lace tightly in her arms, against her breast.

Father put down the bottle, the white brown-tinted froth running over his gnarled knuckles. 'You went and disgraced me!' he said, speaking in an aggrieved monotone, not in anger as much as hurt incredulity. 'You went and disgraced me – you that I tried to bring up decent – that I tried to beat decency into with me heart, boot and fist – you went and settled for a registry office – no better than a Protestant!'

'This is me husband, Da—' Lil, next door to tears, small and slight, beside her tall young man, nervously, defiantly putting her arm through his, holding her lamb-white-lace bundle desperately in the crook of her other arm, against her candy-striped blouse, unsteady in her high-heels. Silence.

'Sit down, man, for Christ's sake!' roared Father, kicking a chair across the room with a gesture of impatient disgust.

Joe sat down abruptly, obeying the command, and just as

quickly getting up again and finding a chair for Lil; she sat down tiredly but with care, huddling the soft lace parcel next to her.

'What's that you're carrying, girl?' asked Father with sudden, absurd suspicion, as if only seeing it then.

'Me son, Da.'

Father did not move for a few moments but methodically pulled another two bottles of stout, carefully this time so that they did not fizz; then as though he was going to the window to look out, he sauntered over and stooped down, peering at the prune-puckered comical face of the sleeping infant; as if not knowing what his right hand was doing he touched its cheek gently, as if afraid he might hurt it, for a moment that nobody dared to interrupt or wanted to end, his face was full of a rare delight, a sorely-puzzled wonder, a craggy-browed, lip-thrusting fascination as he viewed his first grandchild, cocking his head from side to side, looking at it from different angles, almost, incredibly, crooning to it, his lips quivering with the effort *not* to croon to it, the pale anaemic blue eyes so often leaping fire now mysteriously mystified and gentle; then with a sudden jerking back of his head he got his old face back again and darted the same livid-blue glance at the John-Henry wartime-suited young man.

'Yours?' asked Father.

'*Ours*,' Lil interjected quickly with pride and hurt.

'D'you want a belt in the gob, you?' growled Father. 'I asked *him*,' he said, craning his head around sideways, glowering at the new son-in-law. 'Is this your work?'

'I wouldn't be here if it wasn't, would I?' said Joe quietly, blowing the froth off the top of his bottle.

Lil drew in her breath sharply on a note of fear, glancing at the two men, from one to the other, her husband calmly sipping his drink, Father glowering furiously, fingers grasping the bottle as if he was going to let it fly at the studiously indifferent head of his son-in-law; then suddenly he grinned and drank, planting one buttock on the edge of the table.

'You've a bit of spunk anyway, bejasus!' he said with a

87

wipe of his frothy lips. 'What's your trade?'

'Carpenter,' said Joe.

'And what's the screw?'

'Seven notes a week.'

'It'd hardly be a day, man,' said Father sourly. 'That's only can-boy money! You'll never raise a shower of kids on that!'

'We'll try,' said Joe easily, 'and we won't trouble anyone for a penny.'

'Bejasus then you'd better not!' Father said. 'You needn't come whining here for your grubstakes. There'll be no hunger-sliding as long as I'm head of this house.'

Joe moved his chair closer to Lil's and put his arm around her shoulders. 'I married her,' he said, 'and I'll keep her without anyone's charity.'

'That's what you say now, Gunga Din,' said Father. 'You're bloody Darby-and-Joan now, me bucko, thinking the sun shines out of her, but wait till you've a gang of snotty-nosed, shitty-arsed crying little demons around you and see who'll be talking like Valentino then!'

'Da!' said Lil suddenly, looking around the kitchen with a swift onrush of panic. 'Where's me ma?'

'She's not dead or anything,' Father said, finishing off his bottle and groping in the bag for another. 'She's lying with her usual complaint.'

Lil stared, her gentle swaying, rocking motion stilled. 'You mean? . . .'

'Where the hell d'you think she is?' queried Father querulously. 'She's upstairs having her last!'

'Mother of God!' gasped Lil, depositing her infant into Joe's lap and flying upstairs, still in her coat and hat, calling out 'Ma, Ma! over and over, one of her shoes falling off in her haste and rattling down the stairs.

'The shakings of the bag,' said Father with a heavy sigh of jovial resignation, draining his bottle. 'The shakings of the bag. Put your little mistake on the sofa there and come down and I'll buy you a pint. We've something to celebrate, man!' he said, lifting his hat. 'I've ended me days of service

88

to me country, and you've just begun! Come down and I'll cheer you up . . .'

15

A SEA-LAPPING fringe of voices, faces, feet merging and mingling, waves breaking on a broken shore; faces revolving, flushed, serious, simpering; mouths opening and shutting, gobbling, guzzling, leering, swearing, singing, shouting, bawling, calling, emitting animal noises of weeping and laughing all under the single stark electric bulb in the jam-packed, sardine-tight, rollicking midnight house; men sitting jammed up tight against women, haunch touching, hip touching, calloused fingers hard on exposed silky knees; a mongrel dog nosing its way in between the erratic dancers on the floor, its tongue lolling out like a piece of red-raw liver, licking up the remains of slaughtered sandwiches; an idiot boy between his merry mother's knees reciting obscene versions of nursery rhymes to the roaring men around him who slammed pennies into his palm; a fat woman of many chins stabbing her little man to death with her eyes as he talked to a big-breasted blonde in a corner, his speaking hands hovering temptingly over the feminine promontory; Father's stringy windpipe jerking up and down as he swallowed beer in long, deep, educated gulps, standing guard over the emptying crates of stout, guarding them from the avaricious hands that reached unendingly out, like the antennae of an octopus sucking everything towards its huge black hole of a mouth; a girl of no wit bending down to retrieve her severed necklace, screaming 'Jesus!' as some eagle-eyed man swooped and twanged her suspender belt against her leg; someone laced the idiot boy's lemonade with whiskey and he ran in and out barking and howling and frightening the dog itself, his eyes wild, his weak mouth drenched with spit. Somebody started to play the spoons.

People coming in with brown parcels of beer.

'And where's herself, Paddy?'

'O still upstairs, the stitches not out yet, but that's the daughter who did such a fine job on the first grandchild.'

The faded flowered wallpaper steaming and dripping and the floor a churning mess of bashed-in bread and beer; the air popping with corks, brown foam spilling over squat green necks of bottles, knuckly wrists twisting deftly with cork-screws, bottles held rigid between knees; smooth-skinned girls with sleeves of sweaters pushed up to elbows, sitting in whispering little clusters, discussing the free antics of men and the older women, splashing gin into their minerals quickly as the quavering singers sang, the erratic dancers danced, and the waves broke and crashed louder and louder.

> 'She lifted her petticoat over her knee
> And I saw all she wanted me to see.'

'None of that in a Catholic household!' roared Father, plunging his face in a tumbler of stout.

'Just for the time that's in it—'

'Somebody give us "She Is Far From the Land"—'

'And she can't swim a stroke.'

'I knew you'd come out with that, Barney. Your one and only joke.'

'What about "The Fennals of Our Land"?'

'Well, what about them?'

'A fine song, a fine patriotic ballad—'

'So is "The Ould Woman Who Lived in a Shoe".'

'Sure that's not even Irish.'

'Well bejasus, if she had all them children she was Irish enough.'

People bending over the newborn member of the new generation in the carrier cot in the corner by the fireplace, watched over by Lil the child-mother, smiling, polite, unmoving.

90

'A Brown if ever there was one.'

'Not at all – look at its nose—'

Father hearing this with his odd occasional adroitness of hearing even in the midst and melee of animated talking, jerking his head sideways, eyes piercing under scraggy brows.

'What the hell is wrong with its nose?'

'O not a thing, man dear, except that it's not a Brown nose.'

'I say it's a Brown nose, and if you say any different you're going to have a bloody red one, you oul bastard!'

'It's definitely a Brown, Da,' Lil intercepting the anger clouds tactfully, imploring with her eloquent eyes her husband to say the same, who grins and takes the eye-bulging, hair-raising new father-in-law nice and easily by the elbow.

'Any fool could see he's a Brown all over,' says Joe the deft diplomat, observing thoughtfully and with pride, 'with definite overtones of Doyle, be it said.'

'Sing up once more and drink a toast
To comrades far and near.'

Red Magso coming in, newly and happily deprived of life-long spouse, grimly enjoying her widowhood, on the arm of her eldest daughter, black-veiled crimson face, walking with all suitable slowness of recent bereavement, greeted and seated effusively on special armchair close to the cot of the newly arrived, speaking in slow subdued cemetery tones, accepting the instant whiskey wanly, sipping it, to the surprise of the neighbours present who expected her to gulp it, holding her glass in a high, prominent, dainty-handed way to show she has barely touched it, the thin, anaemic, already dying daughter kneeling at the stout black-stockinged maternal knee, already fingering the black beads hanging from the matchstick neck and saying 'Mommy' instead of the usual shrill 'Ma'.

And suddenly there she was by the door in a green jumper and plaid pleated skirt, her hair caught up high on top of her head, leaving the white nape of her neck bare, laughing with a soldier, his brothers' mate; her neck swam up from the ruckered woollen polo-necked jumper curving gracefully and he remembered one burning summer day on the hot grass banks of the canal watching a swan flowing in and out among the green filigree, lifting its long drooping white neck and its black demon little eyes, watching him with frightening intensity, making him tremble strangely with the first fear of all beautiful and unknown things in the world. Her bold green gaze caught him now, swept over him coolly as a breeze, the corners of her mouth curling a little upwards in slight far-off recognition, the thrust of her breasts under the taut green wool causing a tight, painful feeling in his throat, the quick flashing movements of her long nylon-sheathed legs setting up a pounding and a drumming in his blood as she danced with her immense soldier, whose great rough hand lay on the small of her back as he held her in the dance and she laughed, shaking her hips freely against him, her red-nailed hands caressing the rough khaki of his tunic. He looked miserably down at his thin bare knees and the pain and hate that was in him then screamed out for utterance; but he only smiled bitterly to himself and at himself and looked on intently at nothing.

'That one will come to no good,' a heavy-breasted woman said shaking her head, her brass earrings rattling. 'Mark my words. She'll end up on the guinea side of the Green, selling it to them bloody foreign fellas that do come in on the ships from Egypt and Liverpool.'

'Her poor mother was a lovely person,' said a neighbour with terrific sorrow, nursing her dwindling glass of stout. 'She always wore lovely white blouses and her hair in a bun and never troubled a soul. O a lovely woman, and that bloody little teasy-whacker over there destroying her mother's memory!'

'The shame of it.'

'Will you look at the allegations of her! Giving them all ideas. And she's only fifteen!'

'She'll have a litter of them by the time she's twenty.'

Two well-married men close by not taking their eyes off

the spinning girl now enjoying alone the cleared centre of
the kitchen, keeping time to the frenzied playing of an
accordion in a tango that lifted her skirt and loosened all
the brown effulgence of her hair sweeping wild about her
flushed ecstatic face.

'Would you, Mick?'

'Would a cat drink milk?' said Mick, heavy-lidded stare
unyielding, feeling for his bottle of stout. 'Like a knife
through butter.'

'For the love of Jesus I'm drownded!' bawled the earring-
rattling woman as the knocked-over stout spilled over her
blouse and skirt from the mesmerized fingers of Mick of the
myopic stare.

'Terrible sorry, ma'am,' said Mick jumping forward,
sweeping out handkerchief and dabbing at the huge stout-
stained mountain of bosom. 'Me eyesight's not too good.'

'But you're feeling's all right,' screamed the woman
pushing him of. 'Take your hands off me, you lustful oul
demon!'

'I was only trying—'

'I know bloody well you were trying! D'you think I was
born yesterday?'

'Well ma'am, to be honest, I'd say be the looks of you it's
a good many yesterdays since you were born.'

The enormous breasts rose, furiously blotting out the light
and the great shoulders swung as a pudding-sized fist flew
and landed on Mick's craggy chin and he keeled over into
the midst of screaming, laughing women who prodded and
poked at him as he lay on the floor slipping and sliding as he
tried to regain his feet.

'You're no man to insult a poor defenceless woman like
that!' panted the injured neighbour, knotting her fists as she
stood over the writhing Mick. 'Get up till I bandjax the
living daylight out of you!'

'The dirty oul vomit!' yelled a younger married woman,
neatly digging the fumbling man in the ribs with her high-
heel as he scrambled on all fours near her chair. 'Trying to
look up me clothes and me three months gone!'

'Sweet bleeding heart of Jesus!' moaned Mick, blood streaming into his eyes from a gash over his forehead.

'It's cruel hard for a poor widow woman to enjoy herself with a few kind neighbours and the body of her man still lukewarm in his grave,' spoke Red Magso dreamily as if to herself, her many-ringed hand patting the head of her kneeling daughter. 'You never miss the water till the well runs dry. Dry,' Red Magso repeated, looking around for her bottle, finding it empty, and reaching over and taking up the half-full whiskey bottle that stood on the dresser. She drank steadily, head thrown back, red-skinned throat working; she wiped her mouth with her wrist, then looked solemnly at the frightened face of her daughter who crouched at her knee. 'Would you ever go and get a man for yourself?' she suddenly shouted at the girl, pushing her away with a shove of her knee. 'You're like a bloody sticking plaster. I can't fart without you. Here's a shilling – g'wan down to the pictures – you're the spit of your oul Da, never leaving me be for one sacred second!'

'Ah, Ma!' wailed Noreen, her thin nose quivering.

'Get out of me sight for Jasus' sake child and let me enjoy meself for five minutes! O Matt me darling man!' said Red Magso addressing the ceiling with outspread arms, still holding the whiskey bottle. 'I hope you're with God in heaven tonight, but I know in me heart it's down in the quare place you are with a red-hot poker up your arse and you screaming for mercy and finding none!'

'That's a shocking thing to say about your husband,' said a woman with rouged cheeks and some gold-plated teeth in front.

'Whose bloody husband was he, yours or mine, Madame Starr?' asked Red Magso with rising rebellion. 'Did you have to have it every night for forty-odd years whether you wanted it or not till you couldn't call your body your own? Did you have to put up being called hoor and brasser and fornicator as he put child after child into you till you never knew what your own feet looked like with your belly always like that?' making a sweeping gesture with her hands in front of herself, her face glowing like a red lamp, the pins tumbling out of her hair, the flesh on her arms shaking as she shook them. 'Did you ever get it at all, you made-up oul bitch?' Red Magso thrust her face up close to the woman, as if challenging her to confirm or deny; the woman drew back hurriedly, tripped over out-thrust feet, and fell into a man's lap, who laughed and held her with both arms around her waist as she tried with not too much haste to get up. 'Maybe you'll get it tonight, Dolores,' Red Magso roared with great seismic heaves of deep inward mirth, putting the bottle to her lips again.

'For Ireland is Ireland thro' joy and thro' tears;
hope never dies thro' the long weary years.'

Father battled through and pulled Mick into the pantry to bathe his face, away from the bevy of belligerent women who cursed and shouted and giggled at the alleged attack upon their virtue and contentedly went back to their drinks and pigs' feet and gossip as the accordion player toiled bravely on, half forgotten in a corner, a pale young man with a blue silk scarf tied around his neck and fawn-coloured bootees over which peeped violent scarlet socks.

Through a chink in the heavy flowered curtains swam the yellow lamplight outside, falling on the hair of the girl sitting with the soldier and the thunder and lightning of memory crashed down on him now and the old terrible unnameable agony that was yet delight gripped him as from his lonely perch he dared look and see again the white soft sheen of her upper leg where it parted from her black silk stocking under the cruelly careless upflung skirt as she straddled languidly on the straight-backed kitchen chair, head thrown back against the shoulder of her soldier, her throat buttercup smooth softly swelling, her eyes half-veiled under the thick matted lashes; and his heart tumbling from its long womb-like sleep and lashed with whips of pain, told him that she was gone away from him into ways he could not follow, and nowhere in all that bewildering night and

95

morning was there peace for him; only a terrible newness and nakedness.

'Meehawl!' someone was shouting for the most popular singer in the house. 'C'mon out of that, Meehawl you oul bastard, and give us a few bars!'

'Best of order now for the singer!'

'The best of singers come from the north side of the Liffey. Me granny always said that.'

'Then your granny must've been a permanent resident up in the Gorman,' someone else countered, jumping up and waving his glass. 'The South Side forever, me boys!'

'Where the hell is Meehawl?' Father shouted, and ran and captured the bellicose balladeer from between two women and yanked him forward by the frayed cuff of the much-travelled coat he was wearing, so variegated with wrinkles and creases that it was obvious the coat also served as the man's blanket at night. He rubbed a black-nailed hand over his blade-neglected chin with a coarse rustle of sand-paper and coughed.

'Me throat is not in the best of singing order, Paddy,' he said, caressing the shiny elbow of his coat with his palm. 'It's a bit rusty on account of me practising to be a Trappist monk. I made that promise to me poor mother and she on her death bed.'

Father retrieved the almost murdered bottle of whiskey from the huge limp hand of Red Magso as she momentarily dozed in her chair, and thrust it into the quick fist of Meehawl. 'Clear your gullet with that, man, and get on with it,' said Father, shouting a harsh 'Silence!' that brought a gradual hush over the buzzing room. Meehawl finished off the remains of the whiskey bottle, opening his eyes very wide as he drank, as if not quite believing that it was real whiskey he was consuming instead of the usual odious beverage concocted in back alleys and outsheds which his belly had come to accept as second nature. Meehawl was always a gentleman to the last and respectfully touched the peak of his non-existent hat to all the company.

'Would I be hurting the feelings of anyone present be

singing a patriotic ballad?' inquired Meehawl gravely.

Father quietly picked up an empty stout bottle and waited; there came not a murmur of dissent; Meehawl at once began to sing in a voice that was ragged and torn in places but which carried an echo of former sweetness undimmed by raucous Liffey winds or the seeping chill of tenement hallways cat-haunted at dead end of night:

'Farewell to friends of Dublin Town,
I bid ye all adieu,
I cannot yet appoint the day
when I'll return to you,
I write these lines on board a ship
where the stormy billows roar
May Heaven bless our Fenian men
till I return once more.

I joined the Fenian Brotherhood
in the year of Sixty-Four
resolved to free my native land
or perish on the shore.
My friends and me we did agree
our native land to save
and raise the flag of freedom
o'er the head of Emmet's grave.

My curse attend the English spies
who did our cause betray;
I'd throw a rope around their necks
and drown them in the bay.
There was Nagle, Massey, Corydon
and Talbot – he makes four,
like demons in their thirst for gold
they're cursed forevermore.

I laid my plans and drilled my men
in dear old Skibereen
and hoped one day to meet the foe

'neath Ireland's flag of green.
I robbed no man, I spilt no blood
Yet they sent me off to jail,
because I was O'Donovan Rossa
the son of Granuaile!'

Silence; then an eruption of handclapping, feet-stomping, bottles banged on wood, cries of 'Encore! Encore!' as Meehawl all meekness stood under the light, his global face shining with sweat, grasping in both hands and putting under his arms the bottles ·⸍ ..ut t⸍ at came sweeping towards him from hands that thum·⸍ed his shoulder and squeezed his arm and suffering ⸍·cilely the huge moist kisses that descended on him from mothering women whose tears mingled with his sweat as they recognized in him the prodigal son they might have had, the ubiquitous underdog, the worm that turned, the berated beggarman roaming the streets with flapping uppers and bleeding feet singing for his supper with the wind in his hair and the rain in his eyes, leaning over the slimy parapet looking down at his own black shadow in the serpentine river at sunset.

The smell of turf and beer and human sweat was strong in his nostrils even as he lay between the blankets on the great straw mattress upstairs in the back room, dumped there unceremoniously on the hot shoulder of Father without a whiff of warning, but far from asleep, the mercifulness of oblivion which would still for now the turmoil that was in him. His brothers were absent; he had the enormous acres of the mattress all to himself and to his own lonely imaginings. The room became a black box enclosing him on all sides; the noise of the people downstairs rang up through the floorboards beneath him, drilling monotonously into him, needles through his flesh. Faintly above it he heard the wail of his new baby brother or it might have been that of his first baby nephew, a tiny sound of protest lost in all the crashing of music and crushing of feet and the hailstone noises of voices, the hammer popping of corks; everything surged and swept over him, everything known and new, bat-

tering upon him with silence more furious than the downstairs din; and all he had ever known was nothing but an
echo in a shell and only the stars seemed near. Again the
sensation of being held down by chains oppressed him; the
blankets felt as heavy as iron, pinning down his trembling
awakening limbs, keeping him *there*, forever *there*, mute and
immobile, choking the rising voices within him, numbing the
rising stream of knowledge within him which was warming
him now with a new and unknown and wonderful heat; tears
stung his eyes and with a thrust of defiance and despair he
flung off the nightclothes and tumbled out upon the cold
bare boards.

He lay there for long moments, lying on his back, not
feeling the cold, ravishing the stars with insatiable eyes; he
heard nothing but his own heart loud with confusion,
saw nothing but the jewellery spread out and shining in the
black inscrutable sky burning in at him through the square
window panes; and he breathed deep, glad that nobody
was near him and he near nobody.

He crawled out upon the top landing, smelling the musty
oilcloth under him. Someone stirred down in the dark
depths of the hall; he edged precariously upon the upper-
most stair and looked down; light from the street lamp
outside the narrow space of the little squat hallway, making
her hair gleam from under the broad khaki shoulder of the
young soldier leaning upon her, and in a sudden lull of
clamour from the kitchen he heard their rapid breathing
and bated whispering exchanges; the catlike hiss of satin.

'You're terrible heavy, aren't you?' Her hushed, amused
voice. The accordion played again, the voices rang and sang,
the peevish whimpering of a baby somewhere; he crawled
back, blind and naked, into the darkness of his room, into
the great disordered bed, under the cold blankets; and he
heard in some far-off place within himself the clashing of
one gate closing and the painful slow screech of another
being opened.

But nobody could know, and the harsh party voices from
below went on and on until he heard them no more.

16

LYING ALONE in the dismal winter mornings under the
rough blankets and coats after his brothers had gone downstairs to breakfast and away up the bitter windy street to
school, he would get once more the heavy under-the-blankets
animal-human smell lingering, lingering from the night before
and the queer dead-of-night furtive fumblings and stifled
moans and groans of one of his brothers whispering some
day-long-known girl's name, unknowing of him who lay
sleepless and quickly alive to pain in his own wrinkled corner
of the vast floor mattress. More and more often now the same
contortions would precede the dawning juices and secretions
that splashed forth from his own body on the rim of some
fabulous and erotic vision in warm jerked-out gushes
mingled with horrific shame and defiant delight, lacerating
his wavering, quavering new-from-the-depths senses with
bold knifestrokes of pleasure, the exultant fierce leap into
estranged ecstasy, the volcanic shuddering in all parts of
him, the bewildered breathless animal noises emitted in a
swift timeless suspension of thought. Then the gradual
sinking back, the long drop down the chill cheerless stair of
inexorable returning reality, the deadly familiar proportions,
shapes and outlines of the room, the green distemper on the
walls penknife-pricked with his brothers' names, the huge
Sacred Heart over the bed, Christ the all-suffering beggarman with blood-oozing palms outspread in that terrible
gesture of mild-mannered meekness, the first faint fatal seeds
of guilt making the secret victory of a moment ago a hot
shame burning within and withering all sense of pleasure.

His own body became at this time a new and never known
landscape to him and avidly he explored, soaking up its
smells and scenes and sensations, surprised or perplexed or
disgusted constantly by what he discovered; the gradual

100

presence of hair on his lower parts caused him quick fright and alarm so that he wanted to hide this curious body-grass from even his own eyes; yet as his sister one day combed before the mirror and under her raised arms he saw the fine dark under-hair a peculiar throb of pleasure gripped and held him, and it seemed cruel and barbaric when later she shaved her armpits with Father's safety blade, leaving the soft under-arm skin raw and pitted with tiny dark ugly pin pricks where the soft dark sweat-limp hair had been.

He thought with almost affectionate pity of the doomed denizens of his own body, the valiant vermin spawned from his own sweat and dirt moving with infinite dignity and languor under his clothes, of the lumbering lice in his head creeping always in a dark jungle, each blade of hair looming before them like trunks of trees, threatened by the scythe stroke of scissors and cruel steel-toothed combs and murderous probing death-crushing fingernails at bathtime every Saturday night, fatal fellow-dwellers of his flesh.

The vast cloudless blue sky of smokeless summer days terrified him, as did everything of absolute petrified purity, a sky like the face of an idiot scrubbed clean and empty of all wit, anger, tenderness, desire, the pathetic human distortions and disfigurements that alone comforted and captivated him; a sky with nothing in it glaring down in pitiless abundance of power, dense and dead and pure, and the sun in that sky gleaming in the centre like the huge inflamed orifice of some unimagined monster; and summer was not always lovely. It opened up festering wounds and weeping sores in the earth, brought evil smells from decaying food in narrow dark-shadowed streets, made the grass wither and turn bilious yellow and the flowers to wilt, ravished of moisture or scent, on roadside hedges like powder puffs caked with dried powder, like biscuits in shop windows with little mounds of lard-like cream jellied and beleaguered by flies. Once returning from the canal they had come upon a cat dead on the road; somebody got a stick and turned it over gingerly and its ancient wrinkled face grinned and grimaced up at them; its belly was flat where the motorcar wheel had gone over it and a few drops of blood were caked and hard on the rubbery skin; it had already begun to smell; the apples and pears in the orchard behind the high wall on the other side of the road glowed in green shadow.

At night, poised in the in-between land of dream and wakefulness bordered but unclouded by sleep, he could look down to where he had left himself lying upon the great gaunt mattress, and be filled with baffled pity and rage for this lucid nakedness, the dark brown matted hair upon the pillow, the high-flung cheekbones in the skull-like face intent and brooding, inscrutably absent, implacably walled by the intense, absurd, aloof indwelling that dropped sheer as any cliff between himself and the awakening terrors of the touchable world; with curious contortion of heart he saw the hollowed cheeks, the thin pale gauze of closed eyelid tinged with a bluish penumbra, pulsing minutely, the sleep-sweat around the rigid mouth and in the hollow of the jaw, the keen hawk-like arrogance of the features forever rapt on some perfect peak only he could see in that red-bramble land all soft and grey and fine and exquisite as dust and a cold blue splendour of moonlight everywhere and the nets of his wonder gathering dreams from nowhere.

After rain the broad road in front of the house would glisten and mirror the clouds scudding across the pale green evening sky like dark battalions of weirdly shaped horses; the concrete widths were no longer dull, but shone strange and misty like a lake, capturing the leaning shadows of houses looming on the far side of the street, the cars and buses and people passing on bicycles, broken into blurred fantastic images grotesque, unreal, without form, yet more real to him watching from the kitchen window than the houses, the vehicles, the people themselves. Shadows spoke more lucidly to his mind than the substance that caused them. He discerned a life and mystery, a uniqueness in them that he searched for but could never find in the bland open and forever closed faces of people and things. A world at once unknown but vastly knowable welled up to him out of reflected surfaces and textures, alive with magic shapes in which moved mysteries and meanings without a name, yet known to him immemorially, through the alchemy of thought, sense and dream forever returning and receding upon the fringes of his mind with the soft slap of surf lipping a fragile shore, a shell-deep echo of intimate gentle voices vouchsafing him peace and visitations of beauty in his islanded world. His far and fabulous angel would come, not with trumpets triumphant and tumultuous wings, but gently and with a gradual joy; aside and within, he listened for that presence.

The large, loose, knuckle-jointed, work-roughened hands of his father lying for a rare moment passive on dungareed knees or lap filled him with terror and yet a strange burning unnameable longing; he imagined those hands alert and agile with the bricklayer's trowel and chisel, flashing in the weak mocking winter sunshine on scaffolding high above the city, piling brick upon brick with brisk brave strokes, the sinewy wrist moving subtly, magically moulding a patchwork pyramid of cemented rectangles to enclose the lives, loves, labours, passions, despairs of innumerable strangers; those master craftsman's hands turning deserts of empty spaces into jungles of human dwellings, offices, stores, theatres, churches, schools, hospitals, fun palaces, the desperate disarray or organized chaos and convoluted canyons where men and women worked, made love, bore children, longed for heights and strange lands and slowly ceased to dream through a myriad profusion of cement-dry days and nights punctuated by traffic screams and the wail of ships' sirens from the foggy river and feeling again with the far-off shrill of a train in the dark morning the loneliness of being on earth. The broad hands of his father had acted in the making of that immense outer wilderness of brick and block and solemn stone, and they were thus both ugly and beautiful in his eyes and eloquent and noble when, as often, they bled from the bitter winter frost, and ugly beyond endurance when they thundered upon the flesh of his mother and flayed her bestially. In dreams his father's hands floated eerily, mostly menacing and monstrous and falling upon him like

103

flattened sheets of iron, but in rare instances stroking him too with marvellous gentleness and a tremulous strength.

Once, when he had seen his father touch his mother's hair almost timidly, a throb of joy and absurd ecstatic hope filled him; the moment burnt bright and perfect, full of a wild sweetness as when sometimes he fervently lost himself in prayer, the moment dropping into his mind like a first spring blossom; then almost instantly it was gone, broken, washed away on the harsh returning wave of his father's voice demanding his supper. Nothing of peace or charm lasted longer than it took his beating heart to feel it, and he was back once more in the walled garden of his thoughts, chasing the shadows of such moments, listening always rapt and intent for the wings of his ambiguous angel, the touch of felicitous fingers upon his brow that turned always and abruptly to a vicious cheek-stinging slap dashing the tears from his eyes.

Awkward as any animal, and more immensely mute, he was learning to grow and live without being blinded by the stars.

17

'SEAN – you blondey bastard – keep out while I poss out the floor! You have me heart broke . . .'

Mother floundered on her knees, her stout rosy arms rippling bare to the shoulder and the swell of her large pendulum bosom swinging heavily in the ravelled print blouse, deep-clefted at the buttonless top. Flaming with exertion and exasperation, hair all about her face, she raged at the fair-headed sapling of her terrorist son repeatedly running in from the famished front garden mucky-heeled and mad-eyed, to desecrate with splay-footed clay-caked soles the shiny soap-smooth surface of the faded flower-corrugated linoleum she was washing, dipping the thick coarse floorcloth in the basinful of murky water at her side. The no-colour little mongrel dog that the boys had adopted as their mascot and miniature dinosaur yapped and sniffled fastidiously at the dirty basinful of water, yelping back on its scrawny hunkers as the floorcloth came to clout it and Sean called its name from the garden. It slipped and slithered across the wet floor furiously wagging its abbreviated tail and barking in thwarted joy, imprinting paw marks all over the gleaming oilcloth.

'Mother of God, amn't I scourged?' panted Mother, starting on another patch of floor, dragging the basin after her. 'One four-legged pup in here and a two-legged one out there! Sean!' she yelled anew as the dog jumped out through the open front window. 'Sean, you snub-nosed cross-grained bugger – wait till I lay my hands on you . . .'

'Why – what did I do?' a strong cheerful voice inquired as the kitchen door was opened gently and a fair-haired young man stood on the threshold, grinning.

Mother looked up, her face a flaming globe. 'Oh, Father!' she gasped, scrambling to her feet, wiping her hands on her checkered apron. 'I didn't know it was yourself, and me swearing like a heathen – that young Sean—'

Later, on that sullen, still-not-warm Sunday afternoon, Father returned from a trade union meeting in town, trilby at a dangerous angle on the sandy head, bitterly berating his eldest sons for not attending. 'Let me down, they did, the ungrateful lousy bastards, before the whole hall,' he would rave, throwing his arms in the air, taking fierce imaginary swipes, shadow boxing with his own private fury. 'Every man-jack of them sitting there proud as punch with their sons, while mine were gallivanting the city drinking and hoor-hunting – after all I did for them – getting them union cards – putting them into good jobs before they were done shitting yellow – giving them everything – and they turn around and make a laughing stock of me before the whole society . . . It's your rearing, woman!' he finished illogically, and fuming he sat and stared with mad fanatical eyes, with a certain absurd comic unbelief, at the steaming cabbage and potatoes, biting his lip furiously, the pale blue eyes wild and flashing on some inner unseen object of hatred. 'Sweet suffering bollacks!' he burst out with resigned ferocity as if bearing the ultimate humiliation: 'Jesus God – is that any kind of dinner to hand to a Christian? Answer me, woman!' he bawled as Mother stood by, waiting the inevitable blow, the meaningless rage, the murderous onslaught of unmotivated fury. And then suddenly Father stamped out, upstairs.

'Why don't you leave him, Ma?' It was Lil who asked the question, shame and anger in the arch of the beautiful dark level brows as pensively she brushed with her pursed lips the tiny downy head of her sleeping baby wrapped in its shining linen shawl, holding it as if the world might at any moment snatch it away from her arms. 'Why do you put up with it?'

'Take your tea, love, and stop talking nonsense,' Mother said as they all sat around the supper table, the cold-meat sandwiches piled high in the centre, the little cracked egg-cup full of soggy yellow mustard spilling over the sides.

'But, Ma—'

'That'll be all now,' came the parental command. 'You're a married woman now with enough of your own to think about. Just say a prayer for us, that's all.'

'God – if I thought that *you* would turn out to be—' the sudden swift fear starting out of the wide, heavy-lashed, blue believing eyes over the table at her calm-smiling meat-munching husband.

'Drink your tea, girl,' replied Joe, reaching across and taking a fleck of loose wool from her sleeve.

Shortly afterwards the clang of heavy boots up the path, green khaki figures walking through the doorway.

'Lord, forgive them, for they know not what they do,' solemnly intoned the younger of the soldier sons, shoving his fingers through the black serrated waves of his hair with a certain rigid ferocity. 'But I bet *he* knows – I just bet *he* knows damn bloody well!'

'Didn't Nancy look great today?' the eldest son hopefully put in. 'She's all grown up now—'

'You know what to do with your little Nancys,' said the younger brother, pushing back his chair with his knees. And rising, buckling his Sam Browne, he jerked his thumb up at the ceiling. 'It's him up there I want to get at right now – sleeping the sleep of the just!'

'There'll be no trouble in this house on this day of days,' said Mother, putting down the butter knife. 'This is a day of peace—'

'Oh my God, don't make me laugh!'

'He's your father—'

'Don't make me sick!' the rigid-boned fine young head flung back in derision and appeal. 'Give me a dose of Epsom Salts if you want to make me sick, Ma, but don't give me that!'

'Why weren't you at the union meeting today, both of you?' asked Mother. 'He was fuming over that—'

'We were on guard duty, Ma,' the elder son explained. 'We couldn't help it. We meant to go—'

'Oh, any excuse – any Goddamn excuse!' raged the younger boy, turning wild and earnest to her, pressing both clenched hands upon the table. 'We're not kids any longer, Ma. Look at your arms, for Christ's sake – black and blue! And for what?' he asked, lifting his arm and making a wide sweep of the room, eyes glittering. 'For *this* . . . for *us* . . . for having us, and rearing us, and bringing us up the best way you could!' He bent closer, lowering his voice to a trembling, intense whisper, knuckles hard on table. 'D'you know what, Ma? – He'll never forgive you for that!'

Mother, pale, thin-lipped, staring helplessly at this tall broad-backed young man so lately a son she could safely smother in her arms, now strong and implacable and strangely beyond her; quietly the tea was poured out; the wireless was turned up loud, a broadcast of a hurling game in some city stadium; a goal had just been scored and loud prolonged raucous applause crackled over the ether; ruthless tobacco-smudged fingers viciously twisted the knob; silence again; discreetly Lil went into the pantry to breast feed her baby.

There came the creaking of floorboards upstairs, the metallic racking cough of the habitual smoker; Mother started up in a fright. 'Go, in the name of God, son,' she said, picking up the soldier's fallen cap from the floor, settling it on the rebellious black head, straightening the green tunic collar. 'Go before he comes down – it'll only provoke him—'

'I'll provoke him all right if he as much as lays a finger on you again!'

'Will you be seeing Nancy tonight?' the stout older brother asked with all his old unkillable tremulous innocence, plonking his own green cap on and hurrying to the front door, holding it open, glancing anxiously up at the staircase as a door opened above.

'Oh – stuff Nancy!' came back the reply as with a resigned, infuriated, affectionate impatience the younger brother pulled the paunchy pacifist older brother after him. 'You big fat-arsed coward!'

Mother stood at the window, looking after them. 'I hope they're not taking to drink,' she said.

'They wouldn't have the guts, missus,' said Father, sobered up, coming in behind her and peering out with contemptuous screwed-up eyes, rubbing his hand across his scummed-up lips. 'All they can do is play tin soldiers. If they saw some real action like I did—'

Quietly, rubbing her hands in her apron, Mother went into the pantry.

'You can't go in there yet, Paddy,' said the son-in-law as Father made as if to follow her.

'Why the hell not? Who are you to tell me—'

'The chiseller's being fed.'

'Humph!' said Father, turning back and going over to the fire, standing with his back to it. 'There was never anything but bare tits and arses in this house for as long as I can remember.' Then with mercurial suddenness he brightened,

108

standing there in his tie-less collar wide-winged and open, silver studs sticking out of the holes, shirtsleeves rolled up over the thin wiry hairy forearms. 'And how's the second generation coming?' he asked jovially. 'Still stuck in that lousy dogbox on the Quays?'

'Houses are hard to get,' said Joe quietly, rubbing his hands slowly together. 'At least it's our own.'

'Why don't you get a decent job, man?' said Father, warming himself, throwing back his shoulders. 'I was talking to Frank Flaherty just today – he knows the president of your union well—'

'I want no favours,' said Joe, toying with some bread-crumbs on the table.

'And you'll bloody well get none,' said Father glaring, craggy teeth gnawing at his lower lip, stooping forward, bending his buttocks closer to the heat. 'You'll have to work like a cow's melt of a black at this job, but the money's there to be earned if you're not afraid to bend your back. Are you going to kick it back into my teeth like the rest of them?' he asked with quick bitter bile.

'Well,' said Joe, picking a loose piece of undigested meat from between his teeth, 'I'll try anything once.'

Father grinned and went in search of his coat. 'Bejasus, it's good to know someone has a morsel of pluck and grati-tude in them!' he said, finding his coat and throwing it on. 'D'you think you could handle a pint or would it interfere too much with your internal organs?'

'I'll try one,' said Joe, ignoring the lip-thrusting sarcasm and putting on his own coat.

'Then what in the name of Jasus are you waiting for?'

'They're gone,' said Mother, presently coming in from the pantry. 'He took Joe with him.'

'Joe needs no encouragement, Ma,' said Lil, putting her satisfied infant down into its cot with elaborate care. 'They're all men. Sit down and rest your bones, Ma. I'll clear up.' She started clearing the tea things off the table, going back and forth from kitchen to pantry, moving with a new authority, young and strong and purposeful at the beginning of her new life. 'Sure maybe they won't get drunk.'

'Aye – maybe,' said Mother, sinking tiredly into an armchair. 'And maybe if we pray hard enough it will rain half-crowns.' She closed her eyes and soon started to hum a song to herself.

> 'When shall the day break in Ireland?
> When shall our day-star arise? . . .'

18

A SOUND of brass brazen in the hot June air blaring across innumerable backyards. Red Magso lumbering to the open back window, thrusting through it her mottled perspiring face, the coarse moist mouth opening wide on a tremendous trumpet wail of infuriated protest drowning the unwieldy uncertain horn.

'Will yeh go and blow that thing up your bloody arse, yeh bastard!' she roared, her red throat swelling, shaking a clenched fist in baffled fury at the unseen, unknown trumpeter. 'It's crool,' she said, after shaking the languid afternoon with some more blatant blasphemies, rejoining the two other women in the kitchen. 'First thing in the morning he's at it, blowing that thing like Saint Gabriel himself, and the hot weather makes him go mad altogether.' She plonked down heavily in her sprawling shiny-leathered armchair by the wide-open window, loosening another button of her spotted flowery blouse, exposing more inches of her huge unbrassiered bosom, blowing with puckered lips falling wisps of scorched ginger hair away from her pale-lashed eyes. 'Jesus – this heat has me beat. And that bastard blowing his horn out there blasting me ear drums!'

'And you don't know who he is, you say?' spoke the new neighbour, a young plump pretty woman, dressed neatly, her long sleek coils of hair caught up in a bun on the smooth tanned nape of her neck.

'Sure if I knew that,' snorted the widow, opening another button, 'I'd give him a different kind of horn to think about.'

'If you open any more they'll be hanging out altogether!' cautioned Old Essie, winking at the young woman, who was trying hard to avert her startled gaze away from the unfolding white moon-breasts of the widow woman. 'Did you ever see such terrible big things in your life?' chortled Essie gustily, the gumless gap of her mouth creaking inwards with a garish grin. 'A shove from Magso's tits would send you spinning!'

'Men like their women to have fine outstanding fronts on them,' said Magso, looking placidly and with pride down at her nearly naked bosom bulging buoyantly out over her uncorseted belly. 'At least my poor Matt did, the light of heaven on him, for often he said a roll on my dollies was as good as the other thing, and he would play with them like they was toys or something and let on to bite them with his few remaining teeth.'

'A year gone tomorrow!' sighed Essie, pinching another flaky morsel of snuff up each thin nostril. She rubbed her bony transparent hands together upon her dull time-soiled skirt, which wafted forth to even the most insensitive nose a mixed aroma of ancient smells; onions, cabbage water, boot polish, quinine, whiskey, snuff the ever-present; an assault of odours strangely inoffensive, surrounding her like an aura of sanctity. 'Time flies. Here today, gone tomorrow. Will you be putting a memorial in the paper?'

'I suppose I'll have to do that, right enough,' said the widow with fretful reluctance. 'You'd have the price of a naggin or two with what it will cost.' She picked up the bottle from the floor and squinted at its diminishing contents, then drank from the neck, wiping her large hair-sprouting chin with the back of her hand. With increased reluctance she passed the bottle on to Old Essie, who leered

111

ludicrously at them and put it to her loose-hanging lips, opening her eyes wide open to heaven as she drank. 'Go aisy on that, for Jasus' sake!' Magso howled nervously, pulling the bottle away out of the old woman's grasping fingers. 'Yeh greedy oul cow!' she cried, aggrieved, inspecting the bottle once more up to the window. 'You'd drink piss if it was inside a bottle. For an oul one like yeh you've a swaller like a demon!' She looked half with hope, half with dread, at the young woman, not quite proffering the bottle, not quite withdrawing it.

'Oh, no thank you, Mrs Rattigan,' the woman said hastily, interpreting the unspoken inquiry. 'Sure I never once let it pass my lips. I took the pledge for life at my confirmation. So did Rory. That's my husband, you know,' she added proudly, smiling.

'Sure if I had a half-crown for every time I took the pledge, I'd be up to me eyeballs in money like a pig in shit,' Red Magso declared. She dragged herself up into a sitting position, peering out through a carefully contrived gap in the heavy curtain. 'There's them two strolling by like lovers,' she said as a couple passed on the other side of the narrow street hand in hand. 'Mister and Missus High-an'-Mighty with their heads in the air and their clothes in the pawn. They're not as young as they try to let on, yeh know. She's forty if she's a day, with that dyed head on her, and sure he puffs like a billygoat running for the bus in the mornings. Yeh can see straight into their front bedroom from mine, and maybe it's just me bad mind and may God forgive me if I'm wrong, but I think I saw them doing it once in the middle of the day, in full broad daylight, and they standing up too, the way animals do it.' She sank back in triumph, relishing her story.

The young woman went scarlet, but Old Essie nodded her grey head and gave a slow series of grunts of approval. 'I wouldn't put it past them two,' she said, spitting into her palms and rubbing them briskly together. 'One solitary baby after over twenty years of marriage. Sure that's not natural!' She looked slant-eyed at the young woman,

112

fawning and leering all at once. 'No offence, me pet,' the
old woman said, with a rise and fall of disavowing hands.
'I know you've none yourself—'

'No – not yet,' said the woman, then stopped, annoyed
at not having checked herself in time. 'I mean—'

'You mean you're that way at last?' the two other women
said almost together, leaning forward interestedly. 'When
did you find out? Is it starting to show yet? Did you tell
your fella?'

The woman held up her hands as if warding off a buzzing
horde of bees, laughing uncertainly. 'I don't know – I didn't
say – I'm not sure—' she spluttered. 'I only thought –
well, that I was feeling – funny, you know – longing for little
things, like . . .'

'You're up the pole, as sure as Christ,' said Magso,
satisfied. 'Don't I know the symptoms like the back of me
hand? When do you think it happened? What night now,
I mean?'

'I – I wouldn't know,' the woman said in a faltering
hushed voice, her eyes wide, fastened on the widow with
fascination. 'I'm really not certain of anything yet. It might
be just a – a false alarm . . .'

'I had about seven false alarms in me time,' said Magso,
crossing her meaty red-freckled arms together, 'and they
were all true. When I knew it was me time, I just lay down
on the bed and in next to no time it was there beside me
bawling like hell for the breast, its little face all puckered up
like a prune. Whatever you do,' she went on, wagging a
large sausage-like forefinger, 'have nothing to do with your
fella after the fourth or fifth month. It'll damage the poor
little bugger. Water on the brain. If he comes knocking on
the door slam it in his face. You'd want to wear iron drawers
for them, the lustful oul demons! D'you know what?' she
was warming to her theme, sitting more upright, the skirt
stretched taut across her gartered knees, showing glimpses of
pendulous thighs. 'D'you know what it is, child? I never
knew what it was like to wear knickers until me darling Matt
died. Isn't that the gospel truth, Essie, yeh grinning oul bitch?'

Old Essie bleary-eyed and reminiscent, nodding and clucking to herself in the chair. 'Ah, poor oul Matt, he wasn't the worst,' the old woman crooned with luxuriant sadness, skeleton fingers clasped tight over knife-sharp knees, rocking back and forth, eyes closed. 'He made a lovely corpse. So dawny-like that you could see through him, like a petal . . . There wasn't much of him in it at the end.'

'You didn't look under the habit did you?' asked the widow balefully. 'Well, I did, just before they nailed the lid down, and there it was, as large as life and twice as ugly, the same big brute of a thing that had crucified me all me life! Oh, dear God,' she cried on a fresh outburst of indignation, quivering as if shaken by internal waves of fury, 'it's crool what a poor woman has to put up with from the time a man first puts his hand between her thighs and starts talking about the stars! Sure I don't know the end of me comfort now, the whole bed to meself, acres and acres of it, and sleeping right through till morning, with ne'er a dig in the ribs to wake me or the dead weight of him on top of me poking me with his bony knees and calling me every name under the sun for not wanting it bad enough!'

'Oh, now, I don't know,' said Essie knowingly, shaking her head like a mandarin. 'I wouldn't be sitting back there like a queen bee drowning in honey, for you're not past doing it again, I tell yeh. I do see the way that oul fella from up the street looks in at you when he passes . . . Speak of the divil!'

'Who – him?' shrieked Magso, looking out of the window and scowling at a tall droop-shouldered elderly man who politely lifted his hat to her but hurried on when he saw her storm-wrecked face framed ominously in the window square like an angry red moon. 'Oul go-by-the-wall and tickle-the-bricks! Oul Empty-fork!' she yelled after him as he loped hastily away up the street. 'Wait now till I shake me tits after him!' she cried exuberantly, straining out of the window and fumbling at the one remaining button that barely held the blouse shut over her huge wobbling breasts.

Old Essie pulled her back with wiry tenacious strength

114

while the young woman looked on, stupefied in the chair, unable to move, as if mesmerized, her eyes wide and full of astonishment and slow dawning horror.

'Sit down, woman, and don't be making a holy show of yourself before the whole street!' said Essie vigorously, pushing her back into the creaking depths of the armchair. 'You know the way they talk—'

Magso shook her massive shoulders and felt for the bottle at her feet; she drank the last of the whiskey, some of the golden drops spilling out over her large luscious mouth and running in tiny rivulets down her arched protuberant throat. When she was finished she heaved the empty bottle out over the window sill into the front garden, running a large hand extravagantly through her wild red hair, unpinning it and letting it tumble over her shoulders as she sang in the style of the old-time music hall:

'Oh, it's not the fancy label on the jar that counts
but the tasty bit of jam inside.'

'Ah Matt, yeh oul fornicator!' she cried, maudlin now with drink, her voice lifting and falling with fierce bawdy tenderness under which lurked an insensate rage for the whole crude waste of her life. 'Yeh were a man to the last anyway, I'll say that much for yeh! Yeh toiled on to the bitter end doing your bit for your country which yeh could only do by doing me.

'How long are *you* married?' she suddenly asked the young woman aggressively, thrusting her glowing face up close to her.

'Three years, Mrs Rattigan,' the woman answered instantly, drawing back.

'Three years, and not a bulge in your belly yet!' roared the widow, flouncing back in the chair and slapping her thighs. 'What does he do with it – wrap it up in cotton wool?'

'Ah, the young wans of today are more well up than we were, Magso,' intoned Essie, pushing more snuff up each

115

nostril and sucking her breath in with sensuous pleasure. 'They do things . . .'

The woman now sat up, jolted into indignant denial. '*We* don't do such things, ma'am,' she said through primly tight lips. 'We were both brought up good Catholics. We pray to God for willpower . . .'

'And in the meantime the poor bastard has to make do with wet dreams?' said Magso. 'Or is it into your ear he puts it?'

The young woman stared, her face first flaming, then ebbing into paleness. She gathered her coat tightly about her, stepping elaborately between the sprawling legs of the two older women, as if afraid of being contaminated by contact with them. 'I can't stay and listen to such scandalous talk and this supposed to be a Catholic household,' she said in a low quiet controlled voice, looking over her shoulder at the large cracked picture of the Sacred Heart on the wall behind her. 'May God forgive you, Mrs Rattigan, and put you on the right path, for you're not really a bad person in your heart—'

'Me heart, is it?' shouted Red Magso, her face contorted. She ripped her blouse open, the last button flying across the room with the force of her wild fingers, and her mountainous breasts were bare, moving with slow sensuous rippling motion as she thundered on them with her slapping, ringing palm. 'Me heart, is it? This shrivelled-up little thing inside *here*, d'you mean?' she panted, slapping her left breast, gripping it, shaking it furiously as if it were a dog. 'What d'yeh know about a woman's heart? Yeh know bugger all yet, yeh little bitch. You'll soon get to know a man doesn't want a woman's heart – only her breast! That's all we are to them – breasts and arse and legs and bare bodies in the night beside them!'

'Oh, Mrs Rattigan . . .' the woman said in a choked compassionate voice, staring helplessly; then she clutched her hands to her throat and ran blindly out.

Magso fell back in the chair, breathing in great shuddering gasps; Old Essie calmly folded her arms and rocked herself

116

gently forward and back. Slowly a look of almost beatific peace settled over the widow's countenance as with slow un-hurried limp hands she pulled the ravelled saffron blouse loosely, languidly over her breasts.

'Essie, yeh toothless, titless oul hag yeh, there's a drop in the bottle left over from Easter in the bottom dresser beyant, wrapped up in a pair of poor Noreen's drawers . . .'

Her drowsy fluttering eyelids sprang open suddenly in the silence, and she glared with hard intense venom at the cellophane-wrapped bunch of cheap fresh flowers her daughter Noreen had bought that morning out of her factory wages for the year-old grave.

Old Essie snored. In the distance the horn blared out again.

19

A DOOR swung wide along the bleak shrouded street; a young girl stood silhouetted against the sudden lovely yellow light from the glowing kitchen behind her, taking in a batch of late mail from the temporary postman, laughing and wish-ing him the compliments of the season. He sat hunched in the boxcar, knees touching his chin, left stranded and happy, loving the soft snow falling upon him out of the fleecy emptiness, turning his face up to it, feeling it touch his eyes and throat and tingle coldly on his tongue when he opened his mouth. He welcomed the snow, wishing himself naked under its caress some place where people would not see, where they would not come trudging and trampling it with their cruel heedless feet into a soiled dirty sludge. He felt it settling upon his closed eyelids and singing past his ears with a faint, far uncatchable whisper. He heard the sound of the snow everywhere in the air about him, hiding the sores and scars and pockmarks, the moulding, gnarled ugliness of things that hurt and hounded him. One day he would build a snow castle far away from where people could find it and live brightly there for ever with all that dazzle and delight.

The lighted door banged shut with a harsh rending casualness, filling him with dismay, shutting him out, taking away from him that swift exultant sense of intimacy he always felt whenever he passed lighted houses in the night and a door or window would open, that glimpse into the unknown but not unguessed-at life of others, the more thrilling if they were absolute strangers to him, bringing to him images and intimations of the secret lives brooding or seething or ebbing slowly, wastefully away beyond the door or window. He longed to knock and beg admittance to the warmth and mystery inside, to sit quietly and watch those complete strangers laugh, cry, eat, drink, argue, worship, sleep; he longed to share a single intense moment of his existence with them; it would not matter if, the instant he had gone, their remembrance of him vanished too, as long as he had known the moment, stepped over the threshold, savoured the warmth, touched their uniqueness with his own, free of the muteness that chained him and cemented him to the one knowable acre of earth. He longed to fly with the wind and seek the hidden things, the small quiet undying treasured things in the warm hearts and houses of the unknown people harboured by the night and the falling felicitous snow. He sat limb-locked, dream-locked, in the rough wooden tumbril under some blackened bushes by a garden wall, harpooned by this hunger, hearing still the sound of a door being banged shut.

Too soon they came for him, chafing his limbs with rough gentleness to put warmth back into him, vastly unaware of that other warmth that shut out the real and more frightening cold, and with loud hurrahs and monkey tumblings in the snow they wheeled him down the brighter streets where the garish shop fronts threw yellow rectangles upon the glistening pavements; snowflakes swirled around the burning lamp posts in a frenzy; all was noise, hurry, torrential footfalls murdering the snow, the mad, glad, spell-

Something glinted under a street lamp. 'Would this be them?' asked one of the gang, picking up the spectacles with a grin and trying them on himself, imitating the groping gestures of the kneeling boy to the loud guffaws of encouragement and mirth from his leaping, dancing companions. 'Would this be them, Hawkeye?' the gambolling youth asked again, swinging them in the air; then, quite calmly, as if he were dismembering an insect, he snapped off first one ear clip, then the other, flinging each over his shoulder, broke the noseclip in two, and finally dropped the two lenses carefully down the grating of a roadside shore.

'That's for the Holy Mother of God, Proddywhoddy!' the youth shouted, hitching up his pants importantly and running off at the head of the gang, leaving the muddied, distressed, weeping boy to struggle blindly homeward in his own and the night's dark.

The little holly tree stood by the window, boy's height, in its coloured wrapping and box of clay, wired to the electric light, blazing, its tinsel glinting and bright berry globes swaying each time somebody opened the door, making a thin metallic sound, a distant yet distinct frosty crackling sound scarcely heard above the clamour of the children in the kitchen, the hiss of logs in the fire spitting flames. In the pantry the pudding boiled and bubbled on the oven range, wrapped as always in the large flour sack in the big corpulent copper pot, sending up clouds of steam that made the walls weep and clung to the low ceiling, to fall gradually in fat plopping drops. Paper chains spanned the kitchen ceiling from corner to corner, shaped in hearts, flowers, rainbows, funny faces; a big ornate red and gold lotus-like star was tacked onto the old-fashioned mirror over the fireplace; in the corner above the dresser a wooden altar was erected, with a red oil lamp on it; little china figures of the lamb and oxen, the shepherd boy and the three wise travellers were arranged round a crib that had real hay in it, the rather puzzled-looking bearded man leaning on a staff and the fragile lady with lowered eyes, all gazing at the bonny pink infant asleep in the hay. The oil lamp played upon the ceiling and when the light was turned off it filled the kitchen with a red glow.

The two soldier-sons were home on leave, the younger one with his new girlfriend, a tall gay pretty girl named Margie, with dark hair, brown eyes, and a lovely little golden mole on her cheek, who helped Mother in the kitchen, sipped sherry, and sang snatches of songs, tossing back her long loose hair. She got down on her silk-shod knees to play with the younger kids. She laughed deep in her throat, and once she rumpled his hair with her slim nail-varnished fingers, asking him to sing with her; he smelt her clean young smell and liked her. His brother smiled blandly, every inch a cavalier, peacock proud of her, drinking beer with a flourish out of a favourite old cracked mug, eyes on her all the time. The eldest brother drank freely now, with many a huge hiccup, and cried easily for no reason in a sentimental way, and often went in and hugged and kissed Mother as she toiled at the stove, and she would swipe at him with the towel and tell him to be grown up, and the fat foolish likeable rather lost boy who was not yet a man would wander about among the kids, crying happily and laughing, picking the little ones up and nuzzling his steamy wet face against them, playing games with them, getting down on all fours and lumbering about like an elephant, snorting with exertion, making mad outrageous animal noises till they squealed with delight, presently losing wind and puffing red-faced up again to grab his beer and gulp it down noisily.

'Here – wipe your snots and tears, you dope!' the cavalier said with a grin, tossing over a big immaculate linen hankie, showing off. He pulled his girl onto his knee and started to sing 'Margie, my little Margie'. She blushed and laughed with shy delight, tugging at his tunic collar.

From the depths of the ancient spring-loosened horsehair sofa by the burning holly tree, he watched, soaking in the magic, the fantasy that had come to life, the tremulous, uncertain joy in the room and on the familiar faces. Strange stirrings awoke in him with a fluttering and rustle of awakening wings at dawn; he sat very still, only his eyes moving, afraid to stir, as if the loud, clamorous, buzzing little room might in a moment dissolve into the old outlines of dull desolate dread. All was familiar, and all was strange; the gaudy-flowered wallpaper with new bits pasted on to hide the dirty head stains; the ugly ceiling-high black sideboard with the many carvings and cunning little side gilt-edged mirrors, its mahogany scratched with their initials; the queer sodden brown stain on the ceiling that was somehow in the shape of a man's face like the figurings on the moon; the torn edges of the oilcloth scrubbed shiny in parts with the marks of the floorboards showing through; the hole at the bottom of the pantry door that some adventurous midnight mouse had gnawed ... the familiar made strange, the strange made familiar, that which was tiresomely real made dream-like, the dream descending and putting on ordinary garments, an ordinary face, dancing on ordinary feet, beckoning him, saying there was no longer need to hold back from the loud laugh and the lusty stamp of careless life-loving, telling him to come forth from that lost middle-distance, that the chains were not unbreakable, that he might enter their dusty bellowing arena, partake of their bread, share their rough warrior kit, their brawling, bruising, belligerent world, with its wordless loving and quick hating and all its screaming and sprawling mirth, its fights and heedless hurts and its mad, savage, tenacious stranglehold on life. He saw his mother's face framed in the pantry doorway, beautiful with a tired strength and innocence that escaped his groping mind. He saw the sideward-turning face of his brother's girl in the falling glow from the altar lamp, soft and dream-like on a whisper; the broad godlike knees of the splendid lover, the black arrogant head hewn from burnished oak; he saw with the old lurch of heart the sad, comic, harlequin face of his eldest brother all open to the world, full of an absurd belief. He saw all this gay, hurtful life spread in generous haphazard prodigality around him like a warm sea, and he grew weak with tongueless tenderness, with the murderous longing to step over the threshold,

123

through the waiting door, and stay forever beyond the lighted window, and never know the hunger for voyages, never heed the wind-whispered hailing call across impassable seas.

Slowly he became conscious of the hush that had settled over the room. Unwillingly dragging his time-leaping, joy-peeping thoughts back from the never-never land of possible wonder and harmony, he turned his gaze in the direction of their faces, and saw Father standing in the doorway, hatless, collar and tie loose, an expression of bemused uncertainty and confused contrition on the flushed hard-lined face, a curiously boyish look, hesitating in the doorway, as if having entered the wrong house by mistake. Nobody stirred, all talk stopped; everything seemed frozen, arrested, stilled into immobile postures, the click of a camera recording a still-life scene, as in the picture house sometimes when something went wrong in the projection box and the figures would become static and wooden-like upon the screen. Mother, on her endless trips to and from the pantry, carrying a plateful of newly baked scones and apple fritters, saw him, and stopped abruptly. From away down the street some early carol singers could be heard dimly.

'You're back,' said Mother, putting down the plate on the table; her words brought movement flowing back into the room; everyone completed the gesture or motion they had been engaged in before the door opened; the eldest son put down his beer mug, the other dropped his caressing hand from his girl's hair down to her shoulder; the scrambling kids picked up their toys again.

'Don't be minding me,' said Father, coming into the kitchen, carrying a bottle under his arm; he unwrapped it ceremoniously and placed it on the table. 'For the season that's in it,' he said, then clapped his hands. 'Glasses!' he ordered, and when someone had jumped to this command and brought them from the pantry, he uncorked the bottle and poured to the brim. 'A drop of sherry, missus, for the time that's in it,' he said, handing it to her gravely. Mother, too surprised to argue or protest, took it. He turned, noticing the strange girl for the first time, his eyebrows contracting.

'Father, this is Margie,' said the dark-haired sapling son, rising with the girl, linking his arm through hers, brass buttons of uniform gleaming under the electric light. 'We're going out together.'

Father looked at them both solemnly, then grinned and poured out another glass. 'Ah, you've a bloody fine Christmas box there, sonny boy!' he said, thrusting the glass into the girl's hand. 'Give her plenty of kids and she'll be happy.' He stooped and yanked one of the crawling youngsters up into his arms. 'Whoosh-a-la!' he roared, throwing the squealing, terrified child ceiling-wards and only just catching it again. 'Never let a year go by without proving who's boss!' he said, flinging the child upwards again.

'Jesus, Mary and Joseph, he'll kill me poor child!' Mother cried, rushing over and tugging the child from his arms, rocking it upon her breast, hushing its frightened cries.

'I'm as sober as a judge, missus, word of honour,' said Father, swaying back on his heels. 'Wouldn't you know just be looking at me? Ah, me poor woman!' he said with sudden desperate remorse, awkwardly rubbing her face with his thumb and forefinger, his eyes misting over. 'You've been through the mill, haven't you?' He turned to his son. 'If you've got yourself half as fine a bargain as I did thirty-odd years ago, you'll be doing bloody all right, my bucko!' he said, then turned back to Mother and put his arm around her shoulder. 'She stood by me through thick and thin and never begrudged me the price of a pint if it was in it. She has a heart of pure bloody gold, that woman, and none of yous appreciates it! Ungrateful buggers. Ah, me poor woman!' he sighed, nuzzling his face against hers and singing out in a soft unsteady voice:

'Let the great big world keep turning
never mind what may come through
for I only know that I love you so
and there's no one else but you . . .'

'I'll make the tea,' said Mother, edging away, a little

embarrassed in front of the girl and her grown sons. 'Sit down and rest your feet.'

'Me feet!' he said with swift nostalgia, looking down at them fondly, lifting one then the other slowly and carefully in the air; through the day-long cement dust and muck the boot polish still shone hard. 'I once had the best pair of dancing feet in Dublin, boys,' he said to his sons, eyes bright as pale cherries under a frosty moon. 'Ask your mother! Isn't that right, missus?' he said, grabbing her cardigan sleeve. 'Wasn't it me dancing feet that made you be me mot? D'yeh remember when we used to dance to the Magazine Waltz up beyant in the oul Round Rooms of the Rotunda?' He started to whistle the tune of that far-gone unclouded time, catching hold of her hands and swirling her into the dance. 'I'm not beat yet, bejasus!' he roared exultantly, twirling her round and round in ever-widening circles, whistling madly all the time, his face shining and with sandy hair bushy and erect, heedless of her protests, something of summer alive in him still.

'You^{'ll} break something!' Mother gasped, trying desperately to keep her feet as he swept her faster. 'For God's sake . . .'

'He's mad,' whispered the fat eldest son, awed and scared. 'Stone mad.'

'He'd better stop it,' muttered the other tensely, clenching his fists; the girl held on to his arm tightly.

'Nineteen-eighteen . . . the Ancient Concert Rooms they were called then . . . Parnell Square . . .' Father's voice, ragged but rough with reviving memories, broke through the rhythm of his wild whistling, mounting to a shrill crescendo, his boots twinkling, beating out an erratic yet insistent drumming upon the floor, her hair tumbling and flying about her tense flushed face. 'You wore . . . a white dress . . . red ribbons in your hair . . . little black shoes . . . O Jesus, we were young . . .'

The Christmas tree toppled over on its side as they inexorably crashed into it, falling with a bang and hiss of crackling exploding fairylights, its gay little glass globes rolling over the floor, the box of clay splitting and spilling out; the bottle of sherry went over as somebody bumped against the table; the room plummeted into sudden darkness save for the weird red radiance from the little oil lamp on the altar; the children whimpered and began to cry as their toys were stepped on in the sudden chaos of frantic feet and muttered curses, which was followed by a strange and baffled silence.

'Jesus,' said Father softly, hoarsely, sprawled amid the ruins of the festive tree, passing a trembling hand over his forehead.

The carol singers were closer now, almost outside the front gate, clear voices rising in the cold brilliant night air, singing 'Adeste Fidelis'.

20

A BLACK SPECK of a hawk hung movelessly in the unclouded blue afternoon sky high above the gnarled skull's contours of the pithead; it circled slowly, dropped invisibly lower, was still again, then with a sudden and terrifying swiftness plummeted to earth hidden by the tree beyond the cemetery walls. Windows of distant houses opened and glinted in the sun; buses and cars moved along the canyons of streets without sound, looking as small as toys; the dull slap of water could be heard striking sluggishly against the rotten timber of the homemade raft down by the mud-oozing mucky edge of the disused stagnant quarry, a noisy group of boys and a few hardy girls tying the swaying raft with a thin twist of twine to a pointed slab of rock.

'She shaves it every week,' said Charley, stretched out with some others upon a slope that actually boasted some dry yellow grass, overlooking the blackened bowl of the weed-stuffed quarry, chewing a blade of grass and looking through slit-lidded eyes at a tall sturdy broad-hipped girl of fourteen with hip-length tawny plaits. 'I tell you, lads, it's as baldy as a baby's bum.'

'How do you know?' challenged another boy with thick hazelnut freckles and a nervous twitch of his right eye.

'Didn't I see it, you thick?' declared Charley, who had a habit of constantly leering though he might be talking about the Bible. 'First time she let me see it for a tanner one day her oul wan was out. Now she lets me see it for choice.' Charley put his hands behind his head complacently and puffed out his ganseyed chest.

'Is that all – only *see* it?' asked a big boy named Shamie with lazy scorn. 'Jasus bless your innocence – what use is that?'

'Yeah – what use is that?' the others all said in a chorus, taking a cue from Shamie, the obvious elder statesman of the group.

'Well,' began Charlie, uncertain, yet anxious to restore his masculine image; 'that's all it's bloody well good for – looking at. I mean, without a morsel of hair . . . well, would *you* bloody well touch it?' he asked truculently of Shamie, hoisting himself up on an elbow.

Shamie scratched his ear. 'Hair or no hair,' he said, massaging his thigh methodically inside the pocket of his new long trousers, 'a quim is a quim no matter what. Right, lads?'

'Right!' the others chorused as before, looking expectantly at Charley to come forward with some new argument of self-defence. The hawk lifted once more into the sky, gripping something small and dark and limp between its claws.

'Well, yeah – all right,' said Charley stubbornly, 'but still and all – where there's hair there's comfort. I heard me oul fella say that once to me oul wan when they thought I wasn't there.'

'I wonder if it hurts her when she shaves it?' reflected another, a fat boy with a baby-pink skin and a moist boil on

128

his neck, who picked his nose incessantly and, after scrutinizing the contents with absorbed interest, popped it into his mouth.

'Some mots like to be hurted,' said Shamie with a note of immense and mysterious knowledge in his voice. 'Maybe it tickles her. Maybe she likes it better than a fella feeling her.'

'Will you look at the bloody tits on her!' said the fat pink boy, carefully pulling the ragged collar of his shirt down from his oozing boil. 'They'd poke the eyes out of you!'

'She shows an awful lot of arse when she bends,' someone else observed with a relishing smack of lips.

'You know, Charley, I think you're a bleeding liar,' announced Shamie with slow deadly contempt. 'I don't believe she shaves it at all. I don't believe a single solitary word out of your lousy trap.'

'Want to bet on that, you mouth?' answered Charley, getting red and indignant, sitting up and wiping his saliva-drenched mouth with the sleeve of his gansey. 'Bet you a sack of me best bloody cinders—'

'That her fanny's baldy?' asked Shamie with quick interest.

'Yeah – that her bloody fanny's bald as an egg!' Charley said hotly, almost stuttering in his anger and haste. 'Are you on?'

'I'm on!' said Shamie, grinning and sitting up also. 'But how are you going to prove it – thump her and drag down her drawers?'

The parrots all laughed nervously, the young ones glad to be in on such a privileged and erudite adult conversation, but Charley's leer grew merely broader and he ran his sleeve across his nose once more before jumping up. 'Just watch,' he said, buckling his belt.

They watched avidly as he loped lazily down the slope and went over to the small crowd playing around the raft; presently he drew the girl aside and for a time stood talking to her earnestly, waving his arms oratorically; she laughed often and shook her head, her long twin plaits swaying like ropes of corn in the wind; then, suddenly assenting, she

129

linked her arm through his and together they started up the slope; when she drew near the top she halted and scanned each face with a grave grey-eyed stare until she found the tall raw-boned lad in the long flannel trousers.

'Is it you?' she asked matter-of-factly, stepping up and standing square-footed in front of the youth.

'Yeah – why?' asked Shamie, trying to sound contemptuous but his composure now beginning to desert him.

Still staring at him, not saying another word, the girl rubbed her palms thoughtfully downwards over her sides, then quite slowly started to pull up her wide-flared gingham summer dress. There was a general gasp of awe and bewilderment, a quick and loud shuffling and scrambling of feet as, one by one at first, then all in a rush, they jumped up and fell back in disbelief, breaking into a run as the dress rose higher and higher; soon, the only ones remaining were Charley, preening and strutting in the background, the mesmerized Shamie staring as the dress rose inexorably higher, and he who crouched spellbound in the boxcar nearby, unheeded, no longer watching the spiralling hawk.

She had raised the dress hip-high, her straight young legs framed against the brown burnt hillside, and had placed both her thumbs inside the elastic band of her faded blue calico knickers, when with a choked cry of rage Shamie sprang forward and flung himself upon the wide-grinning Charley. Their entangled limbs thrashed and writhed on the ground in furious combat, then rolled down the slope in a blur of flailing boots and fists amid ribald whoops and shouts of fierce encouragement from above and below.

'Serves you right, you horny little buggers!' yelled the girl, nervous with elation, slapping her calico thigh and buttock as if she were mounted on a tempestuous steed, charging and laughing into the breeze, eyes wild, teeth bared and flashing on a mad seething ecstasy that convulsed her. 'Serves you bloody well right, me buckos!' She laughed as if in a fit, jumping into the air, clapping her hands and bawling out joyously the words of a current song mangled under her moist hot tongue:

'Roll me over in the clover,
O roll me over, shove me down, and do it again!'

She stood splay-footed and breathless on the edge of the hill, flinging forth harsh, hurtful man-words into the hot acrid breeze in a bright tumbling tormented torrent, her fine free young body shaking with deep seismic shudders of delicious malice and mirth, her brown face at once ugly and beautiful, radiant with a gypsy abandon. She seemed transparent, a wispy, quivering flame shaken by the elements, wild and wilful and beautiful beyond his slaughtered senses to comprehend, riven like a bright shaft of agony into that burnt-out skull-like cairn.

She turned, brilliant and burning on a smile, seeing him there in the boxcar for the first time, and a sunset look came into her face, a look of sudden remote charm and melancholy as she looked down at him, shading her eyes from the sun and the sky full of the spinning hawk. 'My name is Maureen,' she said, leaning her strong brown hands on the rough edge of his movable cell; slowly her dark eyes smouldered again, an ugly defiance twisted her mouth. 'Do you think there'd be room for two in that thing, young fella?', and without wasting another breath on another word, grinning like a monkey, she climbed over the sides and snuggled in beside him, the sudden warm smell of her humid flesh surging over him like pollen, her queer boyish hoydenish face pushed close to his, her eyes like hard coal diamonds swimming in sperm. She sat crouched with her knees up, grinning at him; then she plucked forth his clenched hand and held it against her breast. 'Ah Jesus – don't be nervous,' she said, licking her lips with the flame-tip of her tongue. 'Spread them out, like this,' she said, trying to unlock his fingers upon her breast. She seemed absorbed with his fingers, then she looked at him slyly from under lowered lashes. 'You're not bad-looking, I mean, for a cripple.' Her voice grew more hushed, her face swam closer to him, her breath warm and peppermint sweet. 'I often thought . . . don't be afraid, now . . . are you like the rest?'

131

She put her slim hand down, along his groin, never taking her eyes from his face, her fingers feeling, probing, finding. Smoke rose into his eyes, the smell of her rose into his nostrils and along his brain like burning leaves, heather blazing under summer, the green glassy fire of grass glaring into him, flame of fabulous unknown summers sweeping the bone-dry, heart-dry tinderwood of his dreaming undergrowth, setting alight the far places of his solitary awareness, beacons winking, wavering, beckoning, drawn out of a long unremembrance, pulled from dragon depths up through the primal dark to tremble perilous on a surge of muted menace and a slow sensuous stab of primal pain. Her fingers insistent, her voice lisping, her face transfigured with a ravaged, curious exultancy, she crinkled and crackled all around him, flaming leaves, June burning in his veins. With dread, with loathing, with old remembered fear and tremulous joy, he felt his core harden, magically, mercilessly, to a throbbing arrowhead of bruised strength and pleasure permeating his belly, shooting flame-like from his groin, burning down there like coal, stirring mysteriously, pulsating with a quick, brutal life of its own. Briefly, life throbbed and flamed brightly within him, hot and helpless under cruel fingers, and summer smoke of her rose and swirled about him enveloping the world.

She pulled her hand away abruptly and looked at him slant eyed, teeth gleaming, forehead glistening. 'As hard as a bloody stick, you are,' she said with clear, derisive emphasis, the slipping sun forming a shadow along the sharp line of her jaw as she held her head at a sideward angle. 'Just like all the fucking rest!'

There came a sudden commotion from the quarry's edge, a loud buzz and flare of frantic shouts, a certain dim yet ominous thrashing and turmoil in the water; an excited murmur, a swelling of voices jabbering in frenzied confusion.

'Nedser's falling in . . . quick, someone – Nedser's falling in!'

The girl snapped up rigid like the suddenly released blade of a penknife, face going pale under the sunburn. 'Jesus my

God – my brother!' she said, not wild or even excited, but with a sort of puzzled disbelief. She rubbed her forehead twice with her hard knuckles. Then, panther-like, she leaped from the boxcar and ran down the hill, brown heels flashing, hair streaming behind her. From the crest he saw unfold before him the deadly little scene, like a cameo in a nightmare, etched with sharp, cruel knife strokes against the placid air, the dull bronzed sheen of the stagnant moveless water; the carrot-headed yellow-jerseyed boy already thrashing and writhing, the buzzing black beehive cluster of boys, petrified cries torn from their throats, crawling along the crumbling cancerous lip of the quarry, forming a human chain that was piteously too short, trying with sticks and poles and whipped-off trousers and jerseys to reach their thrashing, terrified pal who was slowly drowning, their cries for help lost on the gaunt, gruff, still agile but stone-deaf old watchman who had been a powerful swimmer in his long-gone heyday and who could still put many a young chiseller to shame, but who dozed and dreamt all day now in his wooden hut. It was all seen in cold bitter print against the lucid blind sun, and the heart in him turned over in sick outrage, seeing on this broad bland summer's day death taking horrible dominance over all things, feeling the senseless violence of it all, the barbarity of sudden death over young growing things, a knife twist in the guts.

The girl raced sudden and splendid through the helpless weeping throng of boys and, untrapped by thought, untouched by fear, flashed bright through the air, hitting the black surface smoothly and swimming with swift beautiful strokes towards her drowning brother; but he, his dripping shining half-crown of a face all twisted with green slime and terror, had already sunk below the surface. All was now quiet, save for the broken enraged sobbing of Maureen as she crawled on her belly back up the muddy quarry edge and knelt on her bleeding knees, her dress clinging like seaweed to her, lifting her blind wet face to the sun, the rest of them struck dumb as statues frozen in postures of terror and near-comic unbelief, scattered out along the shrunken shore.

133

In the brimming, burning heavens the hawk had flown westward with its prey.

21

'WOULD YOU credit it?' came the awed whisper of one of the women out of the shadows. 'Almost a year to the day since her poor Da died . . .'

The candles flickered in the curtained room on each side of the little iron bedstead, throwing shapes around. The forehead of the dead girl seemed transparent, glistening with a faint sheen, an alabaster shade holding an incandescent flicker. Under the stiff yellow-tinged sheets the body appeared quite flat, only the feet showing a bulge. The lips seemed to be stuck together by a red mucous glue, like sealing wax, the veins on the curved eyelids marvellously defined, as if traced by a blue marker. The skin beneath her fingernails was very clear. A slight oppressive odour hung over the bed, rather like stale grease. At the foot a cat crouched, hissing and purring, its grey back arching whenever someone approached the bed to kneel for a few moments in prayer.

'It would put the fear of God into you,' came a second whisper, 'and she barely twenty . . .'

A faint rustling of skirts, a dry rattling of beads, then, 'God be good to the poor little lamb and all that,' came the cautious whispered reply, 'but she was no chicken . . . thirty, if she was a day.'

A snort full of disbelief, yet gullible enough to be convinced. 'Ah, g'wan with yeh! Look at her lying there like a petal, her poor face not the size of me hand . . .'

'Don't be going by that, Sarah,' the other went on with a profound sniffle, fumbling in her many skirts for her snuff-box. 'I've laid out more corpses than dinner plates in my time, and many's the one I've seen looking like the first May flower all in the brown habit, and them with full-grown sons and daughters and drawing the oul age pension for donkey's years . . .' A snuff-loud cackle hastily smothered in puckered depths of genteel calico.

'Isn't life and death quare, all the same?' spoke the second keeper of the death vigil, with a vague sense of awe and sorrow.

'The bloodstream changes after death, you see, or is it the skin?' mused the other, settling back her skirts. 'But anyway you go back to your youth, kind of, all in the bloom of your younger days, so that the man and woman who put you on the earth would be hard put to it to recognize you . . . Herself will never see sixty again except on a hall door, and sure she had poor little Noreen beyant there shortly after she was married, so there I leave you . . .'

The voices lisped on in the thick curtained gloom, dropping like moist plops of spittle on the bare boards and walls. A sword of afternoon light fell from the landing as the door opened and another sympathizer entered on slippered feet; the cat hissed and rubbed its paw with its fanged furry tongue. They went into the fifth decade of the litany for the dead. There came a crash from the street below as somebody's dustbin went over in a scurry of sprawling, scratching cats.

'Pretty Paddy, Pretty Paddy!' a tall angular woman in an imitation fur coat prattled moistly to her blue-and-green budgerigar as she high-heeled down the street, holding it aloft in a large expensive cage, the huge silk feather in her pyramid hat flopping in the wind. The ice-cream man rumbled by in his squat yellow box pulled by the same ancient worn-out donkey, the bugle lamenting lamely, wheels rickety on the crooked axle. A sudden intense pause in which flies buzzed; then a violent shatter of breaking glass from the house directly opposite as a teapot came flying through the front window, crashing against the iron railings in front of the little golden-priveted garden.

135

'Jesus, it's the judge . . .'

A voice shrill with outraged authority ringing clear in the afternoon. Doors and windows opening surreptitiously; discreet coughs and murmurs of disapproval, nervous giggles of amusement: 'Has she no respect at all for the dead? . . .' Sweeping out majestically down the front path, horn-rimmed glasses glinting, wrapped in a long loose black shift-like dress that flapped about her like the robes of a judge, the plump henlike little woman stood head high and supercilious by her gate, eyes closed in scorn to the buzzes of indignation in the street. 'And furthermore, Oscar, you fornicated, dissipated old bastard, I will not tolerate your insulting remarks any longer, and have it in my power to put you where the crows will most certainly not shit on you . . .' the clear ice-sharp voice echoed out loudly accompanied by a determined tattoo of pointed ladylike foot on the stone pavement as, pointing behind to the skulking shape of her spouse flitting across the window trying to dislodge the picture frame from around his neck, she continued in the same declamatory tones as though from a pulpit: 'I bring you all to witness what a poor abject creature I married, ridden with tuberculosis and God knows what other more horrible diseases, gained from a life of sin and evil days, never worked a day in his life, and yet when I ask him to go on a simple errand like asking his filthy old mother to oblige us with a sack of flour for my poor starving children . . .'

The voice of the bereaved woman ricocheted vibrantly through the street, venomous and bitter. 'The curse of God on you, and me poor daughter laid out in her habit upstairs!'

The bright bird eyes blinked and glinted behind the glasses. 'I'm sorry for your trouble, my good woman,' the greying head nodded, one arm stretched forth, hand held up for silence, 'but I proclaim the right, the God-given right, I might add, to chastise my own family in my own home any time I wish—'

'By breaking pots and pans and picture frames over their heads, you bitter oul cow yeh?'

136

'I have the law on my side, and I warn all of you—'

A concerted shower of voices rising as more front windows and doors were opened: 'Have respect for the dead, Missus Somerville, if for nothing else! It will come all our turn . . .'

'As a rent-paying citizen of this city, I protest . . .'

His black robes rustling weirdly with death and mystery down the street, the priest, lost in his breviary, strides into the vortex, looks neither right nor left, up nor down, brown sandals clapping, until he reaches the right gate. Then with a swift clamp he shuts his book, entering and climbing the stairs to the death room, intoning as he goes the foreign words of prayer, raising a languid fragile hand in blessing on the way; windows closing down in the street; a door banging shut; late afternoon silence. With a screech the cat jumps from the bed as the priest comes up.

'She was a good girl, Father,' said Red Magso with soft lisping grief afterwards, the praying over and the few good cups out on the kitchen table. 'A lazy bloody divil, always moaning, never satisfied, never doing a hand's turn in the house, but she was all I had after Matt died. I'll miss fighting with her and giving her the odd clout.'

'Have you no others?' inquired the priest, refusing tea, polishing his spectacles with his handkerchief. 'All married, Father, bad cess to them,' sighed the widow without the least rancour, large hand moving vaguely in front of her mouth. She squinted up at the priest. 'It's crool, Father,' she continued, querulously, 'and I don't understand it. Her to be taken from me like that –' with a snap of fingers. 'I reared six of them, Father, rough and ready, but never left them hungry or cold, and each in their turn left me and went their own way, all except the poor child upstairs . . . She never left me, Father,' the widow continued with sudden defiant vigour, shaking her head. 'She stuck to me like glue . . . often even when the oul whiskey stood seven foot inside me and I'd be lashing out at everyone for no rhyme or reason . . . she stuck by me like a trooper. Aye, she did, the poor delicate little angel, and the life draining out

137

of her every day before me eyes . . . it used to drive me mad, so that I had to hit out at something . . . Ah, Father, she's in a better place now, isn't she?' The tears welled up, spilled over, ran down the creviced red cheeks into the puckered corners of the mouth, wiped truculently away by a large fierce hand. 'Nobody now but the bloody cat . . .'

The priest, indecisive, out of depth, fitted his glasses back on, folding his delicate fingers together, murmuring unheard words of solace, Adam's apple jerking, then going quickly down the path, taking out his breviary hurriedly, as though opening a door of escape.

'It will be a long night,' said the neighbours, coming together after leaving the chapel, 'and we can't leave the poor creature alone in that house.' Purses were taken out, contents examined, counted, coins shining under lamp posts; snug doors pushed inwards, a slow shuffling of feet across to the counter. 'Two dozen, John . . a baby Powers and God bless you, boy . . . put that on the slate, me little dote, like the decent man you are . . . Sure you might as well make it four dozen while you're at it, and a naggin . . . she's partial to a drop, and God knows she'll need it tonight . . . I always say there's nothing worse than a death . . . I wonder will any of the others arrive on the mailboat tonight? . . .' Feet shuffling away, moving down the lamplit dusky street, bottles clinking in crinkly brown parcels. 'Ah, she'd be the first to do the same for you . . .'

They had started on the umpteenth decade of the litany for the dead, the cat now back at the foot of the bed, licking itself fastidiously, the two old vigil keepers drowsing in their chairs but fingering their beads tenaciously, lips puffing in and out with prayer instinctive, the widow by the empty fireplace below in the clock-ticking kitchen, clicking her false teeth meditatively, rocking in the sagging armchair. Brown parcels plonked on table, bottles yanked roughly out, several corkscrews discovered all at once. Moist pop of corks, brown porter cascading into tilted tumblers, golden amber of whiskey gleaming from depths of jug, thrust warmly into hand of ambivalent widow looking with jaded

138

eyes into scarred remnants in fireplace; taking slow sorrowful sips, tilting the jug higher, the old coarse murderous
gaiety sluicing through her grief.

'Tell them to stop praying upstairs and take a sup, for
God's sake.' The umpteenth decade interrupted, slow gurgling down uplifted corded throats, stairs creaking, feet
descending, a fire in the grate now for the long night ahead.
Sliced sausages slapped between thick cuts of bread; lips
smacked loud in relish; a greased pan spurting blue flame
in the pantry. 'Is there any serious harm in a sing-song?'

'They do say there's singing in heaven, and sure as God
that's where the poor darlin' is now, singing her heart out,
snug as anything—'

'Noreen couldn't sing a bloody note,' the widow said with
a bitter snort, 'not even in heaven, and she a saint itself.'

'Meaning no disrespect,' garrulous wrinkled mouth opening wide on lickspittle intake of breath, eyes whiskey
rouged, sunken deep in valleyed skin, gnarled fingernail
scratching at walrus wart on chin; 'but there's a lovely
song I useda sing in me courting days, oh, well before the
rebellion . . .

> 'I took me love on the bus to Bray
> all in the month of June
> and the lovely things we said that day
> we forgot all too soon
> For he was from the Rathmines district
> and I from James's Street
> and like the west and the far, far east
> never the twain could meet . . .'

'You're bringing the hot tears to me eyes, Gertie Rooney.
It was kind of yeh to bring me up a sup.' The widow's
words slithered wetly out from smacking lips, blowing nose
in apron, holding out her jug, rosy wrist supple, top dentures
dropping down with thin metallic click, pushed back up into
place by broad-domed thumb. 'Them poxy things was
never the same since Matt hit me with the poker the

Christmas he got pensioned off,' and then with a burst of anger, 'Essie, yeh greasy oul faggot yeh, the smell of snuff off yeh would kill a horse.'

Rashers sizzling on tin plates, onion filling the room, crusts of bread dipped lusciously in brown fat swimming gravy. An old woman hunched in a corner praying aloud, Hail Mary, full of grace. 'Jesus, can't yeh shut up for a minute and take a bite and a sup?' Sausage sandwich and mug of porter shoved into the praying hands. 'That oul wan would give yeh the pips with all her praying.'

'She has a daughter a nun.'

'I've a brother a coalman, but do I go round bawling at the top of me voice all day?'

'The men will be coming up any minute, full of their oil and eating all before them.'

The pan spitting flame again, neighbours coming in with lumps of brown dripping, coils of black and white pudding, pigs' tails, cold collage of sheeps' head pressed between two plates, tongue, liver, slab of pigs' cheek wrapped in newspaper; meanwhile furious platter and plash from the pantry. 'Has anyone got a shilling for the bloody gas?' 'We'll be eating high and dry for the rest of the week, but sure we couldn't let the poor creature down and there not a man in the house. O Jesus, is that oul wan at it again?' Anguished the inquiry as loud lilting prayers issued from the corner. 'Give her another sausage, someone, for God's sake, and a sup of stout, to shut her up.'

'Mind her bloody halo, Sissy.'

'Hail Mary, full of grace. I wish to God you'd shut her up.'

The widow's weight on the stairs, moaning and creaking of timber, lumbering up the stairs, two women behind standing guard should there be a tremendous mishap backwards. Stumbling through door into darkened room lit only by the wax-corroded candles guttering in bottles and thin slice of lamplight through curtain slit. It will be a small enough coffin, God love you, and I could carry it meself all the way down to the graveyard, for there's not a

140

ha'porth of you lying there between the cold sheets, and how big you once made me look! Sitting on the edge of the single bed, face dreamy, fat fingers loose and limp on sheet, gold wedding ring gleaming in candle glow, puffing noisily through wide wet lips. They will be coming over on the mailboat now, God curse them, coming to cry crocodile tears and mock me in their hearts for the smell of whiskey off me breath. 'Noreen, were you always so weeshy?'

No tears now on the flaming cheeks; the florid flowing face bent lower over the pillows, full of a huge dim wonder, a puzzled head-shaking confusion; thick forefinger placed tentatively on the cold dead lips, as if the gesture might part them, glued for all time. 'Noreen, I didn't know you were that good looking.'

'D'you think we oughta lave her up there on her own like that, her with a sup on her and all—?'

'Lave the poor creature. It's little time she'll have alone with the poor child now, and she being coffined first thing in the morning.'

'Isn't it a wonder none of the family is here be now? What sort are they at all and one of their own lying dead with a widowed mother?'

'Ah sure that's what we're breeding now, Polly – bloody heartless bitches and bastards with not a morsel of nature in them.'

'Did she send word to any of them?'

'She sent a wire to Sadie, the eldest, soon as it happened. I lent her the price of it meself till the insurance came through, though there's little enough of that coming, Christ knows.'

'You'd think one or other of them would be here be now, and not lave everything to the poor unfortunate woman.'

'Only for her neighbours she'd be in a quare state, God love her, little enough though we can do for her.'

'God, it would turn you against having a family and crucifying yourself rearing them, to be left like this at the latter end of your days.'

'She was a hard woman in her own way, but many's the time I saw her tripping to the pawn in the bitter frost

141

with things she was after getting on a Jewman's cheque, to put food in their bellies. It wasn't all drinking and carousing for poor Magso, let me tell you.'

'It will be a crying sin if none of them come home for the funeral.'

'Oh, don't you fear – they'll be here hot-foot in the morning or sooner to collect their policies, for they all knew poor Noreen was delicate and not long for this world.'

Gertie Rooney fondled her ferocious wart, stroked her hairy chin and shifted restlessly in her corner seat.

'Bejasus, it's like a bloody wake in here.'

'So it is, yeh stoopid oul cow yeh!'

'But sure we're not all dead, are we? First no prayers, then no sing-song. What d'you expect us to do – sit around and gawk at one another till we're all only fit to be buried?'

'Respect the dead, now, Gertie Rooney!'

'Ah, shit on your sanctimonious oul kisser!'

The cracked ragged stringy tones began to rise in the turf smoke, lulling resentment away, easing conscience, making old heads nod and hands pause and chairs to creak under the slow swaying of remembered rhythm:

'I have a true love if ever a girl had one
I had a true love and a brave lad was he,
he was true to his country and fought for her glory
and went out to fight for to make oul Ireland free.
So it's all around me hat I wear the tricoloured
    ribbon-o
it's all around me hat until death comes to me
and if anybody asks why I'm wearing that ribbon-o
it's all for me true love I ne'er more shall see . . .'

Old voice lifting tenaciously over cracked rim of mug triumphant above the splutter and splash of burning dripping spitting in pantry.

'Ah you can't whack the oul songs, girls. Such lovely words, such lovely sad words . . . they make me fill up whenever I hear them sung.' Gurgle of brown porter into

142

mug and memory-moist eyes all unconscious of the boisterous irony.

The widow upstairs coming unwillingly back from her reverie to the dim oppressive room, cat purring nervous and rigid-ribbed against her foot, needle prick of late night lamplight boring in from outside through torn curtain, the encore-echoing throatful kitchen throbbing below. She got heavily to her feet and crossed to the window, looking out at the unchanging scene; a courting couple in the dark of a garden wall locked in a world of moveless embrace; a group of boys tossing pennies twinkling under the lamp post; a man fiddling with the engine of his dilapidated motorcar under the raised bonnet a few doors down. Then a knot of men came into sight strung out in twos and threes, carrying familiar brown parcels under their arms, talking loud, laughing, quieting slowly as they neared the house, opening the rusty-voiced front gate, stepping up the narrow path with elaborate tread, tapping carefully on the hall door.

'Will yous be quiet in the name of God?'

'Sure we heard yous all singing coming up the street!' one of the men said in an aggrieved voice, pushing through. He stood out from the others, a short, strong-limbed ruddy-faced man of about forty, with close-cropped wirelike hair, authority and agility evident in his every movement, eyes blue and sharp and fully alive crinkled in an almost constant smile that was often half a grin, ghoulish because of its steely assurance. His jaw was strong and his mouth thin-lipped and sardonic. He plonked his twin parcels on the table and turned round jovially to the women, rubbing his hands. 'I feel like a lion tonight, girls, so if any of yous want to be savaged . . .'

'Whacker Dunne, this a house of mourning, and don't be using that kind of language here,' said a spidery restless little woman, taking over as manageress and shooshing the men into their places around the room.

'And may the poor child rest in peace with the Man above this blessed night, ma'am,' replied Whacker, chaffing his square-fingered hands together with irrepressible bonhomie,

143

winking broadly to several younger women at once. 'But it's hard to keep a good man down. I'm lost without the oul hen. She's away in Liverpool helping to bring our first grandchild into the world, and it's bloody hard on a fella like meself, still in me prime and full of the hot juice of life—'

'Ah, can't you cut it bloody well out, Whacker?' one of his companions reasoned.

'What – and have me bleed to death?' answered Whacker with mock horror, swivelling around on his heels away from the women and holding both hands cupped downwards between his legs.

'Jesus, he's a terrible man – like that all night – nearly had us all bleeding well barred down in Madigan's—'

'Ah, I know his kind,' spoke up another, twisting his mouth contemptuously as he removed his trilby and put it on his knee. 'All blow and no balls.'

'I don't know all the same – I wouldn't trust him with me cat. He'd screw anything on two bloody legs, that fella.'

'Oh Jasus – he's at it already, lads!'

'Does he never come up for air?'

'And how's the oul puss-puss tonight, Delia me darling?' inquired Whacker, sitting tightly down beside a plump young woman with a round stolid rather cowlike face who was staring woodenly into space and absently scratching her thigh. 'You look bored, Susannah. Did you miss me that much?'

'Like a toothache,' the woman replied without turning round. She sighed heavily as he inveigled his hand under her thin nondescript skirt, feeling for her thigh. 'Jesus, Whacker, will you stop mauling me or I'll spit in your eye,' she said in the same weary voice, languidly pushing his hand away. 'I know your type, I do, thinking a girl's all right because she doesn't object now and then to having a drink with you. You can't be sociable in this country.'

'Ah yes, sure I was forgetting you were a sociable creature at heart,' said Whacker, reaching for a bottle of stout, 'and you a permanent visitor to the lock hospital. Ireland needs more of your sociable kind, me oul flower.' He brought his

144

mouth up against her ear. 'You're getting respectable – you're wearing them tonight!'

A feigned half-playful half-snarling slap from the woman, who settled back in her chair and henceforth seemed completely oblivious of the heavy hand roaming under her skirt, shielded by a terrace of dull-clothed backs and shoulders as she munched dreamily into her sandwich and now and then sipped her inky mug of beer.

Sods of wettened turf were stacked on each side of the fire, banking it up for the night. A clatter of boots in the pantry, men milling round the oven, ravenous, raucous, avaricious hands reaching out for sandwiches, lumps of meat, rings of pudding, returning with cheeks swollen with food, looking round wolfishly for their mislaid bottles and foaming mugs of stout, some staring ceilingwards with immense and comical sympathy, eyes liquid, as if communing silently with the dead and the bereaved in the darkened room above, filling their mouths unerringly with food and beer.

Slowly as more bottles popped and talk buzzed and grew animated, a kind of instinctive order crept over everything. The men gradually separated from the women and sat in groups on the opposite side of the room, slipping jokes, jibes and secrets freely to one another from behind mouth-concealing hands, heads cocked to one side, canine-fashion, stooping and belching laboriously to retrieve fallen half-eaten sandwiches from the floor, faces shining, famous and familiar with each other, locked in the rude rollicking companionship of men, eyeing the women with mock in-difference, with pretended disdain, with long laconic lewd looks, the jaded fatuous comic hunger of men strait-jacketed in the domestic mould.

The women came in from the gas-tainted pantry and sat down in hunched huddles, flopping into chairs with ex-aggerated groans of exhaustion, finding their abandoned mugs and cups, unpinning their hair, poking impatiently at the slow-smouldering fire, bending face forward to each other, fingering absently clips, brooches, ear-rings as whispers deepened and grew yet more intimate, broken frequently by

145

swift giggles and breathless spasms of hushed mirth, quick sideward flash of amused inquiring glance over shoulder at the steadily swilling men.

A floorboard creaked in the room above; sudden hush, faces upturned, questioning, listening; then the slow settling back to tongue-wagging, hand-lifting, the intermittent popping of corks as the long night of the vigil lengthened, the turf glow mellow, and chairs scraped on wood as they were pushed back from the spreading encircling heat. The plump young woman munched lazily on, eyes half closed, placidly permitting the rough-knuckled hand to move under her skirt, against her bulging thigh, as she probed with her little finger for a piece of meat trapped between her teeth.

The widow tumbled from a sudden soundless slumber that had come upon her without preamble, groped about in the dark and pulled an enamel washing basin out from under the bed. She lowered herself pendulously over it and urinated noisily into it, mumbling long-unmentioned words of endearment, humming a ghost-laden song to herself.

A loud tattoo on the hall door startled the cosiness within; it was opened to reveal, washed in yellow light from the jam-packed kitchen, a girl in a black skin-clinging sweater and mauve woollen skirt, her tears making the mascara drip darkly from her reddened eyes.

'I'm only after hearing about Noreen,' said the girl, stumbling on the top step as the back strap slipped from her high-heeled shoe.

The spidery little woman who had opened the door stared, squinted, then drew back as if from some apparition. 'May-May Gunn!' she exclaimed, both surprise and distaste in her voice. 'Where in the name of God did you come from?'

The girl did not seem to have heard the question. 'Poor Noreen!' she wailed, leaning her head against the door for apparent support, wiping at her eyes with the back of her wrist. 'I nearly died.'

'It's a bit late to be calling on people in sorrow,' the woman said, not stepping aside, neck rigid with disapproval. 'Almost one in the morning and the poor woman prostrated—'

146

'I'm only off the bloody boat from Holyhead, ma'am,' said May-May with a sudden flare of temper, brushing past, head held high and haughty. 'I felt it me Christian duty to come and pay my respects—'

'Christian duty!' a woman said loudly from somewhere in the room. There was a certain immediate stir, a frigid uneasiness among the women, a quickening lift of interest and expectancy from the men.

'Where's Mrs Geraghty?' asked May-May. 'Can I see her?'

'No, you can't,' said the little woman flatly, folding her arms and standing sentinel at the kitchen door. 'She's had more than enough of upset and can't be disturbed—'

'Sure I don't want to disturb anybody, Mrs Quinn,' said May-May sweetly now that she was safely inside. She stood on the fringe of the gathered guests, one red-nailed hand resting lightly on her outflung hip, looking around, half smiling. She was taller than any woman present, about twenty-four, with tawny shoulder-length hair and very fair skin; she was very handsome in a startling brazen way, but already her eyes, quite blue and long lashed, had dulled over as if some once essential fire had gone out of them, and her vivid crimson mouth had a sullen sensual droop. Her slim long legs were sheathed in expensive dark nylon stockings and many rings glinted and flashed on her hands.

'May-May Gunn,' whispered somebody in awe.

She stood there staring boldly at the faces she remembered, savouring both the famished hungry glances of the young and old men and the venom and resentment and sudden panic in the looks of the women. A glow of private inner feline satisfaction seemed to come from her, softening briefly the hardness in her face; then, seeming to remember the sorrowful errand she had come on, her eyes filled up again and she lowered her head, fishing a very clean hankie out from under the sleeve of her sweater. 'I can't believe it,' she cried, wiping her eyes and dabbing delicately at each nostril. 'We went to the same class, meself and Noreen, up in the convent. Sister Fidelma's class – I even remember that.

God it's terrible, all within a few years, and she not much older than meself . . .'

Unthinkingly a kind of passageway was made for her, and she walked slowly up to a hastily vacated seat by the fire and sat down, still crying softly into her hankie. Whacker slowly withdrew his hand from the plump woman's lap and straightened up, a new light in his alert eyes.

'Is that the famous Gunn one?' he asked side-mouthed of the man nearby, not taking his eyes from the girl, whose thick fallen hair now hid her face from his view and shone copperish in the turf glow.

'Aye, it is,' the man answered, teeth gnawing hungrily into lip, 'and they say she comes off like a gun, too.'

'That,' said Whacker slowly, both hands now on knees, powerful shoulders erect, looking straight over, 'that I intend to find out before this night of prayer and lamentation is out.'

The women began to buzz and hiss, drawing themselves away from the girl, mouths rigid and sour with revulsion.

'The cut of her, the shameless bitch, ringing with jewellery and half bloody naked . . . the skirt up to her thighs!'

'Why couldn't she be decent and come without a stitch on?'

'How long is it now, Florrie? Six years?'

'Aye, and the rest of it. She had to go away, you know.'

'Sure I remember well. The man next door to them, old enough to be her father.'

'She never left the poor man alone, forever going into the house on some excuse whenever the wife was out, bursting out through the few clothes she wore.'

'She was always well developed for her age. What happened exactly?'

'Need you ask? A baby before she was sixteen. They do say that she even tried with her own brother . . .'

Words heavy with swollen hate crushing the tiny thin vessels of compassion, drowning even the vague resemblance of pity, crashing down on the lowered tawny head.

'Noreen was a lovely person,' said the girl suddenly, lifting her head up, eyes bright and hard as she faced her accusers,

148

As if drawn by a magnet, as if mesmerized, his bottle-free hand slowly lifted and stretched out towards her, then paused in mid-air, just inches away.

May-May took a step unevenly backwards, the mirthless smile seeming to be pasted on to her face, like a mask, a thin ghastly gauze plastering her taut facial contours; slowly her eyes travelled down the front of the man's corpulent body, stark in their purpose. 'I see nothing there, mister,' she said, voice thin as a razor blade. 'I see nothing there at all.' She craned her white neck forward like an inquisitive bird until her forehead was almost touching his. 'Did you forget to bring it with you, by any chance?'

From where he stood in the pantry doorway, arms crossed, leaning easily against the jamb, Whacker watched intently, the smile never leaving his face but his eyes hard and glinting. The fat man's face screwed up in rage and he raised a pudding fist as if to strike her, then the others laughed and roared raucously, slapping their thighs, and the man's anger ebbed and he grinned sheepishly, falling back and lifting the bottle to his mouth, flinging at her a belly-shaking good-humoured obscenity devoid of malice. May-May swayed dizzily in the midst and press of the jeering, jiving, jovial jesters of men crowding avidly in on her; she put her hand up to her eyes in a futile effort to shut out the barbaric knife strokes of light falling upon her, her brief triumph gone, swaying helplessly as if buffeted by relentless waves; a red-knuckled hand reached out of the swirling smoke behind her; there came the metallic rasp of a zipper being opened; a sudden sheen of pink silk at her hip through the skirt. Whacker moved powerfully forward, a scythe slicing through wavering top-heavy wheat.

'I think I heard a knock,' came the quavering voice of the praying pregnant woman in the corner; nobody heeded her, and for once shaking off her timidity, she made her way through and opened the hall door. 'Yes?' she asked uncertainly, peering short-sightedly into the night. 'Do you want someone—?'

'I happen to live here,' replied a cold feminine voice.

153

A hush fell over the clamorous kitchen as the young couple appeared suddenly on the threshold, the man laden with two heavy suitcases, the fur-coated cheek-chafed woman holding a carrier cot, the handle looped under her arm. Their faces were strained and lined with travel fatigue, and the eyes of the woman swept slowly over the crowd with hostility and supercilious surprise.

'Where's me mother?' asked the young woman, accusingly.

Mrs Quinn, the spidery restless little woman, rushed forward effusively, both hands outstretched in greeting. 'Sadie Geraghty, for the life of me!' she gushed, rushing over her uncertainty. 'And Frank Kinsella himself, no less! Oh, it's years—'

'Where's me mother?' repeated Sadie in the same cold tone, ignoring the welcoming handclasp and stepping back, taking the carrier cot out of the elderly woman's reach. 'Where's me mother, and what are all these people doing here at this hour of the morning?'

Mrs Quinn squinted up, puzzled. 'People?' she echoed. 'Sadie, don't you recognize your old neighbours? They came as a mark of respect.'

'Respect!' said Sadie, shooting out the word like a dart. Then her eyes fell on the bemused, somewhat bedraggled figure of May-May leaning against the table, hair tumbling into her face, the side of her skirt wide open; Sadie's mouth tightened. 'Do you show respect by bringing prostitutes into my mother's home?'

May-May's head jerked up as if she had been upper-cut, and the two women stared across the heat-filled body-packed space of the room at each other with a resentment known before between the two of them and now resurrected like dead tissue touched by a fiery current.

'Hello, Sadie,' said May-May with an odd twist of her mouth, sweeping back her hair rather wearily. 'What's new over there in the Big Smoke?'

'Get that – that *thing* out of here!' muttered Sadie, her eyes sharp as the points of knitting needles.

'Hold on, love—' her husband began, trying to catch

her arm, a thin dark stringy-throated man in his late thirties with a dark-blue chin and a quiet air of resignation.

'You keep out of this, Frank!' snapped Sadie, flinging his hand off, 'This is my mother's home, not a brothel.'

'Let there be peace, for the love of God, and the corpse lying upstairs,' said Old Essie, shoving her way through with her thin elbows. 'Ah, Sadie, I'm surprised at you!'

Sadie turned on the old woman like a tigress. 'Fine neighbours you turned out to be, singing and shouting till all hours like it was an August Bank Holiday instead of a wake, and then bringing the likes of *that*' – pointing a rigid finger at May-May – 'under my Mother's roof! What sort of neighbours are you?'

Old Essie folded her arms over her flat chest and faced the nervous anger of the young woman with calm implacable dignity. 'Your mother's upstairs with the only child she had that was worth rearing,' she said, her sleek silver head gleaming under the light, her skeletal features serrated in slanting shadows. 'Come down off your high horse, Sadie Geraghty. If it wasn't for her neighbours your Ma might be getting coffined in the morning along with poor Noreen for all the care or help she ever got from her family once they went to England, for it was only state days and bonfire nights any of yous ever bothered to send her home a farthing even after your father died!'

Sadie's eyes faltered before the old woman's piercing stare. 'Mrs Boylan, I – I didn't mean to be . . .'

Old Essie's face softened and she clucked her tongue gently. 'Tie a knot in that tongue of yours and go up and see your mother.'

The husband took his wife's arm firmly now. 'It's the travelling and loss of sleep,' he said quietly. 'We're both fagged out. C'mon, love,' he said, leading her to the stairs, 'your mother's waiting.'

Sadie held back, tired and fearful, clutching the Moses basket. Old Essie gently loosened the woman's grip and took the carrier cot from her. 'Go up now,' she said, 'I'll see to the baby.' The couple walked slowly upstairs.

The fire by now had been dying steadily, long unattended; snoring had been coming from many parts of the room, faces hung limply back, ceilingwards, hands quiescent in laps, the drugged sluggish movements of people back and forward as if in slow motion; the hall door had been opening and closing softly as others slipped furtively away to their beds; talk now hummed low enough to allow the clip-clop clatter of an early morning milk dray to be heard rumbling down the dawn-still street. The gathering had dwindled.

The drowsy dull-lidded hiatus was shattered by a scream down the stairs. 'Jesus, somebody – come quick!' came the shrill cry of Sadie.

A startled stunned uncertain hush, heads jack-knifed upwards, slack mouths incredulous; then a scrambling feet-entangling rush to the foot of the stairs, chaotic climbing upwards, tumultuous thud of feet across the groaning floorboards above.

'What in the name of Jesus is wrong?' Whacker wanted to know, wiping his mouth and putting down the now empty gin bottle.

'Maybe somebody's been raped,' suggested one of the men hopefully, rubbing the back of his boil-encrusted neck.

Mrs Quinn bustled back breathlessly into the kitchen, two red-mottled blobs of excitement on her parchment cheeks. 'It's Magso herself, God help us,' she announced, quivering like a bird, her eyes rolling with comic wonder. 'They found her lying in her own blood and vomit, not a stitch on her, sprawled over the poor corpse!'

'Great bollacking Jesus!' somebody whispered with profound awe.

They carried the widow into the back bedroom, throwing a sheet over that huge time-ravaged nakedness, the mattress shuddering under her massive weight, placing her on the long narrow iron-framed single bed where Noreen had slept, sibilant sighs and moans and long-forgotten words of endearment echoing raggedly from the cavernous depths of her. A man mounted a commandeered bicycle shakily and wobbled uncertainly off down the chill unlit morning street in search of either doctor or priest. Sadie cowered back in a corner of the bedroom with the whites of her dilated eyes shining in the gloom, horror, disgust and fascination etched into her face.

'Mother! Mother!' she cried hoarsely, stumbling to the foot of the bed, her skin-taut fingers clutching the iron rails.

Red Magso's eyes flickered briefly open, slow recognition stirring in their dim depths. 'God's curse on you,' she said softly, wearily, then her head dropped sideways and she lapsed into unconsciousness.

In the kitchen the clock ticked loudly above the faint lisping embers in the firegrate.

'Dear Lord, I feel sick!' mumbled May-May, clutching at her throat, eyes watering, stumbling past Whacker into the pantry. She bent over the sink, retching violently, her shoulders shaking, her groans gradually faltering to a low sick animal whimper.

'All right, love?' asked Whacker softly, stepping up behind her. He reached out and flicked down the light switch on the wall nearby, leaving them in blue dawn-tinged darkness.

'Please, mister . . .' moaned the girl, trying weakly to twist away as his arms fastened around her waist.

Whacker laughed quietly, holding her easily, pushing his hand under the waistband of her sweater, flashing upwards, finding the hard satin-clad cones of her brassiere, exerting an insistent rhythmic pressure.

'Oh God,' she moaned softly as he backheeled the door shut behind them. 'Oh God,' her voice tremulous with involuntary response.

'Easy does it, love,' whispered Whacker soothingly, feeling the cool rasp of her fingers sliding over him in a frenzy. He caught her strongly and, half lifting her, eased her gently down on top of a musty pile of old clothes crammed into the narrow enamel bath fitted along the wall behind the door. She slumped back, her arms still clinging round his neck, and gingerly he lowered himself down upon her, moulding his body to the widening triangle of her thighs.

A small group of men remained seated around the lifeless

hearth, swilling the black beer round in their mugs, listening with ironic casual amusement to the hastily stifled deep-throated sounds of fevered pain and pleasure escaping from the dark closed pantry.

One of them grinned and fished out a large old-fashioned watch chain from his waistcoat pocket. 'He should be nearly there be now, lads,' he said, holding up the dial. 'Three minutes flat.'

'I hope he brought his rubbers with him,' another said. 'Durex is a man's best friend.'

'It's a terrible thing to be doing and a corpse in the house,' said an older man with grey locks, shaking his head mournfully. 'I mean, there's a time and place for everything. It's like doing it in a chapel.'

'A standing one has no conscience, Larry,' said another, grinning. 'I bet yours is standing out a mile this minute!'

'They say she's got a one as wide as Dublin Bay.'

'I hope Whacker likes swimming.'

'Eh, tell me, Dinny,' said a youngish man, leaning forward with brow-puckered interest, hands clasped over one crossed knee, 'have you got a horn, be any chance?'

'No,' said Dinny, laughing. 'This is just a bottle I have in me trousers pocket.'

A hand was raised to quell the laughter that followed, and once more they all listened intently.

'Good oul Whacker!' said the florid Dinny, slapping his own swelling maleness with comradely fondness. 'Give it a final twist for me!' Then, yawning, stretching, feeling for cigarettes in their pockets, they got out a soiled deck of cards and began to play a game of four-handed 'dawn'.

22

'YOU COULD have killed the poor man, Essie,' said Mother, after hearing the old woman's rambling story. 'You should've been more careful, like, before putting them into the pot.'

'But Jesus, I didn't mean any harm,' said Old Essie, holding her hand up gingerly to her discoloured eye. 'Me oul eyesight's not what it used to be, and the wallop he gave me is only after ruining it altogether, bad cess to him. Jesus, he gave me an unmerciful belt, all because of a little mistake.'

'Little mistake!' said Mother. 'Ah now, Essie, you've got to be fair. You might've poisoned him. It isn't every man that gets boiled tulips for his dinner. You wouldn't expect him to make love to you.'

'But I could've swore they were onions!' Essie said stubbornly, twisting her skirts into place round her protruding knees. 'That oul bitch next door had no right to grow bloody tulips right in the arsehold of her onion patch. It's looking for trouble—'

'But, Essie, you had no right to take her onions—'

Essie snorted and drew herself upright. 'Ah, she knew bloody well I've been slipping in under her back railings for years whenever I'm making a stew for the oul fella. Sure she wouldn't miss a few bloody onions and she with half a yard full of them. Some of them were bloody rotten into the bargain. I think the oul cow did it on purpose, putting the bloody tulips next door to the onions, them looking so alike and knowing me sight wasn't too good. I'd put nothing past that wan, let me tell you. Sure how could she be any use and she from Belfast? She was supposed to turn when she married poor Paddy Kerrigan, but anyone can see she's still a black bloody Protestant at heart. Tom is always saying that the Belfast people is worse than the English themselves any day.' Her husband's name made the old woman remember, and she winced. 'The little murdering fornicated oul demon! He nearly took the eye out of me.' She began to laugh without warning, holding a hand to her mouth, convulsed on the chair. 'Jesus, d'you know what I'm going to tell you? The oul bastard turned blue ... blue as your fucking dress, bejasus!'

'It's no laughing matter, Essie,' said Mother, but unable to repress a smile at the outrageous mirth of the other.

The old woman did not seem to have heard and went on breathlessly guffawing into herself, one hand across her mouth, the other slapping her knee in a riot of private glee. 'True as Jasus, not a word of a lie ... blue he turned, and the purple froth bubbling out of his mouth every time he tried to say something ... and the eyes jumping out of his head as if he was looking the divil in the face ... they was like coloured soapsuds coming out of his mouth, running down the front of his lovely white shirt ... "Ah, that's a powerful smell, Essie," he says coming in well nourished from the pub and taking a look at the big pot bubbling like bejasus on the gas. "Is it nearly ready, for me belly thinks me throat is cut."' Her eyes rolled up in remembered relish. 'Ah, it was lovely looking, all foamy white and luscious-thick, the best-looking bloody stew I ever saw that would make a cripple run a mile to get at. I'm telling you, if you saw it yourself—'

'But what about the smell of it, Essie?' asked Mother. 'Wasn't there a strange smell off it?'

Essie shrugged. 'How the hell did I know? Me oul smellers is as bad as me eyes. And I was after putting that much pepper and mustard and peppermint on it—'

'Peppermint?' Mother interjected, incredulous.

'Peppermint,' repeated Old Essie, unperturbed. 'Grand for the indigestion. Well, there was that much pepper and stuff on it that Tom couldn't smell anything strange either, and he was that side-lepping with the hunger that he would have ate a farmer's arse through a hedge. I lifts him up a bloody big bowl of it and sets it before him, and off he starts leathering into it like he never had a bite before, and me sitting there looking at him pleased as punch, seeing the way he was attacking me cooking. It went straight to me heart to see that ravenous look on his face, for a woman likes to see her man enjoying her cooking. And then bejasus, right there before me eyes, as God is me judge, didn't he start turning blue ... not blue exactly, more of a *puce* colour, half blue and half mauve, sort of, and when he tried to speak the white bubbles started flying out of his mouth like a fucking fountain ... I just sat looking for a time, for the colours were gorgeous, and it took me back to me young days when there was this fountain up in the park and they used to put different dyes in the water to make it like a rainbow ... I could see he was near choking be then, his oul face like a red balloon, and the stuff all fizzing out of his mouth, so I jumped up and got a bar of carbolic soap from the scullery and stuffed it down his throat to make him sick, and in next to no time the floor was swimming with the contents of his belly and the quare colours had gone out of his kisser. I was helping him up off his knees when he ups and gives me a rare bloody haymaker right in the eye that sent me spinning, and me after bringing the life back into him, the oul bastard.'

'But you could've been up for murder, Essie,' said Mother.

'Murder bedamned!' Essie spat out. 'A fucking service to the nation, that would've been. It'd take more than a bunch of stewed tulips to send that wicked oul bastard to purgatory. So now I'll have to buy me onions, for I'd be in fear and dread of me life doing the same thing again, and he wouldn't believe it was an accident the next time. He'd cleave the head off me if I did it again. He would've slaughtered me if it hadn't been for Magso hearing the row and rushing in. He knew better than to argue the toss with *her*, for one swing of her tits would send the little scut sprawling.'

'Is she any better?'

Old Essie's wrinkled countenance drooped. 'Ah, poor Magso!' she said, her head falling back against the chair, sucking in her wide flabby lips over her gums, the hollow in

161

her turned-up chin deepening. 'I was full sure she was going to join oul Matt and poor little Noreen when she had the attack that time. The Sadie wan and her husband were no sooner left Mount Jerome after the funeral than they were off catching the next boat to Holyhead. That's feelings for you! And did you hear what happened when they brought the coffin to the chapel?' Before waiting for any reply, the old woman jerked herself suddenly forward in her chair, shooting out a bony hand and gripping Mother's arm, chewing her gums fiercely. 'Wait till I tell you! The coffin was no sooner put up on the altar and the few prayers said, when your bould man Father O'Rourke slips over to poor Magso in his sandals and says into her ear loud enough for all to hear, "That will be two pounds, please, Mrs Hannigan." Now I ask you, was that a right thing to say to any mother in her hour of grief? It might have been the only two pounds she was possessed of. I'm as good a Catholic as any, but bejasus, that's making a mockery of death altogether!'

'Sure it costs money to come into the world and it costs money to go out of it, that's the gospel truth,' said Mother.

'Aye, but in the house of God . . .' Old Essie glanced sideways at Mother, a look of sly cautious abandon on her face, as if weighing the effect of what she was going to say. 'D'you know, it would make you sit and wonder if there's any sense in religion at all. You'd be better off not going to church or meeting, for all them priests ever ask for is money. If it's not for this it's for that and if it's not for that it's for the other, and them living in the swank houses with maids and housekeepers and valays, playing bloody golfballs on a Sunday and driving around in bloody motorcars like De Valera himself.' The old woman, seeing her words had not invoked a sudden and inexplicable seizure or brought down the wrath of the heavens, grinned and rubbed her fingers in her outer skirt. 'D'you know what it is? You'd be better off sometimes being a bloody Protestant!'

Suddenly she jerked her head up towards the window and hastily clambered to her feet as she spied a figure crossing

162

the street. 'Oh, bejasus, here's Balls from Dalkey!' she said, shuffling her old coat on about her shoulders. 'I'll be going in the name of God—'

'Sure his dinner's ready,' Mother said, with no great effort to detain her. 'There's no need for you—'

'Now no man likes to eat his dinner in front of outsiders,' insisted Essie, hobbling to the door and opening it before the person outside had reached for the key that was always in the latch, her flapping mouth opened on a grin. 'Ah, there you are yourself, Paddy,' she croaked, sliding past him. 'I was just going . . .' As he grunted out a greeting and turned his back on her to enter the kitchen, the old woman stuck two of her fingers up in a V sign very close to her nose, then shuffled off down the steps.

'What was that oul wan doing here?' asked Father, scraping his boots on a faded green mat full of holes near the kitchen door. 'Ating the living flesh off someone per usual, I suppose?'

'Ah, poor Essie,' said Mother. 'Sure God help her, she's harmless and a great oul trouper in need. She'll stand on her head to help anyone.'

Father gave a derisive grunt. 'That would be something to see, all right – a chimney brush turned upside down! Bejasus, the fingers nearly fell of me with the frost up on the scaffold today,' he said, taking off his heavy ancient overcoat and hooking it up on the back of the coalhouse door. 'The winter's setting in hard and fast, and it's only October yet.' He went over and stood by the fire, feet wide apart, warming his behind, rubbing his hands up and down over his hips and flanks. 'Bejasus, it's fucking hard graft in the winter, this bleeding building trade. There was a wind out today that would blow the balls off a brass monkey. What's keeping you with me dinner, for Christ's sake? Me belly thinks me throat is cut.'

'It's nice and warm over the gas,' Mother said, going into the pantry, picking up a towel.

'I hope it's not turnips again, missus,' said Father, having warmed himself and flopping down into one of the large

163

sagging armchairs that perpetually flanked the fireplace. 'If I eat any more turnips I'll turn bleeding yellow.'

'Ah, don't be always giving out,' said Mother, smiling, coming in holding two steaming plates between her hands, setting them down on the big round mahogany table with the great curved serpentine legs that had been drawn up before the fire. 'I've something here that you like—'

Father grinned and slipped the braces off from his shoulders. 'Bejasus, ma'am, you always had that,' he said, slapping her hardily on her behind. 'It's still a fine oul arse you've got there, thank Jasus, in spite of everything—'

'Ssh! The children!' Mother shushed fiercely.

'Sure I'm only saying me prayers,' said Father. 'You're still a fine-looking woman, and maybe there's a final fling waiting to be flung yet. Last of the Mohicans . . .'

Mother looked at him with a suspicion she could not suppress. 'Is it drink you have on you?'

'Drink!' Father snorted. 'Where in the name of Jasus d'you think I'd get drink in the middle of the week, woman? I only work for Sisk – I don't own a fucking share in it.'

'I thought maybe you got the sub,' said Mother, going to the dresser and taking out a pot of mustard and pepper and salt.

'The sub!' Father echoed again with another nostril-flaring snort, dabbing great globs of mustard all over his plate. 'God bless your innocence. That frosty-nosed bastard of a Corkman wouldn't give you the sub not if you told him your crippled mother was dying with the holy stigmata. A bleeding culshie for your life. He'd build a nest in your ear and sub-let the other.' He piled his fork high with cabbage and shoved it into his mouth with annoyance. 'I come home with the fingers dropping off me with the cold, and you ask me have I a drink on me!'

'Well, I mean – you were that good-humoured,' said Mother, seemingly without thinking.

'Suffering God!' said Father with heavy resignation, putting down his fork. 'Can a man not come home in the evening and pass a pleasant word or two with his wife without being pissed up to the eyeballs? It's enough to make a man lose his bloody appetite,' he said with absolute disgust, shovelling another forkful of cabbage and potatoes into his mouth.

'Ag, g'wan and eat your bit and don't have so much to say,' said Mother, anxious to placate him and preserve his rare mood. 'There's more in the pot if your belly can hold it.'

She put a big mossy-green log on the fire; it was years-old-dry, and soon the flames were hissing out from it like serpents' tongues, darting ferociously up the smoke-blackened chimney. The poor little thin-ribbed mongrel dog, more gifted with longevity than any cat on the street, lay curled up like a ball of dull brown wool on the other side of the fireplace, for once upon a rare time unmolested and basking one-eyed-awake in this infrequent freedom, the other eye all watchful on the mortar-tipped boot reposing upon the hearth inches away from its tingling nose. A quarter to dusky six said the clock, arguing quietly with itself on the mantelpiece, but already the dull, many-times-dyed curtains were drawn tightly against the early dark of October. A row of children sat in tiers upon the shiny age-honoured horsehair sofa, gobbling up their school books, scribbling hasty ill-considered sums into their ninepenny exercise jotters, secretively elbowing one another for more space, their truculent squeaks of protest and rebellion instantly silenced by a look full of menace from Father.

The utter absorption he always gave to the functional faculty of eating was both fascinating and obscene; no talk was allowed, even when it did not concern or involve him; the radio could not be turned on; nobody present could go either up or down the stairs; if there came a knock all unwelcome on the front door his dark thick brows would clash together ferociously and, laying down one hand on the table and gripping the fork rigidly, veins standing out to attention, he would wait grimly for the buzz of conversation at the front step to be over and the door shut, before twice as grimly resuming his meal. Even the thin faraway scraping of the cheap metallic nibs on the exercise copies was enough

165

to provoke an explosive cough of imminent peril, and the pint-sized offenders would look up with crestfallen guilt on their faces and hold themselves fear-stiffened still, waiting for the marathon meal to be at an end, flashing looks of resigned martyrdom, their sighs of long-suffering docility and patience hastily stifled by yet another thunderous look from under those tremendous brows.

Now he laid aside his knife and fork, grunting with satisfaction, loosening the brass-buckled time-smooth leather belt around his waist and leaning back in his chair. There ensued the gradual restirring of activity in the room once he had finished dinner; the sudden relieved laugh and nervous giggle, the tumbling outflow of words that had been dammed back while the knife and fork rose and fell, glinting in the firelight; the renewed elbow pushing from the over-burdened sofa, the high-pitched exclamations, the scrape and thud of boots and shoes in flight and pursuit across the floor. The radio was switched on; a rumba pounded forth into the kitchen; two of the girls jumped gleefully to their feet and started dancing to it, jigging and wriggling their hips, throwing out their bellies, clicking their fingers above their heads in ludicrous imitation of the exotic Carmen Miranda of the famous talking torso. One of the girls slipped out of her older sister's many-sizes-too-large high-heeled shoes and bumped loudly against the dresser, making the delft go swinging on the metal hooks. She glanced fearfully over at Father, but he just went on reading the evening newspaper and chewing remaining bits of gristle, legs spread-eagled upon the hearthstone, his slack rough-clothed loins soaking in the warmth. The two rumba lovers went on with their shadow-flinging gyrations, mocked at and pelted with screwed-up balls of paper by their grinning brothers hiding behind their schoolbooks and other paraphernalia of assiduous learning. Father looked up finally, laying the newspaper down across his knees. 'Eh, you,' he said, pointing to one of the boys. 'You, what's your bloody name—'

'Me, sir?' said the boy, coming over at once.

'Aye, you,' said Father, fumbling in one of the pockets of his waistcoat, the few coins jingling therein. 'Go and get me a North Light safety blade and be quick about it.'

'Yes, sir,' said the boy, galloping out of the front door.

'Will you put on a sup of water for me, missus?' said Father, getting up and stretching himself, rolling up his shirtsleeves and scratching his hairy forearms.

Mother looked in from the pantry. 'For the tea, you mean? Sure it's nearly drew—'

'I want a bloody shave, woman,' he said, rasping his thumb and forefinger along his bristling chin. 'I'm going around looking like an escaped convict.'

Mother, looking uncertain and apprehensive, came in, wiping her wet hands in her apron. 'It's only Wednesday, sure,' she said. 'You never shave until Friday at the earliest—'

'Sweet bleeding Jasus,' Father said, exasperated. 'Can't you boil a saucepan of water for me when I ask you without wanting to hear me confession? It said fuck all in tonight's paper about the Dublin Waterworks going on strike.'

A look of reluctant enlightenment crossed Mother's face. 'Oh, you're going out?' she said in a faltering voice.

Father glared at her. 'Going out?' he mimicked grotesquely, thrusting his face forward. 'You don't think I'm going to the bother and expense of shaving meself just to sit on the other side of the hob all night gawking over at you? Have you a clean shirt handy, or do I have to go out looking like a bleeding knacker?'

'There's a clean shirt ironed and all, but—'

'And you,' said Father, yanking one of his sons off the sofa. 'Get me the boot polish and the brushes.' He got down on his knees and pulled out his good pair of brown brogues from under the dresser. 'Where are you off to, mister?' Mother asked at length, moistening her lips.

Father sat down on one of the plain wooden straight-backed chairs, pulling off his work boots, upending each of them in turn and shaking out bits of grime and cement from them on to the hearthstone. 'Did I not tell you?' he said, grinning with sudden sly ironic amusement. 'They made me a shop steward on the job. Can you beat that? I didn't want to take the job, for them fellas all have a bad name with the men, but they all voted for me, so I couldn't bloody well refuse, now could I?' He shook out the other boot. 'It's a terrible temptation, though, minding all that money.'

'What – what money?' asked Mother feebly, gripping the edge of the table hard.

Father seemed not to have heard her, for he shouted out to the errand boy in the pantry. 'Are you making that bloody polish in there? I have to be out by half past seven, and if I'm late I'll make your bloody arse sing with the leathering I'll give it!'

'What money, mister?' Mother reiterated, unwilling, yet determined to learn the full extent of her impending doom.

'You little shit,' growled Father, grabbing the polish tin and brushes from the boy and swiping at him with his other hand. 'What are you on about?' he asked Mother impatiently, shoving one hand into the boot and holding it out in front of him, beginning to polish vigorously. 'The bleeding Union money, of course, that I collected off the men.'

'The . . . the Union money?' came Mother's awed whisper.

'Will you stop talking back to me like a fucking parrot, woman?' he roared with goaded annoyance, balancing the polish tin on his knee. 'Are you deaf or what? I'm after telling you a dozen times already. I'm a shop steward. Most of the fellas were out of benefit with the Union before they appointed me shop steward. Since I took over most of them are back in benefit.' He shook his head, highly pleased with himself, yet still bemused. 'They trust me, bejasus. I may be a narky bloody bastard and all, but they trust me. They know I'm no fucking latchico or general foreman's lick-arse. But still,' he said, shaking his head and sighing profoundly as he began polishing the second boot; 'it's a terrible responsibility, holding that much money for other people . . .'

'That much money?'

'Aye,' said Father, his sense of responsibility and importance making him forget to be annoyed by Mother's faltering repetitiveness. 'Thirty-five quid, nearly five weeks' money. I'll be glad to hand it in to the committee tonight.'

Mother stood at the table, no longer even looking at him, staring dully into the fire. 'You'll be wearing your good suit tonight, then?' she asked.

He nodded. 'Aye. Wouldn't give any of them committee bastards anything to talk about.'

'And you left the money in the suit?' Mother went on, as if merely stating something which she already knew to be a fact.

'Where else?' said Father, oblivious to the peculiar tone of her voice. She seemed no longer tense or taut; she just stood there leaning heavily with the undersides of her palms downwards on the table, a remote look on her face, as though she had only just then been hit over the head with a mallet. Father put down the shining boots and got up, going past her towards the kitchen door.

'There's no use going up for your suit, mister,' said Mother with a kind of dead calm. 'It isn't there.'

Father stopped and turned round, staring. 'What do you mean it isn't there?'

'It isn't there,' repeated Mother, toying absently with some breadcrumbs on the table. 'I took a loan of it this morning.'

Father's breath went in and out, his stringy windpipe jerking up and down. 'You mean you pawned the fucking thing?'

Mother nodded dumbly, still not looking up.

His hand fell away from the door handle and he took a few shuffling steps back into the room. 'Well, you could've told me you were taking it,' he said, forcing himself to grimace in a grotesque imitation of a grin. 'I'll tell them I was working late and hadn't time to change.' He came up to the other side of the table, a sick kind of look on his face that made the attempted smile all the more hideous and abortive. 'I'll go as I am. Just tell me where you put the money.' She did not answer, appeared indeed not to have heard him, and he leaned forward across the table, lifting his voice. 'The money, missus! Where did you put it?'

She lifted her hand and brushed back her hair wearily from her sweat-moist forehead. 'I never touched it,' she said. 'I never knew it was there. You never said a word about it. I took the suit as it was. You know yourself I never look in pockets . . .'

Father's face crumpled incredibly and he tottered back into the armchair, staring up at her, vast and ludicrous disbelief chasing anger and fury across his craggy countenance. The mongrel dog sniffed anxiously, then obeying its own well-tested instincts, slithered quickly under the dresser, its bony head thrust between its paws, peering cautiously out. Father's eyelids were rising and falling rapidly over his eyes like blinds being jerked up and down, the dark-blue pupils glistening like black berries out of the glazed fog and frost of his gaze.

'How much . . .' he stopped and drew in his breath once more. 'How much did they give you on the suit?'

'Thirty-five shillings,' Mother said.

'A shilling for every pound,' echoed Father wonderingly, rubbing his wrist across his dry mouth. 'Do you hear that?' he said sweeping his arm in a wide circle to include everyone in the kitchen. 'I swear to Jesus, it's a madwoman I married! It's a madwoman you have for a mother! She pawns thirty-five pounds in return for thirty-five shillings . . .' His mouth twisted sideways with the effort to speak, he pulled himself up from the chair and stood wavering and flapping his arms about like a demented windmill run amok in a freak thunderstorm. 'Sweet sacred cunt of all the female saints in heaven! What did I ever do to deserve this? Jesus God almighty, what did I ever do? What am I going to tell the Union – what am I going to tell the men? That me missus pawned me suit with their money inside it? Woman, woman, you're after fucking me good and proper, do you know!' he roared, not so much in fury as in baffled wrath and bewilderment, tottering back and forward from table to fireplace, kicking at everything in his path with lost, childish savagery, his knuckles hard knots of congealed anguish in his pockets. 'What a bleeding bollacking jackass you're after making of me before the whole Union! Oh Jesus Christ, why did you put her before me in the first place? Her belly fills up with another bastard year after year, and me working like a hungry poor cunt for the lot of them till I'm nearly blind and bollaxed, and what does she do? She goes and pawns thirty-five bleeding pound for thirty-five lousy clap-happy shillings, the fat-arsed, big-diddied oul madwoman . . .'

He stopped halfway between table and fire, halfway between jagged broiling fury and defeated impossible desolation, eyes bulging enormously; then he dashed forward like a projectile fired from a cannon, and Mother flung up her arms instinctively, to ward off the inexorable assault, but instead he rushed past her and grabbed at the radio, a neat set in black imitation oak, lifting it above his head and holding it aloft, a pathetic Samson shorn of his mythical strength striving mightily to bring down the roof of the world upon his tormentors; the sounds of Latin-American music crackled crazily from the airborne radio as his head shook violently from side to side, then he flung it with a long loud shattering curse against the wall and stamped on it, crushing in its satin-covered volume box, the electric wires and plugs jerking loose with a queer fizzing noise.

He fell into the armchair and lay slumped in it for a long while, arms sprawled over the sides, feet twisted on the hearthstone. The life seemed to ebb visibly out of his face until it was empty and ravaged, like a deserted shore after the tide had gone out, pitted with the ugliness and debris of his own wasted strength.

'Get me my tea, woman,' he said, putting his hand to his eyes, seeming suddenly and frightfully to shrink into himself.

23

'ARE YOU not well, mister?'

Father looked up from the sagging depths of the supine armchair, eyes flaring fiercely and briefly with something of their old fire.

'Why, am I not going bleeding quick enough for you?' he answered Mother, gnawing his toothless lower gum.

'You look terrible, that's all.'

'Don't worry, missus. There'll be a strike on at the grave-yard when I go.'

He got sluggishly up and went to the front window.

'I can spare you the price of a pint.' Mother rooted in her big apron pocket, face flushed and steamy from the ironing.

'Keep it to light a candle for my soul.'

Away from the window, brooding, pale eyes hidden under hairy cliffs of eyebrows, staring at the crumbling white turf ash in the grate. Clock speaking quietly, monotonously on mantelshelf.

'It's not like you to say no to a pint.'

'Don't be annoying me, woman.'

He switched on the new second-hand radio. Grand Hotel. Mayfair, the heart of London, ladies and gentlemen. And here to entertain you for the next hour. Vibrating violins serenading Vienna. Hands rummaging in heaps of musty old rags in the bath, pulling out bottle. 'Moses in the desert finding a fucking well.'

Swift twist of wrist, tin cap spinning off, bouncing on the concrete floor of the scullery. Back to the armchair, drinking from bottle, squinting one-eyed, dark green shade on slack cheek.

'How is that fine dainty daughter of yours, missus?'

'How could she be, and she expecting any day now?'

'Serves her bloody well right. Could tell what was in that fella's mind all along. One thing. Two up and one to go. A bare three years married. Jesus Christ.'

'You're a fine one to talk. What did you ever think of yourself?'

'I was drunk every time. Dead bloody drunk every time.'

'You'd get out of hell itself. That lad is very good to her.'

'Oh aye. Good as gold, and him bone idle.'

'It's not his fault he can't get work. Footsore he is, tramping all over Dublin looking for a job.'

'Putting a daughter of mine in that bloody hatbox on the Quays. Big hairy fucking rats running all over the kip. The smell of stale piss everywhere. Oh aye. He's good to her all right.' Glint of pale green glass lifted in vein-thick knobbly fist.

'People in glasshouses. You forget yourself, mister. We started out that way ourselves. Every young couple has to struggle to get on their feet. And they never trouble us for a crust of bread. You must be fair, mister.'

'Ah, fair me arse. If I knew what I was letting meself in for I'd have jumped in the Liffey the first time I saw you.'

'You were no first prize yourself, let me tell you.' Angry thump of iron on groaning table. 'I wish to the Little Flower I had me life all over again. I should have gone into the Sisters of the Poor, for I've been poor since the day I married you.'

'You should've stayed with that fat oul bastard of an uncle of yours. Up to his oxers in pig shit. Giving money for Masses with one hand and the other stuck up the skirts of his servant girls.'

'Mister, you have a rotten mind. You'll never see the light of Heaven.'

'Ah, fuck you and the light of Heaven.' Groan of chair springs. Bottle dropped on to the hearth. 'Where's me hat and coat till I get out of here before I do something drastic.'

'Where are you off to, may I ask?'

'To light a dozen candles. Give me that few shillings you were forcing into me hand a while back.'

173

Tinkle of half-crowns. 'I got a borrow—'

'I don't want its bloody life history, woman.'

'Don't come back here like a raging lion.'

'Sweet jumping Jesus. You must be mad. I won't get bleeding drunk on this.'

She stood at the window, looking after the trilby hat bobbing up and down jauntily until it disappeared. She pressed her forehead against the cool pane, trying to soothe the migraine that was starting. She felt the cold, wet nose of the mongrel against her shins. It whinnied nervously. She knelt down to pat it, her fingers feeling its craggy skull.

'Poor little fella. Let's see if we can find you a bone.'

She went into the scullery, but the dog did not follow. It sat on its hunkers, whimpering softly. She stood at the scullery door, puzzled. 'What is it, boy? Come here and tell me what it is.'

She patted her knee, calling, but the dog remained where it was, looking at her with big mournful brown eyes, as if trying to speak with them. It crawled under the dresser and sniffed at a pair of Father's old working boots. It cringed, then began to howl. 'Jesus, Mary and Joseph.'

Mother came back into the room, sat darning socks by the fire, the mongrel now curled in a ball at her feet. She kept glancing between stitches at the clock, her eyes worried, full of unwilling foreboding. The ironed clothes for the morning lay stacked on the dresser, ready for school. She half listened to the radio at her elbow. Your Hundred Best Tunes ladies and gentlemen. 'Love's Old Sweet Song.' Paul Robeson singing 'O My Baby my Curly-headed Baby'. The sweet Shannon voice of McCormack's 'O Snowy-breasted Pearl' flowing like thick sweetened sugar around the fringes of her mind warming her with an old-wine glow. The high-ceilinged living-room facing on the wide esplanade of Smithfield Market and the beloved high-collared uncle at the brown-oak piano singing in the coloured mists of his memories 'O Take a Pair of Sparkling Eyes'. And behind in the broad sties the pink pigs grunting querulously, sticking their sensitive snouts into ripe mounds of pig food.

174

She laid aside her darning, stirred the smouldering peat ash, threw on more hard sods. It was cool enough indoors. O cool enough for the midsummer month that was in it. She went into the scullery, filled the time-smooth kettle with water from the tap, put it on the gas jet under a low glimmer. No hurry. He wouldn't be home in a hurry from his darts and his rings and his foaming pints. She brought out the slaughtered remains of that Sunday's corned beef and cut a few sandwiches. She heard rumblings from upstairs. It was hard to get them to sleep these bright nights. If he came home and found them not asleep yet the belt would be in action and he up lark-wise for work on the Monday.

When she came back into the kitchen Lil was there.

'I know it's late, Ma—'

'Sit down. Here, near the fire, such as it is.'

'We were up with his people. His father brought him down for a pint. I'll catch the last bus easily.'

'Any news?'

Lil eased herself carefully into the armchair, slim fingers pushing back the hair from her forehead in under her scarf. Her belly was very large. 'I saw the doctor again yesterday.' She looked up, her blue eyes large, a little frightened, yet humorous. 'It might be twins, Ma.'

'God's will be done. Just take care of yourself.'

Mother back at the oven, raising the gas, kettle coming to the boil. Dear God, she's only a child still, thin as a peeled stick and the fear and pain of it all looming in her eyes. Yet she was a woman O long before she knew what it really meant. Coming to me all eyes and the frightened mouth of her the very first time. Mother, there was no blood at all this morning. How many short years ago was that, how many long mornings?

'Twins!' said Lil, with wonder. 'Do they run in the family, Ma?' Mother poured the tea, brought in a plate of sandwiches. 'Your Aunt Mary had two sets. Someone else had four sets. How are you feeling, apart from everything else?'

'Oh, not too dusty. Bit weak on me pins. Do you think I'm

175

big enough to be carrying twins, Ma?'

Mother's eyes, quick, knowing. 'You're big enough.'

'God, I never thought about twins.'

'What does Joe think?'

Lil bent over her tea. 'Ah, you know men, Ma. They don't like to talk about such things.'

'Is he not working yet?'

Lil looked defiant, on guard. 'It's not his fault, Ma, honest.'

'I never said it was. I keep telling you to come here. You won't be stall fed, but you'll get share of what's going. You're too proud.'

'It's not that, Ma.' Lil's forehead glistened slightly as she drank the hot tea. 'You know how it is.' She leaned back in the chair, kicking off her shoes, wriggling her nyloned toes in the slow heat. 'I feel awkward before the boys, and me like this.'

'They're your own flesh and blood, for God's sake, child. Where's the shame in it?'

'I know it's foolish, but I can't help it. Just feels like the other day when I was one of them growing up here, and now look at me!'

'But how are you managing? What they give out on the Labour wouldn't keep you in salt and pepper. Think of the other two kids, God love them. They must be lost.'

'They're very good neighbours we have. Share their last loaf of bread with you.'

'I don't like any child of mine depending on charity when you can get share of what's going here in your own home.'

'Don't be worrying, Ma. Joe's in the way of doing a few nixers. He's doing an extension for Mattie Madigan. You know, the pub on the corner. We won't starve.' Lil paused, rubbing the rim of her cup against her lower lip. 'How's Da? Same as ever?'

'He's not. I don't like the look of him at all lately. Almost had to force him to go out for a pint.'

'He must be real sick, Ma!'

'That's what I'm telling you. He's not well at all. I wish

he'd see a doctor, but it's like getting him to go to confession.'

'Oh Ma, it's yourself that needs a doctor.' The large, luminous blue eyes were flashing. 'You're hopeless, Ma.'

'When you've lived with a man for over thirty years, you can't help feeling concerned. I'm terrible worried.'

'It's just the beer, that's all. Just the bloody beer.'

Mother looked up quickly. 'Is Joe at it heavy?'

Lil looked tired. 'Oh, he's no saint, I tell you. I never wanted to marry a saint.'

'He doesn't knock you around, now does he? Tell me.'

Lil took a quick gulp of her tea. 'You know what men are. Just big children. Best in the world one day, then the next you want to murder them. Joe's not the worst.'

'You're crying.'

'I'm not.' Swift, angry dash of hand across eyes. 'It's just the tea. It's scalding.'

'Are you happy Lil? I want to know.'

A sigh, eyes on the fire, tired. A look of pained confusion. 'I don't know, Ma. I don't understand words like that. How do you know if you're happy or not? Bit late now to start asking meself questions like that. I suppose I'm just as happy as most people. That's all.'

'Your father was asking about you, just tonight.'

Quick rise of head, eagerly. Then down again, eyes clouded. 'Was he now? Does he miss me sweet voice telling him off?'

'Don't be too hard on him, Lil. He can't help being what he is.'

'Oh, I know. None of us can.'

'He often talks about you, asks how you're managing. And even when he doesn't I can tell he's thinking about you.'

'Getting sentimental in his old age. Do you ever hear from that divil over in London?'

'Now and then. Never thought I'd see a son of mine in that uniform. Lied his way into the army here, then into the RAF over there. Your father will never forgive him. He'd

177

go berserk altogether if he ever saw him in the Queen's uniform.'

Lil smiled, bitterly, her mouth tight. 'Da hasn't changed a bit, has he? It's still God Save Ireland for him, isn't it? No bloody surrender. To Hell or Connaught. Oh Ma, he'll be like that till the day he dies!'

'Yes,' said Mother, quietly. 'I know.'

24

FATHER MOVING homeward through narrow corkscrew streets at dusky pub close of evening, the comfortable weight of the half-dozen under his arm, the naggin snug in his hip pocket. The slate as long as a countryman's mile, a blessing and a curse. They knew his strength, knew he always paid up sooner or later. He kept the place alive, pouring out his lungs for them week after week. He had a good voice in his young days. Still could sing the old songs well, remembering Dan Lowery and his famous variety theatre. That wasn't today or yesterday. 'Speak to me Thora, Speak from your heaven to me.' Not much of a pub, to be sure, dwarfed as it was in the sombre shades of the ancient cathedral. That was where your man Swift ended his days. The man Dean. Founded a hospital for the alcoholics of Dublin town, the decent man. Not much of a pub. Bare wooden floors, thin partition walls of a diarrhoea green, dog kennel of a front snug. Still, sound people they were, once they knew your strength. Long-jewelled Dublin matrons dipping into deep apron pockets. Wasn't that terrible about poor Liza's babby born all stiff and blue on the steps of the Municipal Gallery and she not a stone's throw away from the Rotunda? Just shows you, the hand of God. Upstairs the wide living-room, reminder of a gentler age, the tall black piano in the corner. Vista of the perfect little park directly opposite through the beaded window panes. Timeless clock forever tolling, telling you how many more murderous hours you have left. A right bloody mess these streets are and a mile between every lamp post, a breeding ground for corruption. The corporation again, never did anything right. No need to go to London. Bombs on the far North Strand not enough. Look at them doing it bare-faced in open tenement hallways, like animals, and the kids looking on. In his day a man couldn't as much as kiss a girl in the street without somebody running for the priest. That whiskey had an extra horsepower to it tonight. A break away from the home wars. The trees in Mount Jerome dripping with rain in the young dark winter. But they would probably bury him out in the wilds of Glasnevin in an unmarked bloody grave. Let the daisies grow undisturbed. Not that it mattered where they buried him. He could never understand why some people were so particular about where they were to be buried. No matter where they dug your hole, the worms got you in the end. Maggots had to live too. Poor under-the-earth creatures, as lost as the over-the-earth ones. And soon we were all lost.

The woman of the house. Alanna was her name. A lively, dark young thing and the quaint Northern brogue of her. Great big brown eyes. There was something about a North of the Border brogue that caught the heart unawares. Pert and pretty in her crisp apron, pulling pints better than any trade-union barman. The dark head of her bent over the taps, cascading the brown creamy stuff into tilted tumblers. The young and old men at the bar not missing the soft valley of her fine high-flung breasts as she bent, waiting for them to pop out over her low-cut dress, all white and dimpled and the nipples fat and dark, maybe. Not long ago he would have fancied her a bit himself, but that kind of thing appeared to be dead entirely inside him now. Good strong legs on her and the wide hips made for carrying babies. Four already and she looking as innocent as a nun professed yesterday. Your man knew his onions even if they were

179

Spanish. A shrewd customer he was, slippery as an eel, foolish as a fox. The round shining bald head of him, the eyes pale blue never straying far from his gay long-legged wife or the monotonous click of the cash register. Not far from the wrong side of the border. You could always tell by their canny little ways, famous for the minding of mice at the crossroads. A homely little pub, just the same, home away from home for many a man weary like himself from domestic warfare. The cream of the citizenry. Sure a man needed some sort of escape, a trapdoor to open suddenly under him, letting him get away for a while. The drink made him forget the terrible headaches that seldom left him now. Made him almost blind, that pain, made him appear half-jarred and him with maybe not a drop taken all the week. It pressed down upon him like an iron fist, squeezing, gripping, never letting go. He felt like tying a bandage around his neck and pulling it tight, tight, until the pain stopped. Never a day sick in his life, not even from the drink. Up with the lark he was, every morning, no matter what hour he put his head down on the pillow. That was something they couldn't take away from him, though the volume of his sins filled the sky itself. The young men of today couldn't say as much. Women was all they ever thought about. The opening between the thighs. Gateway to paradise. Moy-ah. Christ, if they only knew the trouble it led a man into, they would let the poor bloody cock sleep. The hot young stallions of today, keeling over dead drunk after a couple of pints, the leer and grin fading from their kissers. Not a patch on their fathers, the men of his generation. Pale amber whiskey or the black velvet pints came all as one to him and the men like him. Hard they lived and hard they died. Hard grafters, hard drinkers, hard men in bed with their women, begetting themselves bloody kids who sprang up all of a sudden into men and women and went their own way, disremembering all the backbreaking years of toil and sweat a man went through to put food in their bellies and clothes on their backs and the fear of God in their mean little hearts. Pain they were coming into the world, pain going out of it. And the way they just happened, the bloody thoughtless, casual way they just kept on multiplying until a man found himself in next to no time knee-deep in them. Rabbits. Jesus Christ. Let a man think about that for a while, and he would soon tie a bloody knot in it. Lil. Twins. Sweet suffering God. That time when he was working, renovating some donkey-years-old houses along the Quays, he had come upon a nest of baby mice under the rotten floorboards. He felt bloody sick, just looking at them, squirming about in piles of old paper, little raw pink things, no eyes, no mouths, no hair, nothing but glistening lumps of boneless raw flesh. Rabbits. Mice. Rats. Kids. He had poured the scalding contents of his billycan over them, almost hearing them bleat, and nailed back the floorboards again in a hurry. That day at the break, he couldn't eat and threw his lunch over the Liffey walls for the gulls to make a feast on. She's too bloody skinny to be having twins. Must be a mistake, a false alarm. What did that bastard think he was up to, putting twins into her? Didn't he know she was too bloody skinny? Thank God the missus was past all that. The last shakings of the bag, that last kid. Begetting them was just as hard as bearing them. That was something the women didn't understand. They thought it was just a matter of putting it in and taking it out. It wasn't that bloody simple. If only it was. What you put in wasn't *just* that, but something else. A deeper part of you. Adam's rib. Each kid that came kicking and bawling into the world took a part of you with it, made you less and less, weaker and weaker as a man, as a person, till the time came when a man was left with nearly nothing, not a bloody rib, not a bone, not a muscle, not a particle of gristle that he could call his own. He felt now as if everything inside him had been pulled out, extracted, like the guts of a chicken, leaving only a carcass. Every time a man poured his seed into a woman, he poured some of his heart's blood into her as well, the sap of his muscle, bone and sinew, his animal strength, and each time, he got less and less, weaker and weaker, till there was just a shroud of skin hung upon a

181

frame, shaking and bending in every wind like a bloody scarecrow.

Lil. Twins. Pale dungeon face of her, blazing her defiance. He staggered a bit, corrected himself, leaned against a wall, hoisting the beer parcel into a safer position under his arm. The dark womb of a woman, waiting to open up and engulf a man. A baker's oven. The flour, milk, yeast, a man's blood, sweat and sperm. Juices of his body drained away till he was sucked dry, thrown aside, discarded, like a well-sucked orange. Take away the womb and you're okey-doke. Dive in as often as you like. No hidden little fishes swimming in that deep dark pool. A woman didn't take too kindly to having her womb cut out, strange to say. A bit like cutting her heart out, maybe. Probably made her feel bloody useless, a garbage bin for her man to empty himself into. But a man never knew, when he was pouring himself into a woman, what he was letting himself in for, what he was starting. Work. Bitter winter mornings, the knife-winds slicing through his clothes, frostbitten on the high city scaffolds, blood in the veins like ice. Work. Blistering high days of summer, the shirt sticking to a man's back, sweat running into his eyes like vinegar, thighs and legs scalded as if he had pissed in his trousers, burning the skin. No, a man never knew. And even if he did, it still wouldn't stop him, it still wouldn't hold back the ocean of his lust. That was the terrible thing about it. A man had to be dead or bloody castrated to hold himself back. It was good to lie between the soft thighs of a woman, to feel the softness of her coming to you on a trembling wave, drowning you, breaking warmly over you. Nothing better in this wide and weary world. Take away that, and what was left but dumb little gods and lonely little deaths every hour you drew breath. A man felt the need, somehow, no matter how the years kept slipping behind him, no matter how empty or jaded. You never got to be *that* gutless. A good enough woman in bed she was once, God knew, Oh none better in her day. Small, plump, but firm under the softness. God, she was small, nothing of her in it he used to say to tease her, covering her body entirely with his own. Till the kids started to come along and she started to spread out till he could barely span her waist with his two arms. Oh quiet enough when she had to be and him with the whiskey devil in him, yet even when she was still and wordless, he felt the life throbbing all the time inside her, like electricity, burning quietly in her eyes.

Sometimes he would reach out and touch her roughly to pull her out of her day-dreaming, to pull her back to him, and he would snatch his hand away as if he had touched fire. Promise of the morning. That was how she had been for him in the first years. A flower opening for him petal by petal, shedding herself for him, all open to him and the world. He had not known the strength behind the petal, the gentlest of flowers with strong dark hidden roots that he could not pluck out though he tried with all the raw rage in him. First in a warm golden way breaking down the barriers of his young lusts and suspicions. Picnics out on the broad bright acres of the Broadstone, the ornamental ponds, the dreamy ducks gliding by, fern lying on the water like fine green silk barely moving. Pricked her finger on a thorn and gave it to him to suck. Her warm blood sweet on his tongue, trusting him with her live green-shaded face under the singing leaves. Lived then with her aunt in one of the little council cottages not a fiddler's fart away from the old Linenhall RIC barracks. Funny-looking sort of spiky things across the middle of the street. That far soft hazy sky of Easter spitting fire all of a sudden. Blood everywhere. Blood running down the gutters, spattering on walls like scarlet fingers, oozing red and thick over the white puttees around the khaki legs of the British soldiers. Give it to them, boys. Long live Ireland and this strange-sounding new thing called the Republic. Wrap the green flag round me boys, to die 'twere far more sweet. Eireann's noble emblem drowning the pain-ridden scream of a boy with blood gushing out of his belly and throat. To be his winding sheet. He felt bloody foolish in his Fianna Eireann scout uniform, like some excited boy dressing up for a party or parade. She'd be sure to be there watching for him marching by and she in her fine black lace mantilla and her blue eyes all proud and shy on him. Alive and glad to see him spring up into a man that smoking, fiery, thundering morning going to fight the British huns and the big guns on the Liffey black and venomous breaking down the walls of this jaunty little Jericho of a town. Britannia's huns and bloodhounds. He felt afraid, a green lad catapulted into pain and terror and the terrible need to hate and destroy, when all he wanted to do was sit with the other lads on the bottom steps of the tenement up in Dorset Street and play cards, drink from secret smuggled bottles of brown stout and joke about the girls skipping outside.

Yet with the memory of her long-lashed leaping eyes on him he could have faced the whole murderous band of Black and Tans single-handed, taken the tumultuous town of Dublin in both hands and gone singing lustily up the wide windy blood-red alley of the sky. He felt the sap of his manhood rising, felt a power and majesty in his limbs he had not known before. He was not fighting for any bloody Sinn Feiners, not fighting for any bloody country. He was fighting for her, his soft girl, his child-bride, his lissom little love barred from him by contrary-minded old maiden aunts and uncles who viewed with tight-lipped disdain his rough clumsy strength and warm lust for living.

Don't be seeing that drunken bowsie, her black-shawled little ferret of an aunt would say. He is no good for any little girl, he'll bring you nothing but salt tears all the days of your life, child, mark my words. He will drag you down into the gutter with himself and die in the foaming horrors of drink like his demon of a father before him. Her lovely orphan child being tainted by the low likes of him and she a prize for any respectable young man and all the comforts of money and good breeding behind her. That auntie of hers, oh, that curse-of-God auntie of hers all wrinkles and wisdom, a bloody gypsy looking into a crystal ball and spilling the beans about the future, spoiling it all before it even started. Are you out of your mind, Bridget, to go out with the likes of that cornerboy, and that clean well-mannered young man from Irishtown who has eyes for yourself only and him with every prospect of getting his father's grain business? What would your poor dead mother say, my own sister that was killed when the row of houses beyant in Church Street collapsed on them all and you only a toddler sent with the grace of God out on a message a bare few minutes before?

Oh that ferrety little fairy of an auntie blackening him in her eyes at every hand's turn. After the first few years, the first few babies, it was all as good as over bar the crying. He always thought she cried a lot. He thought all women cried a lot. Yet on looking back out of this windless June night several lifetimes later he realized with a dull dismay that she seldom ever cried at all. Or maybe he just didn't see. Each new baby came regular as a winter cold or a summer chill. So bloody unfair it was, God taking it out on him just because what he had down there between his legs was warm and real and alive and not entirely useless. He had parted the whiskers too often, maybe, but in God's name what was a man made for and why was he made the way he was if not for that? Up the pole with you my good woman and no hemming and hawing about it for this is the way the poor people live and they say the grace of God shines on us each time we make a child. Lilies of the fields. Flowers of the earth. Poor bloody him. Poor bloody her. Poor bloody people. There was this wildness in him that got in the way of everything he had ever tried to do, snarling inside him like a mad beast, clawing the breast out of him till all he saw was red. A whole sea and sky of red swimming before him like blood and the hammers inside his head crucifying him with a blood-red, beer-black, sperm-thick uproar . . .

'Are you all right, mister?'

A voice falling down the night sky, little white moon of a face swimming above him. Oh dear thorny-headed Christ.

How the bloody hell did I get down here? he thought, looking up. And then he saw the brown-green bottles all smashed and gleaming in the moonlight and the dark sluggish river of stout flowing into the gutter, plopping over

185

the edge of the kerb with a slight gurgling sound. The face above him went out of focus, dissolved, whirled crazily, then sharpened again, floated back into its clear cut even contours. Young, thin, anxious, a little scared.

'Lil. Is that you, Lil? Help me, for Christ's sake.'

'I'm not Lil, mister, but I'll help you.'

She stooped, taking hold of his coat sleeve. He struggled to gain his feet, but couldn't. She linked her arm through his and pulled, panting a little with exertion, for she was small and slight and just about reached to his chest. He was leaning with his back against some wall, and he tried to slide himself upwards along it. His boots slipped in the murky beer.

'Hurry, mister,' said the girl urgently. 'There's a rozzer coming up the street.'

A big black shape loomed out of the darkness. He tensed himself, about to roar, to charge, a red flag being waved at a bull. He saw the girl's face, pale, worried. He slid himself upright. The policeman stopped. 'Everything all right, miss?'

'Oh, grand, thank you, sir,' said the girl quickly, still clutching the coat sleeve. 'Just me Da. A few over the mark. I'm taking him home.'

The colossus in uniform stepped closer, silver buttons shining. 'I can phone for the squad car if you like—'

'Ah sure thanks all the same, but I can manage. We don't live far from here.' She tugged at his arm. 'C'mon now, Da. Sure we're nearly there.'

The policeman peered down at the carnage of stout bottles.

'Oh that!' The girl quickly knelt down, gathered up the broken glass in the soggy brown paper and laid it carefully at the side of the kerb. 'Out of harm's way,' she said, taking a handkerchief from the side pocket of her coat and wiping her hands.

'Goodnight, so,' said the policeman reluctantly, moving on. 'Sure you can manage now?'

'Positive sure, sir.'

The girl sighed, pushing her hair in under her spotted headscarf. 'That was close!' she said. 'Them buggers do be only waiting for any excuse to pull you in. Are you all right now, mister? Do you live far?'

'The contrary side of the moon, love. I'm okey-doke now.'

'That's grand. Well, goodnight,' She put her hands deep down in her pockets and started to walk away.

'What's your name, me girl?'

She stopped abruptly, twisting around her face angrily, a gesture he seemed to know well.

'Look, mister, I only tried to help.'

'And I'm thankful to you. I only wanted to know—'

'Look, mister, if you think I'm just another pick-up—'

'Suffering God. I have grown-up daughters of me own.'

The girl laughed and her voice was hard. 'So what? They're the worst kind of all.'

He sighed, shook his head, ran a hand over his mouth. 'Run on home, love. I meant no harm. I'll get the missus to say a Hail Mary for you in the morning.' He felt in his hip pocket, half in dread, but the naggin bottle was intact. He took it out, screwed off the lid and drank. It ran into his guts, burning him, bringing him alive, steadying his reeling head. 'Jesus Christ. A life saver.'

The girl laughed more easily, now curious. She came back a few yards. 'Why can't you say a prayer for me yourself?'

He looked up, surprised, not expecting her to be still there. 'Who – me, is it? Sure what would I know about praying? That's the wife's department, love.' He took another long sip.

'You're funny. Just like me own Da.' She came up and stood beside him at the wall. 'I didn't mean to be sharp, mister, but a girl has to look out. Say a kind word to a man today and he thinks he's on to a good thing.'

'That's very grown-up talk coming from the likes of you—'

Her head went up. 'I'm eighteen,' she said proudly. 'I'm no fool. You can't be in this city.'

'Do you take a drop yourself, miss?' he asked, uncertainly holding out the bottle.

'No thanks. Seen too much of it all me life, first with me Da and then with me brothers. Me name's Connie. You might know me Da. Barney Cadbury. Used to work in the Corpo. A plumber.'

'I might, at that.'

'Drinks down near the Iveagh, he does.'

'A good place to drink, to be sure. Well, Connie, can you kindly tell me what in the holy name of Jesus was I doing sprawled out on my mouth and nose like that?'

'Sure I found you like that, mister. Thought you were dead. Gave me a terrible fright.'

'You were a brave girl to stop all the same and give me a hand.'

'Oh, it's nothing.' She laughed shortly. 'I often found me Da in the same condition. Paralytic. I only hope someone will give him a hand some night and him coming home not knowing his own religion. If the rozzers find him it's the Black Maria for him.'

'A most ungodly vehicle, I can tell you. First time I ever passed out like that.'

'Maybe it's a warning from the Blessed Virgin, mister.'

'Aye, Connie, maybe it is, at that.' He lifted the bottle again, took a quick noisy gulp, wiped his mouth.

'But men never take warnings.' Her face was suddenly overcast, a cloud passing over the young moon. She stood head bent, chin tucked into the folds of her scarf. Her eyes were dark, veiled, terribly known to him. For a moment, briefer than it took to breathe, longer than he dared to hope for, it was Lil who stood there by his side in the wide moveless moonlight, speaking quietly with a sad wisdom beyond her years. He heard her words with a thrust of familiar hurt.

'God put women on this earth to suffer. That's what my Ma always said. She was right. That's all women can do – suffer. With their men and with their babies. Men are sometimes worse than babies. Twelve of us my Ma had by the time the eldest was twenty. She died last year giving birth to the last. A little boy. He lived, but he's all twisted and deformed. Can't talk or walk, can't feed or dress

188

himself. Dribbles all the time. They say he's mental. They want to put him in a home. But I won't let them. I know he's not soft in the head. I just know. In here.' She laid her index finger gently on her left breast. 'He speaks to me with his eyes. I won't let them take him away from me. By God I won't!' Her voice was suddenly defiant, strong, the voice of a woman facing the world, defying the world in defence of something she loved. The face she now turned towards him was charged by that strength and that love. It was luminous, transparent, fired from within. 'Don't you think I'm right, mister? Not to let them take my brother away? I'm right – oh, amn't I right?'

He could only nod numbly, could only mutter 'Aye'.

Another night, long ago. Another long-ago girl, quite small, quite breakable, comforting him, daggers drawn, face all on fire, putting herself in his path, afraid, yet daring, sacrificing herself to his wrath. 'You can kill me, Da, but don't hit my mother.' That face, that same defiant delicate face, meeting him squarely and all the senseless hurt and savagery of their looted lives, was turned towards him now in the cruel alchemy of moonlight, wise vulnerable and murderously young, afraid, desperate, more indestructible in its fear and desperation than the shrillest fishwife fury. He shivered, and closed his stinging eyes, and wished to whatever God was living beyond this dull earth that he could cry. But always he lacked the gift of tears. Oh cry, damn you. Cry and empty yourself of the hard dried-up concealed grief lying in your heart like dead blood. Cry and be cleansed, be purged, be rid of this black poison drying up your arteries like dead canals cutting you off from the sweet broad air of mercy, entombing you in your shrunken carcass. Oh cry now with the weeping stars from the debris of your life. Let your soul be kissed by tears for a love that turned to carnage. Oh cry, damn you, cry. Until men become as children.

When he opened his eyes again, he was alone. He looked down at the whiskey bottle in his cold fingers. It slipped noiselessly to the ground. He started to walk. He walked

189

very straight, very slowly and carefully, eyes wide open, seeing everything, every shape, every particular shadow that lurked and beckoned from doorway, alleyway and side street, hearing his own footsteps fall hollowly in the near morning. Past blind shop windows, faceless tenements, the tight-lipped shuttered fronts of pubs famous and derelict, boots striking on cobblestones. Rattle of milkcarts in the distance. He came to a bridge and leaned on the frayed parapet looking down at the river. Broken bits of the moon swam about down there. He thought he heard a child wailing somewhere. Or was it something inside himself that was crying? Crying for some unnameable thing unnameably lost down all the speechless years. He crossed over the bridge, down under the drooping trees on the other side. Leaves shook and spoke quietly overhead, yet he felt no breeze. Trees and people were much the same. Trees, too, had to talk between themselves, though nobody understood what they were saying. Maybe not even other trees. Dull sluggish green water sliding past like oil, thick and slimy, polluted with mud and dead decaying things, a heavy stench lifting in the air. This river winding through the night, winding through so many lives, a serpentine corpse foul and fearsome, yet from which sprang the pearl-breasted ballerina swans. Flowers from the dull, the indiscriminate earth. High gaunt skeletons lean and narrow-ribbed against the ink-blue sky. Beehives of human habitation. The river talking, arguing with the night, seeping into the marrow of the people, nourishment of their bowels, the poison in the blood, foul and wretched mistress of the mind. Love newly risen from filth spawned by greed and irony. Cry, damn you, cry. The gift of tears more precious than pints. Could tears come with porter he would drown himself in the salmon-brown flood. No more parting of the soft whiskers for him. Life now a tightrope running out. Leave it for the industrious worms. The wasteful wilds of Glasnevin. Even lust itself no more, his help in ages past. A wide depthless chasm was opening up inside him. He no longer heard the lonely fall of his footsteps. The river, the pavements, the trees, all seemed to burn in the moonlight. He felt a stranger, an alien, an outsider. A voyager come home, seeing home for the first and last time, through the eyes of a stranger. The fire of moonlight blinded him. A silver cat slinked swiftly between the silver trees. Parting of the phallic ways. The lowlands and the uplands of love, lust, hunger. A wide lonely landscape pitted with hidden ravines. One false step, and down into the darkness with you. A woman's body the endless plain over which a man strayed all his life and sometimes lost himself. Theirs the power and the glory, the triumphant pain. Never to lie between her thighs again and cascade his life into her. All that behind and gone, nothing in front or to come. He had given nothing, nothing had taken all, all, down all the mindless years. He would never again fall into the trap of her tenderness and Oh it was bitter, bitter. He was free of her, free of the old insatiable hunger crawling under his skin like fiery ants eating him away, eating up the days and nights in a long voracious revel of his senses. Free now of all that once hunted and hounded him, the woman-hunger drowned at last in a high tide of porter and whiskey washing away the last tenacious tentacles of his lust. And his freedom now was bitter, for it too had come too late, it had cost too much, and nothing remained alive in him any more except the echoes of that rare and forked violence that alone had kept him alive all these years, wrath feeding upon wrath until it had devoured itself in savage self-cannibalism.

The years down which he had walked were burning now with the same cold fire as the long silver avenue of trees, fire that blinded and blighted but did not warm, did not comfort, did not touch. She was a good woman, a good wife, a good mother, the rich wine fount that had anointed and flooded his life out of which he had drunk deeply and reeled away drunken and defeated, raging against her tenderness, her knowledge of him, the terrible innocence and clarity of her through which he saw finally his own utter weakness. Love grown surgeon with scalpel cutting through the unwilling mind, laying bare the thin secret cancerous membranes,

191

probing to the final level below which lay nothing but the dense dark and desolateness of self. The burning moonlit trees, the speaking river slithering past, the stones over which he walked, feeling nothing, not even the throbbing pain that he somehow knew was going on inside his head, pumping behind his eyes. He seemed to float above even that. The chasm was widening, was opening with a cruel, grinding sound, and he was falling down, down, with no fear, no foreboding, with a large and peculiar calm. A strange thing to be happening to a man on his wayward way home after a few jars. As if drowning and him seeing his whole bloody life passing before his eyes. Who was that girl back there in the moonlight, and what was this that was happening to him now? He just wanted to go home, to go to sleep, a long sleep in which he hoped to God he would not dream, and forget work, forget the tyranny of clocks, the cold and heat, the kids, the pain, her quiet eyes shutting him out and all the lost things that lived in their depths. He wanted now Oh most in the world to sleep that kind of sleep and forget everything under the bronzed bruising breaking bells of morning.

25

A DARK red-skinned woman crawled towards him on her knees, spreading her thighs for him. She was huge and hairy and legless. Her yellow eyes lapped him up greedily. Her broad wide-nostrilled nose spread halfway across her grinning face, dented deeply in the middle as if a hammer had smashed into soft putty. Thick lips opened out over glistening teeth from between which slithered the fat red-raw tip of her tongue. As she waddled towards him the great bronzed globes of her breasts swung heavily up and down almost with a soft swishing sound, the nipples large as pears, her naked torso twisting in sinuous, sensuous rhythm, dripping with sweat, shining like dull copper. A great hairy sporran draped down between her thighs like the shaggy beard of a giant; tufts of strong hair sprouted from the black pit of her navel. She left a thick glutted trail of blood behind her from the raw stumps that rasped over the hard ground like jagged glass. She reached out her huge rippling arms to engulf him, swaying from side to side, moaning weirdly, the sweat and stench and spermy heaviness of her sweeping over him in a strong gushing flood. 'My poor little pet,' she gurgled deep in her heaving throat, drawing him to her as he shrank back. 'Let me warm you in my pelt.' He felt himself sinking into the core of her as if drawn by some terrible gravity, drowning in a whirlpool, pulled down and down into her dark abyss by some fierce unstoppable centrifugal force. He thrashed about in a frenzy, feeling her mountainous flesh closing in on him, swamping him, burying him alive, the domes of her breasts swinging menacingly in the air like clanging bells, thudding against his head until stars flashed in his head. He was sinking in the sucking sea of her flesh. Then a fine male tenor voice started to sing 'The Indian Love Call' somewhere in the distance. A shudder ran through the tremendous torso that was entombing him, and with a great inner throb of disdain she ejected him from her as if spitting out an apple pip and he went toppling backwards, reeling and rolling over and over, banging into icicles on the way yet feeling no impact. 'I am coming, my love, my lover, my master, I am coming, I am coming!' the legless half-woman incantated as she slithered off into the darkness, leaving blood behind her like a snail's slime.

'Testicles quite handsome for a boy of his tender years.'
  'I think that is the general opinion, Genocky.'
  'Ah sure he was always big for his age, sir.'
  He was lying on a green plush billiard table under a great luminous arc that blinded him sorely. He perceived vague

formless shapes on the periphery of light, but could see no faces as the arrow beam of light bored down into his paper-thin skull. He heard voices, precise, clear, clinical. Hands touched his bare body calmly, probing, exploring, finding. Men and women with voices that were fantastically familiar to him and he longed to see the faces, but he was blinded by the pitiless glare above him.

'He questions the existence of a Creator, I believe. Now that we cannot tolerate in a staunch Pope-loving little family circle like ours. Which of his abominable glands must we manipulate in order to bring about an acceptable change in his heathen mentality, Dr MacGillicuddy?'

'The old pineal. What else?'

'Poker hot enough, yet?'

'Just about.'

'Well, this is it, Sundown.'

'Ah sure you won't hurt him too much, sir?' His mother's worried voice lisping on the fringe of darkness. 'He's all I have . . .'

'And it isn't much, is it, God help all the poor souls.'

'Mother, do not weep for him. Into our hands he has commended his body and soul, not realizing that even as we plunge the burning iron into his creepy-crawly flesh he is sleeping quite soundly between his brothers on the great mattress in the back bedroom at home at this very point in time, quite probably about to piss in his sleep.'

'Then what is he doing here, brother Genocky?'

'He fell once more through the trapdoor of his hot lustful thoughts, seeking release from conscious shame in the unconscious act of involuntary masturbation, the silly little sod.'

'Begging your pardon, sir, but what's that awful big word you just said? Is it some disease?'

'An apt if inaccurate description, my good woman. You have an unerring proclivity for cutting through to the hard core of truth through the lightning bolt of your intuition, a quality I have noticed often in ordinary and otherwise uneducated people. Now hear you this.' The erudite voice

194

boomed suddenly as if speaking through an amplifier. 'A dream is just as real as the five fat fingers on my hand or the hair growing out of my nose holes. Oh indeed yes. Dreaming is merely the irrational and totally unbound side of reality. It is, if you like, the absolute reversal of the external experience—'

'Oh shut bloody well up and get on with the job. I want to hear him scream as his flesh fries.'

'Oh Jesus, Mary and holy St Joseph, don't hurt him, sir.'

A large thorny murdered head swam over him, his father's face gazing sadly down at him, still chewing his unarmed lower gums. A muscular forearm appeared, fingers gripping a white-hot poker with pulsating circles of heat extending halfway up its length. He tried to wrench his clenched jaw muscles apart to scream, to identify himself, but could not. He watched in terror as the poker descended and paused an inch or so above him.

Father's voice, melancholy. 'This hurts me more than it hurts you, son. A time for bravery, to be sure.'

At the very moment when the sinewy wrist and fingers flexed for the downward stroke, a high-flung scream swished like a knife through the air. He thought it was himself screaming, but then almost immediately he knew it was not. He observed with an aloof, lordly surprise the poker embedded in his flesh and felt its comfortable heat spreading along the canals of his body. The scream echoed again.

'Who's that screaming, in the name of Satan?'

'Someone in mortal agony, surely.'

'In mortal ecstasy, more likely. See them over there, the brutish couple? He goes into her with such admirable efficiency. Not a movement wasted, not one ounce of unnecessary energy expended. They say that at the extreme point of the coitus the woman screams out in primitive exaltation after the fashion of Mother Eve when Adam first injected her with his dark honey. Hedge up there you inquisitive shower of bastards and let me behold my handiwork. Oh it was a good stroke indeed. Rare Ben Jonson.'

'Not to be confused with rare Al Jolson, folks.'

195

Father's devastated face floating above, sorrowful and lonely as a late, late moon.

'My son breathes in me as I in him. Brave, oh brave. He never uttered a whimper.'

He felt a violent volcanic eruption take place directly under the billiard table, flinging him high into the air, and he felt himself falling, fearfully falling in precise, regular revolutions like a demented hawk, swooping in swirling loops round and round, nearer and nearer the unseen ground, his heart bounding madly over and over each time he performed the static somersault, his brain rattling like an oversized marble inside a tin box.

'My good God, Holohan, but that was an almighty fart.'

'It nearly destroyed my back passage, to tell you the God's honest truth. Beer always does that to me. Great man for the freeing of the bowels, the beer. The missus won't let me sleep with her after a feed of Guinness. Says I stink her out of it. Get your arse fumigated first, she says, before you get a bit off me. God, marriage is a trial, a vale of tears and beery farts.'

'Where are we now, can you tell me, in God's holy and much abused name?'

'Indeed I can and why wouldn't I? Up from the arsehole of the country you'd think you were, Charlie Genocky, and your poor late lamented mother one of the original O'Shaughnessys from the Coombe. Lift up your hangdog head you sod and behold the dirty dilapidated defamed face of Trinity over there crouching like a dejected lion warming her little brood of scholars in her abdomen. Any minute now they will be swarming through the gates, the purse-proud Protestant lads and lassies with books stuck under their oxers, heading for the cheap eating houses along the Quays, those deft denizens of Hatch Street and Ely Place. The lads will be striding out manfully, their coloured scarves streeling after them in the wind, and the girls will have pale, airless faces and big dark eyes sunk in their sockets with the learning, and walk on fine straight legs, the gorgeous non-conformists.

196

'For you may say Hail Marys till you're dumb
But you can't beat a bit of Protestant bum.'

'Oh, it's true, my Lord, it's true. I once fell in love with a
Protestant girl and for one squeeze of her slim narrow thighs
I would have kicked the Pope himself, may God forgive my
heretical heart. It wasn't Guinness I thirsted after in them
days, but the warm white milk from her nutmeg breasts.
Up in the Hollow we would lie on a Sunday after dinner and
she'd drive me that mad I'd forget she was a Protestant and
start calling her by all the angels in heaven. A Trinity girl
she was too and me with as much learning in me as me
poor uncle Jamesy who died only last year in the Gorman
still believing he was Tom Thumb.'

'Ah, yes, there is something about us working-class blokes
that attracts the females of the higher social orders. Our
uncouth minds and rough-and-ready hands, no doubt,
soiling their soft fastidious limbs and laughing at their
pretended horror. But sure wasn't Wolfe Tone a great man
and him from the Black North? Ah, here they come,
MacGillicuddy, the great surging horde of Luther's children.
Let us stand here now and abuse them with our rabid
Catholic minds as they stream past.'

'With a Protestant lass now it's like doing a Jewess.
Deliver me not from temptation, O Lord.'

'The sun shines bright on our little dirty souls.'

He sat on the chill pavement under a brown burnt-umber
sky of noon, and a soft-eyed collie dog with a womanish
face came and lay at his feet. He patted the animal's head
with a free unhindered hand, his eyes swimming with
absurd tears, for thousands of thronging feet filled the
streets and all he saw from his lowly niche were the frayed
turn-ups of trouser ends, well-worn uppers, and the mud-
spattered ankles and insteps of women clocking primly past.
Nobody paid him or the dog the slightest attention. The
sardonic sun shoved aside the ink-bottle clouds and blazed
balefully down on his wobbly head, drying his tears until

197

they became caked like hard little knobs of gravel upon his cheeks. He looked down and saw an army of big red-backed fleas swarming numerously through the forest of the dog's shaggy fleece. As he watched intently the fleas turned cannibalistic and began to devour each other, gobbling each other up voraciously until only the victors were left, and these were so swollen from gorging themselves on their brother parasites that they were replete to the point of exhaustion and just fell off the dog's back on to the pavement, where they lay twitching their thin red legs in the air with gluttonous futility until the collie dog lazily flicked out its porkchop tongue and licked them up. He slowly raised his eyes from his lengthy naturalistic study and saw the great grey columns of the college slowly drip and melt like sugar-sticks in the trumpeting midday sun.

'I'm telling you, Holohan, I'd be an agnostic myself this minute to be in there feeling all them lovely listless Protestant mots under their tartan skirts.'

'Wait now till that one gets up on her bike.'

'Ah yes indeed. Oh see how her lower extremities creep shyly into view like a timid half moon in the muddling month of May. Up and down, down and up goes her beauteous rump, fitting snugly into the bicycle seat.'

'Mine is an elephant's trunk by now.'

'Down, boy, down, before you cause a public disturbance. Let us now recite three decades of the rosary for our sinful meditations.'

A shadow fell out of the sun. He looked up. A heavily pregnant woman stood before him against the scarlet sky, hands folded complacently over her belly hump, thick wooden clogs on her stockingless feet, her head in a shawl, her long gaunt frame draped in shapeless grey clothes. Her skin was wrinkled and sallow, and as he looked she seemed to grow taller and larger, until the buildings in the street were dwarfed by her height and width. The front of her swollen stomach was transparent, like a sheet of plateglass in a shop window, and inside he saw the unborn infant curled up within her, shaped like a question-mark, gently floating inside her womb held safe to harbour by the glistening umbilical cord attaching it to the mother flesh. He saw to his unique surprise that the face that stared out at him and at the world from within the translucid womb of the woman was his own; thin, hawk-like, intent and alive with fear and wonder. The eyes were large and alert and already wet with tears. Slowly the woman sighed and pointed a finger at her unborn child, a look of great sadness on her face.

'I feel him turning over and over inside me, poor dear,' the woman said, clicking her large loose teeth and nodding her head on the stem of her long neck like a big top-heavy flower swaying in the wind. 'Uneasy he is already. Quiet, my son, quiet.' She folded her arms over her belly and began to rock back and forth on her heels, crooning softly, head nodding forward.

'Don't let me be born, please,' the baby whimpered, its voice muffled as though coming from under the sea. 'I don't want to be born. I have seen what it's like out there and I don't want to be born. Surely the child has a say in such matters?'

'It is a man's fate to be born, my son,' the woman declared in a melancholy voice, her fingers tapping softly upon her abdomen. 'To be born, to live, to work, to love, to suffer and to die. All these things are a tragedy, and the first and greatest tragedy is to be born.' She grimaced with birth pangs as the infant kicked woefully within her and keeled over, banging its head against the wall of her womb.

> 'The womb is my tomb
> Golzolantha
> my delight and my doom
> Golzolantha.
> We are in this together
> come fair or foul weather
> So hedge up and make room
> Golzolantha.'

The sun spun round and round and swam and swung in the sky and the woman melted away into its red turbulent core on the dying end of her wail. A great dazzling esplanade of yellow sand opened out before him, seeming to fill earth and sky. He heard the soft sonorous roar and snore of waves and saw far out the hard blue glitter of sea. White bleached shells winked up from couches of ruffled sand with here and there an emerald blaze, an orange splurge, a crimson cloudburst. Silence dense and impenetrable hung over everything, crashing down on the sands like an avalanche, beating every living moving thing into a palpitating pulp. Nothing seemed to stir, to breathe in all that huge stillness. The glassy gulls were frozen against the sky. A red-topped lighthouse pointed upwards like an accusing finger. A staircase of solid rock dropped from an unseen height to the sea, the lower steps slipping under the waves, dissolving magically and spreading out in white flaky slabs under the brilliant sun-scorched water. The horizon burned like smoking glass and sea and sky melted into one. Soon even the distant dialogue of the waves lapping upon the lipping shore could no longer be heard. Clouds of incense rose up from the simmering sands, filling his brain with a terrible sweetness like roses crushed under the hard ruthless hands of a lover. He recalled frail unnameable things, sensations long buried, beyond the deepest memory; milk in a deep cool blue-rimmed jug, a frayed blue slipper peeping from under a chair, a slim gloved hand reaching gently for a gleaming bronze doorknob, a saw cutting cleanly through timber, the yellow shavings curling on the dark carpet like leaves . . .

A young woman, tall, slender, draped in a neck-to-ankle madonna-blue robe, barefoot, glided along the shore against the blazing sky, singing in a beautiful bell-like voice, a liquid sound floating on the air. The robe caressed her perfect form, the hood loose upon her shoulders, her long hair flowing behind like golden smoke. Her feet were small and pink and did not touch the sand. She yearned forth with both arms exultantly to embrace earth, sea and sky, her delicate face lifting, satiny throat curved thrillingly. As she came closer, carried by the amorous wind, the words of her song gushed up round and clear from her honeycombed depths.

> 'There's a bricklayer down our street Molly Bawn
> and he swept me off my feet Molly Bawn
> when he got between my legs
> 'twas then he fertilized me eggs
> now I'm stuffed up to the teeth Molly Bawn.'

'Don't you know your woman screeching her lungs out like the banshee?'

'The ghost of Margaret Burke-Sheridan, would it be?'

'God bless the mark, but that's the little hoor from down around Cornmarket. Clappy Maggie Dunnalot, the best investment for a wife-weary man this side of the Dardanelles. A bottle of Red Biddy and you're right. Must be at least ten inches before she's interested. Are you off for a stroll by the seaside, Maggie me lovely hen? Are you bringing anyone?'

She turned her radiant face upon them, the long-lashed painfully lovely blue eyes clear and empty as a cloudless June day.

> 'Isn't it grand on Dollymount Strand
> with only the gulls around us
> and I'm off to find my own true love
> and knit again the ties that bound us.'

She smiled, dazzlingly, beckoning to some unseen figure.

> 'O button up your flyhole love
> in case the wind gets at it.'

'Clap-giver or not, she has a powerful voice, Genocky. A great loss to the Irish operatic stage. She would make Melba sound like a street hawker in Moor Street, and well-jarred at that.'

'I never knew she had a lump on her back, though. It somewhat spoils the image.'

201

'Get your eyes tested. She's up the pole again, you see, and instead of carrying it in front she carries it behind.'

'He must have been a Chinaman that did her.'

'Ah sure we're all Chinamen under the skin, General-issimo.'

'They shall inherit the earth, the meek bastards.'

She vanished down the shore, her low tremulous notes shimmering on the air and was last seen riding upon a pearly porpoise, trailing her long, pale, languid fingers in the green water.

'Sure she'd ride anything, that one.'

'Give me the binoculars, for God's sake, Genocky.'

The old man crouched alone and naked under the great elm tree, cracking huge walnuts between his bony fingers, carefully picking the luscious brown core out and popping it into the black cave of his mouth, crushing it with his craggy teeth. A thick yellow furze covered his tongue. His bare hairy flanks shivered on the cool grass. Fronds of dirty matted grey hair fell down into his eyes. Thin little forests of foliage ran along the razor edges of his cheeks and jaw-bones. He masticated with insane relish, jawbones crackling. His bent head and shoulders were lathered with leaves and speckled yellow-and-grey bird droppings from the capacious canopy of the branches overhead. His eyes were so sunken in his skull as to be invisible, but from time to time they would glitter abruptly, twin torches flaring from deep-delved caverns. Every time he drew a long despairing breath tongues of flame would shoot jetlike down each nostril, singeing the encrusted folds of his beard that drooped dis-mally down to his lacerated loins. His long-toenailed feet were locked together, the criss-crossed soles split and oozing blood that hardened at once. His voice boomed sonorously as he cracked the doomed nuts.

'Anna-Pola, where are you
this raw and bitter day?'

202

Bongo drums beat out a rumba from behind a low livid bank of clouds. Several many-headed couples sway from between the trees to join in the dance, while Spitfires in a wide V roar in the sky ejecting luminous streams of bullets. Big Ben chimes in the blood-bright background against a stage drop of tangled steel girders and fallen masonry.

> 'Anna-Pola my pretty little poppy
> loving you is all so heavenly.'

'Who's your man all holes and leaks, O Matthias Mac-Gillicuddy of the roaring Reeks? Come now Matthias randy and wild, leave off lusting after the poor prick-happy child. Forget your impulses biological, and give us your opinion genealogical. We ask you again with voices three – who's your man sitting stark there under that tree?'

'An original Irish primitive, so help me God, destroyed with an unholy lust, the dirty oul sod.'

Mother's voice of charity: 'That poor old man so God-forsaken, sir? Ah, surely you're sorely mistaken, sir?'

'Your mercy covers a multitude of sins, ma'am, but let me start at the point where the story begins, ma'am.'

'By God, you're absolutely right, oul fart. No better place to begin than the start.'

'I wish them bloody bombs would only stop falling, and that bloke bawling out This is Germany Calling.'

'That can be put right double-quick. Just switch the bloody radio off, you thick.'

A sharp unhesitating click that is heard all over the land, sky and sea, and then pastoral peace once more. The dancers turn into marble statues, locked in a moveless embrace. Once again the dominant sound is that of the old man crushing the nuts. The speakers are seen seated around a kitchen table, a bottle of wine between them, a lighted candle stuck down the neck of an empty beer bottle, its flare a gaudy orange against the sombre shades of the trees.

'That nodding nudist over yonder is Lord Luvabit of old, and the Lady Anna-Pola was his only child, a girl of purest

203

gold, whom he loved in a most unpaternal fashion. In short, a rash and forbidden passion—'

'Ho-ho said the giant as he ruffled his hair. I smell incest in the air.'

'We ask of you, and tell us true. What became of the poor darling child? Was she left to wander homeless in the wild?'

'Did she escape from a fate worse than life, and become a decent man's faithful wife?'

'Aye, for she married the local poacher who poached more than rabbits, and he eventually cured her of all her bad habits. From her Daddy's wrath they had to flee, and they sailed third-class to Araby. Why third-class don't bother to ask us, but they then took the camel route to Damascus. Her husband took great care of her the decent fella. She had seven sons for him and gave them all to Allah. She had just the one daughter as white as nannygoat's milk, and she gave her to the local merchant for a bale of precious silk. She converted many a native the darling salvationist. Her Da would have a fit if he knew and him a staunch Calvinist. Thus concludes the story of Anna-Pola. I hope you all heeded well. So never cast lustful eyes on your daughter or you'll end up in Hell.'

'He deserves a fate more dreadful and grim. Sure hell is too good for the likes of him.'

'Ah now hang on there, Genocky, and hold your horses, and meditate a while upon history's courses, for didn't peerless King Rameses of the Nile without a leer or double-meaning smile, a most regular habit make the best-looking of his daughters as brides to take? And hadn't he a great mind all-seeing and keen, lord of a civilization the best the world has seen? Now I don't myself hold with the ramming of daughters, but that sort of thing goes on in the best of quarters. That's an impure historical fact that no amount or arguing will be dimming. For in them days there were no husbands and wives or fathers and daughters, but only men and women.'

'Bejasus, Genocky, the truth he has spoke it, so put that in your bloody pipe and smoke it.'

'That's all very well. I'm not disputing the fact. But there's no whitewashing a dirty bloody act. Now what the Egyptians do we needn't be troubling, but you can't have that sort of thing going on in Dublin. That Rameses fella was a raving headcase, and sure aren't them Arabs a bloody unnatural race, the way they run their unnatural lives. Sure they can't tell their daughters from their wives. Now what they do is neither here nor there, but when one of our own tries to do it it's too bloody queer. I believe in our holy nuns and priests, and your man is not good enough to be thrown to the beasts. So them that are with me, hold up your hand and let's hang the oul bastard from the highest tree in Ireland! Let there be no hedging, let there be no fuss. Up with the oul decoyer and so say all of us!'

The frozen statue figures come suddenly to life again and swoop down on the old man, joining hands and dancing round the tree as savages round a totem pole.

> 'And so say all of us
> and so say all of us
> for he's a dirty oul bastard
> he's a dirty oul bastard
> for he's a dirty oul bastard
> and so say all of us
> Hooray!'

'Let he who casts the first stone—'
'He won't bloody well be alone.'
'Let's demolish the oul destroyer!'
'Let's castrate the dirty oul daughter-decoyer!'
'Ireland holy is Ireland free, forever!'
'Dan O'Connell forever!'
'St Laurence O'Toole forever!'
'Blessed Oliver Plunkett forever!'
'St Bridget who mantled the plains of Kildare with her plaid shawl – forever!'
'Not forgetting poor One-Eyed Jamesy McGurk forever!'
'Who in the horrendous name of Jesus crucified was he?'

'I know all the Irish saints and their claims to fame, sir. But never did I come across a saint of that name, sir.'

'And you won't ma'am, God have pity on us all. But down in the Fish Market Jamesy had a stall, and he gave fish away for little or nothing to everyone who came, but especially to the oul age pensioners from the Golden Lane, and wrapped the cod and plaice and herrings in papers spotless clean and trim. So may the all-purifying light of Heaven this day and always shine on him.'

'Ah, may God in His wisdom reward him for all his good work. Three cheers and ten Hail Marys for poor One-Eyed Jamesy McGurk!'

'Leave the poor unfortunate oul man alone. Can't you see he's only just skin and bone?'

'And after all, he's been eight hundred years and more under Old Nick's flaying, so it's a prayer for his sin-stained soul we should be saying.'

'What a bloody long time to suffer lust and damnation. Let's offer the poor oul soul our commiseration.'

The dancers cease to be malevolent and instead kneel reverently down in front of the nutcracking old man and make the sign of the cross with large slow gestures.

'It reminds me the year of the Eucharistic Congress and the whole nation kneeling bare-headed in O'Connell Street and beyond in the Phoenix Park and the lovely lyric voice of poor John MacCormack over the loudspeakers singing 'Panis Angelicus' and all the young and old women crying with tears streaming down their faces and some of the men too, God help us, on account of the grand stirring occasion that was in it. A glorious June week it was, thank God, oh never another June like it for many a year, and it seemed as if the Holy Ghost had descended upon Dublin city, filling us all with love . . .'

He sat on a high wall overlooking a deserted courtyard. The day was drunk with sunshine under a blue sky terrifying and vacant, yawning endlessly and invisibly. The colonnaded front of a cool marble pavilion rose up serrated by dense blue-grey speaking shadows. In front of the steps upon a marble plinth reclined a naked female figure, resting on one elbow, face half hidden from him, one leg arched over the other, a hand reposing upon the rounded hip, a laurel crown girding the smooth forehead, hair thick-coiled and sleek. She gazed away from him, towards a far boundary wall, beyond which spumed many-tinted spirals of smoke from a compact toylike train that kept chugging in blunt-nosed desperation but which remained stationary. Tall blackened roofs of factories, warehouses, churches, the squat flattened domes of gasometers, the phallic spires of electric pylons soared like a frantic foraging forest beyond the wall, the sky thick and teeming and soiled with the grit and grime and gangrene of living, of industry, of power, of commerce, split asunder by the high, hoarse, furious, pleading cries of lovers, merchants, politicians, poets, philosophers, dreamers, profiteers, the builders and the wreckers, the husbands and wives suddenly strangers looking at each other across an impassable sea; the saved and the damned, the naked and the lonely and the lost, the scarlet sinners aping in grotesque mimicry of love, the childless women praying in their little thigh-white hour of love for a son to come forth, a flower to bloom in their desert, the maimed and deformed screaming to an improbable and unheeding heaven their anguished eloquent maledictions to the God who had created them thus in an inattentive moment. Turmoil, the agony of living, the thirsting for love, for lust, for prayer, passion, faith, martyrdom, for the death that is never ultimate. Turmoil, the sky bruised by the unyielding earth, stained, defeated, defiled, polluted by the hungry hawks of devastation, deception, massacre. The sky a desert of furious furore, black with the winged wrongs of puny, precocious, pretentious, predatory parasites grinning, grimacing, deriding, destroying, living and dying in ignorance of life, of death, crawling into little square holes in the waiting earth, the crazed of heart, consumed of mind, convulsed and condemned of spirit. Turmoil abroad everywhere, tremendous and tyrannical because unspoken, unvoiced, unfaced, shunned, pretended or bought out of knowledge by all the tricks and masquerades of the unwilling heart, encountered only and always in the night of self that cannot be held back. But within the courtyard all lay hushed under the warm cloak of peace. With a rare marvelling he saw clearly his own lengthening shape detach itself from himself and creep nearer, nearer to that imperious, impeccable form reclining upon the marble plinth, saw clearly the subtle muscular landscape of the perfect limbs, the smooth horizon of hip merging in dazzled space with the half-glimpsed half-moon buttocks. Silence saluting the deeper silence, beyond the clamour of life, the loud dawn of desire. Unseeing, all-seeing, the unparalleled eyes gazed far out beyond his own fitful little life crackling dully inside him like a damp fuse.

And he heard his voice, his words, moving like deep waves within him. 'Who are you? Where am I?'

And her voice from far within him. 'I am without a name. You will seek all your life to find and name me, until you too are lost and nameless.'

And not a breath, not a muscle stirred in that cool-limbed, all-alive and lifeless perfection, and still the wonderful eyes stared out, impenetrable and remote, facing towards chaos. And the ruthless sky rained down mad, mocking tears, the despair of not knowing, the terror of knowing, if love or loss awaited him out there where his lunatic life cried for him to join it. He shut his eyes tight, in a convulsion of fear and foreboding, the rain burning his skin, abject and abandoned.

'Ah, will you look at him the poor bugger, without even a name, fiddling his flute on the high wall of his shame.'

'Open your eyes my dear brother and pal, and behold what's taking place along the Royal Canal.'

And now on the narrow towpath overhead a neat crisp-linened nursemaid walked leisurely by, wheeling a glittering gold-and-silver perambulator ornamented with intricately worked chromium bars in the shape of the zodiac, from the depths of which cooed a beautiful pink infant as the starched young woman read aloud to it snatches of nursery rhymes from an incandescent book she was holding in one languid hand, green-eyed snake charm-bracelets, gleaming round her wrist and ankle. Clouds of golden dust rose up round her sandal-sheathed feet as she walked along the graceful tree-lined pathway reciting in her strong cool voice:

'Everyone in Dublin town is friendly and civil
but if you run around the Black Church thrice
you're sure to see the divil.'

A bird dropped from the branches overhead and alighted on her shoulder, pecking delicately and amorously at her ear, from which hung a tiny golden goblet filled with scent. Another bird parachuted softly down, folded its wings, and cuddled in a brown dream in the folds of the infant's cherubic neck.

'Here we go round the burning bush
one, two, three.
Suffer little idiots to come unto Me.'

A hawk-faced ghost of a man in a ragged flapping robe teetered over the swaying bridge, holding his long-shaped sepulchre-skulled head in his vein-loud hands, his countenance contorted with anguish as a scream went through nature, hurting the very stones of the earth, the very crevices in the ancient sunburnt bricks of the old houses, sending the bloodied waters scurrying invisibly out of vision through a large jagged crack in the blazing horizon, emptying the canal like a running sore being drained of its foul pus. The sky screamed in vengeful unison, vast valleys opening up, split down all their length by a long livid yellowish-red streak jarring jaggedly over the devastated plains above the lava-loud land. And hungry black hawks fell, zooming, swooning, fuming, pluming, their wings strapped cruelly to their bodies, beaks gaping wide on terror, little yellow needle-eyes gleaming garishly like frozen points of amethyst. 'Dear God,' cried the mangled

man on the bridge, tottering from side to side, face fixed
in folds of horror, fingernails digging into his parchment
skull against the pain and panic that everywhere pressed
brutishly about him, in the air and on the ground, the
merciless scream shattering over everything like breaking
glass. 'Dear God, where is home?' And tears of bright-berry
blood were oozing out from beneath the man's rigid eyelids,
dropping slowly over the gaunt promontory cheekbones, to
fall with an audible burning hiss upon the crooked and
crackling stones of the bridge, spreading quickly out,
forming into great tangled maps and continents resembling
contorted human faces mashed and maimed out of existence
under ruthless surging feet in furious ferment and pursuit of
things perishable as a dandelion's breath upon the wind.

> 'Cross over the bridge
> where the weather is nice.
> All change here
> for Paradise.'

A little ragamuffin group of boys sat dirty-faced, dirty-
jerseyed on the peeling parapet of the low wall that fringed
the swirling waters of the canal, complacently fishing for
pinkeens with huge barbed-wire-strung nets in which, as if
by accident, human infants wriggled and squirmed in lieu of
fishes, their soft pink limbs plucked asunder and harpooned
by the dagger ends of wire, swarming in a flood of torn
flesh within the inescapable nets. The youths swung their
chopped feet happily in the water and jostled each other in
ribald bonhomie as they sang:

> 'Oh show us the way to go home, dear Goddie,
> for we're tired and we want to go to bed.
> We had a few girls about an hour ago
> and rode them nearly dead.
> No matter where we go
> Stoneybatter or Pimlico
> we can always get a few birds to screw

So show us the way to go home, dear Goddie,
show us the bloody way to go home.'

The man's face was breaking up, crumbling, dissolving in waves of agony, weird and ghastly under the yellow serpent glare of the heavens. He stumbled, fell to his knees, crawled like an animal until he had almost reached the end of the bridge, then shuddered and lay huddled in the long shroud, his face pressed against the earth. Slowly, like a snail putting forth its horns, iron spikes began to grow out of his bent head until they formed a circular girdle laurelled with large blood-red poppies burning darkly. From time to timeless moment a spasm shook the shrouded form and the eagle-taloned fingernails sank convulsively into the earth. A young woman appeared on a sigh of wind and stood over the crumpled carcass in the robe. Shyly she unbuttoned her gleaming emerald tunic and, kneeling on one knee, offered her round white breast, supporting its soft weight on one slim supple wrist, squeezing the dark nipple gently.

'Come, Master, and drink of my milk and be strong. See.' With a gentle pressure of her fingers she brought forth a drop of dazzling white moisture from her dilated nipple, and it fell on the shrivelled, shrunken head pressed earthwards before her. 'Come, Master, my milk is warm and pure and will set your loins alight.' Another peerless drop fell, and a strangled groan of mortal agony came from within the robe.

The sing-song boys looked on with wise, weary, ravaged young faces, slyly nudging each other's ribs.

The sky moved away and it was dense darkness once more, save for a faraway glimmer of light that beckoned and drew him movelessly, yet he was exquisitely aware of the fine freedom of his limbs upon the air. He knew the place then, felt its dark welcome rush upon him with a wild, tremulous beating of wings. The heavy sadness of the trees, spreading their arms invisibly upon the night, the dull sheen of tomb-stones gleaming like so many ghostly foreheads. A bell boomed out from behind the huge granite archangel high

211

up on the church tower, and black craters opened up and split the face of the moon, ink flung upon marble. A chill, delicious dread dawned in him as he felt soft wet wings touch him and whirr blindly about his head, making mournful noises. Black engraved lettering spoke to him from the sunken tombstones, telling him the dull short histories of those who lay recumbent beneath them, sighing below the earth, mingling in a loud sea-song murmur, revealing the closed little volumes of their lives. Once in the time above the earth how they had walked through all their seasons, loved, hated, desired, lost, were touched by calm fingers, the sun singing in their veins, the friendly grass cool on their noonday limbs. The walls of their houses had once been strong, shutting out fear, doubt, deception, and hope had not yet died. Now their bones spoke their own sad eulogies. The rain fell on them and they did not feel it. They lay trapped and foolishly defeated in this teeming stillness. Happiest were the children who had died. They had never stopped playing with the toys of life and knew none of its traps, and their small bones sang in the earth forever.

A tall cloaked figure appeared, holding high a fiery torch, moving between the tombstones, clutching upwards with hard merciless fingers, catching the blind bats and thrusting them brutally into the long-necked sack he held in his other hand. The trapped creatures bleated piteously, scourged inside the netted bag, moving in a seething mass of shattered flesh. The man spoke softly to them as though to children. 'Hush, my blind beauties, rest in the bounty of my soul.'

'Bone and bosom, wing and feather
I will crush them all together.
Thrush and robin, sparrow and dove
come and be crushed in the net of my love.'

He felt himself being drawn inexorably towards the glow that faintly called in the drowned dark under the old ivy-covered, weather-worn wall beneath the tremendous shadow of the archangel. Icy sheets of sweat clung to his skin, and a sick hopeless dread grovelled deep in his guts; he tried with all his will to hold back, but inescapably he was pulled nearer and nearer towards what he feared but did not know. And then he saw it. A neatly dug grave, rhymed with wild thyme and lit by a strange radiance, and in it sat Father, naked, reading with familiar absorption the sports page of a newspaper, occasionally scratching one bare bony knee thoughtfully, as though he were at home in bed or sitting in the old loose armchair by the fire. As he watched, helpless, repelled, fascinated, there was a slight rustling movement, just behind Father's ear, as though something inside was scrabbling to get out. It grew and grew like a huge mastoid, swelling under the faintly gleaming skin, pulsating, throbbing like a living creature. Father went on reading, making small absent-minded sounds under his breath as he always did while reading. At length the taut skin broke with an audible dull plop, and the head of a huge rat pushed through, its red-orbed eyes glittering balefully. It wriggled until its fat brown body was lodged halfway in the jagged flesh hole behind Father's ear, squealing with exertion, torn shreds of flesh flapping from its fangs thrust out over its vicious mouth. A terrible physical revulsion gripped him, heaving momentously in his belly; waves of sickness swept up into his throat, leaving a bitter tang burning. He longed to shut his eyes, to scream, but he could do neither, could only watch as the obscene creature sturdily gnawed its way out of Father's skull, its sleek fur glistening with blood and slivers of brain membrane. When it was free it stood for a while cockily on Father's deep-hollowed shoulder, glaring up, blinking its red eyes owlishly. He felt himself the intruder, not this murderous sharp-snouted thing so casually devouring the doomed flesh of his father. It scurried down Father's spine and vanished in the gloom of the grave.

A hounded sob broke his muteness. The figure in the grave seemed to hear, but did not turn or look up. It merely sighed and the head rolled from side to side slowly and sadly.

He heard the voice he knew so well, speaking in ordinary,

unsurprised tones. 'Don't shed any useless tear. I've been dead and gone this many a year. You mustn't worry about the rat. Sure they too have to eat and get fat. Let them gobble me up for all I'm worth. I'm more useful now than I ever was on earth. Don't fret, Sundown.'

He longed to speak, to leap across the oceanic spaces, break the frozen waters that stretched between them, to cry out his horror and rage, to reclaim this calm, defeated ghost and warm it at the gutted fires of his love, feed it with his pain. But the implacable silence held and the ghost had already forgotten and discarded him. He stood in a field of frail white flowers under the small soft rain. One star alone possessed the sky, hanging low over the trees. He heard only his own loud chaos and nowhereness, saw only the tangled ways of his exile, the mouth of night engulfing him, the key forever turning in the lock, the lonely footfall forever turning upon the hill, the leaf falling in the forest, all the fierce, bright faces beckoning, fading before him, and flowers burning through merciless walls. His limbs were now chains trapping him, locking him immutably in darkness, and goaded unbearably by fear of his loneliness he thrashed wildly about, until the world rocked and rang and terror broke down on him in a torrent . . .

'What is it?' he heard someone whisper, a tousled head etched against the glimmering rectangle of window.

'Nothing,' his brother whispered back with fierce disgust, settling down under the bedclothes again. 'The bugger was just having a wet dream.'

26

THE SNOW had changed to a brown slush under the weight of the city traffic, but on the pavements and along the gutters it still crackled underfoot like breaking glass. It lay hard and gleaming on slanting rooftops. A thin, brittle frost hung in the air. Christmas still pervaded the city, although the year had turned; the endless greetings still echoed around every street corner, salutations volleyed forth in a verbal cascade, warm, half-chafed hands reached out in a goodwill grasp, shoulder-thumping, back-slapping, arm-pulling in through the nearest doorway of a rollicking tavern. The revelry was a little jaded, a little forced from over-enthusiasm, but the revellers were full of a grim-jawed determination to squeeze the very last drops of seasonal joy and good cheer both from their glasses and themselves before buckling down to another long, hard journey through another year.

Horsecarts rumbled by in the evening dusk, piled high with pyramids of shrivelled, shrunken holly trees and dead mounds of mistletoe; thick coils of old rags were wrapped around the hooves of the horses to prevent the beasts from sliding on the icy surface. Gangs of ragged, funnily attired, red-nosed urchins milled around corners and outside public houses, whining voices raised and hands outstretched entreatingly as they begged and pestered the still convivial crowds for pennies: 'We got nothin' this year from Daddy Christmas, mister – me Da is out on strike ...' 'Me poor Da got a septic toe, ma'am, and we only had spuds to eat at Christmas ...' Coins fell plenteously upon the pavements, squat brown threepenny bits, horse-faced half-crowns, even occasionally big silver florins; there would be a mad elbow digging, kicking, biting, cursing scramble of squirming bodies in the snow as frantic fingers clutched and clawed to reach the treasure first.

As dust quickened, glad lights blinked on, bringing alive the sombre-faced houses; street lamps flickered and shone, and the snow that had temporarily ceased began falling again, making the trees along the banks of the canal droop, top heavy with their soft burden. Shapes moved across lighted shopfronts, shadows upon a screen; faces instantly glimpsed, instantly gone, eager, remote, young, old, ugly, beautiful, alive, dead, streaming past along their private paths or out of the anonymous city seeking or shunning brighter lights, deeper shadows. Stand-still, haltered horses spread their urine, gushing from them in a greenish shower, and the snow hissed under them. The good woody smell of burning chestnuts hung over fiery stoves, drawing people, the young and the old, like moths to a brilliant candle, gloved or bare hands outstretched towards the billowing warmth. Like latter-day horses of Troy, buses trundled past, deep-bellied and truculent, and the passengers entombed inside them seemed somehow weird and mechanical, sitting like zombies or automatons staring blindly out at the dim white world through their own reflections.

The noises and drone of the city came only distantly into the stillness of the cemetery; through the sparse trees tombstones gleamed dully like ghostly foreheads. A pale thin moon roamed behind snow-thick clouds, glinting upon the plain unvarnished coffins which Joe and Jem were carrying upon their shoulders up the shrouded avenue, pausing from time to time to let the two women catch up with them from behind. They did not speak, the men breathing heavily but evenly with their load. The slight creaking of the coffins and the soft thud of footsteps sounded loud, broken at curiously paced intervals by the howling of a faraway dog. Against the grey sheen of cloud the spire of the chapel rose slowly into view. They left the path and made their way carefully between the haphazard labyrinth of sunken headstones, coming at length to a clearer area of the graveyard, where the coffins were slowly set down. Knowing their way, the men found a spade and pitchfork in a small ramshackle workman's hut huddled against the ivy-clad wall, and began to dig.

They dug steadily, still without a word being said, the tools cleaving cleanly into the packed earth; soon the deeper yellow clay showed, but still they dug until they had made the holes deep enough. They laid aside the spade and pitchfork and walked over to the coffins, lying side by side on the ground, already thinly sheeted with snow. They looked towards their women, their faces grimly chiselled, etched in the swirling snow; then they stooped, gently lifting the small boxes and turned back towards the awaiting black trenches.

'My God,' whispered Lil, swaying a little as the coffins were lowered. 'My God.'

Mother moved closer, holding Lil's arm, saying nothing.

The earth was smoothed and stamped flat. The men finally went back to the women. Lil moved forward, but Joe caught her arm gently, restraining her.

'There isn't anything more to be done tonight, love,' he said. 'Let's go. You'll catch your death of cold here.'

Mother moved and took Lil's other elbow. They started back down the dark tunnel between the trees, hearing again the lamentations of the distant dog. The crudded snow crunched underneath their feet. Suddenly close by there came a slight swishing sound; a figure loomed out of the darkness, walking towards them, face obscured beneath a cowl. Lil gave a soft gasp and tensed.

'God be with you,' said the priest. ·

'And with you, Father,' they rejoined.

The priest lifted his hand in blessing and was gone into the night. They looked at each other, somehow relieved, reassured, less obscure in their sorrow, and passed through the cemetery gates, through Harold's Cross, over the canal bridge and into the city.

They came in from the dismal cold to the turf glow of a welcoming fire reddening the soot-encrusted walls of the huge stone hearth in the quayside tavern not far from the tenement house where Joe and Lil had a room. The owner,

217

a big loose-bodied jovial man, bald head shining pinkly under the fluorescent bars, beckoned over Joe as they came in.

'Anything you want, Joe, on the house,' whispered the publican, absentmindedly wiping the counter with a beer-brown cloth as he spoke. He had a thick West of Ireland brogue.

'Thanks, Colum, it's decent of you,' Joe said awkwardly. 'But you've done enough for us already, putting up the money for the coffins and all . . .'

Colum stopped wiping and leaned on his elbow, picking his few remaining teeth with his forefinger. 'If it makes you feel any better,' he said patiently to Joe, as if placating a child, 'you can consider it as a loan. There. What do you say?'

'Fine, Colum, fine. As soon as I get on my feet—'

'Oh, shit, man,' said the publican mildly. 'Take the drink and hold your whisht. The women look like a drop of brandy might do them both the world of good.' He began to load the tray.

Joe nodded. 'I had to nearly drag them in here. It was bitter cold up in that cemetery tonight.'

'They're bleak and bare bloody places at any time, the same cemeteries, never mind at this time of year. Tell me, Joe,' said the publican, leaning forward intently like a priest in confessional, 'was it bad?'

'Bad enough. It would have been bad enough had they died at birth or shortly afterwards, but rearing them to nine months old, and then all of a sudden—'

'I know, I know,' said the publican, sighing, nodding his head. 'It's bloody heart-breaking, right enough.'

'It's herself I'm worried about,' said Joe as the pints were slowly and expertly pulled and placed on the tray. 'She was scared as hell when she knew for sure it would be twins. Then when they came all fine and healthy – well, it was like a kid with two new fancy dolls. Couldn't get her away from them for very long. I don't think she really knows yet – the shock is still on her.'

218

'Aye indeed,' the publican agreed. 'It's the women who suffer the most when all is said and done.'

'And things the way they are with me,' Joe said, looking down at his amputated index finger and pursing his thin lips. 'Out of work with this blasted thing. It will be months before I hear anything about workman's compensation, never mind being taken back to work. If it hadn't been for you?'

'Oh, shit, man,' said Colum again. 'You make me feel like Vincent de Paul. What is it you want now, Mick?' roared the publican as another customer yelled impatiently from the public bar behind the partition. 'Another special pint?' Lil stared straight ahead, unstirring, as if she saw nothing. Her face was thin and ill, sparse under the dark head-scarf. She wore no make-up at all. Mother's high-feathered hat wobbled as she bent towards Lil, picking up the untouched glass of brandy.

'Here – take a sip of this,' Mother urged. 'It will do you good.'

Lil turned her face away. 'I couldn't, Ma – honest. I feel sick.'

'Take it,' Mother insisted, almost forcing the quietly glowing amber liquid between Lil's chattering teeth. 'For God's sake, before we have another corpse on our hands.'

Lil spluttered as the brandy slid down her throat. Her shoulders shook, she coughed, holding a hankie against her mouth; tears swam in her eyes and she took some long gasping breaths, but slowly colour rose in her cheeks, the dazed, glazed look left her eyes, and for the first time that night and all that heart-twisting day she looked around, alive and seeing things, a little bemused and wide-eyed, like someone awakening from slumber. They looked at her anxiously.

'All right, love?' Joe asked, pausing, the pint halfway to his mouth.

'Yes.'

'Are you sure now?' Mother pursued, uncertain.

'Yes.' Slowly Lil looked around her, at her husband, at

219

Jem, finally at Mother, and then the sobbing started, racking her convulsively. 'Oh, dear God!'

Without saying a word, Mother drew Lil against her, patting her head, her heaving shoulders, wiping her eyes with the hankie, as if time had rolled back and Lil was a little girl again coming to her for solace and safety against dark and fright and pain she could not understand.

The two men looked on helplessly, Joe grave, a little crestfallen, Jem looking desperately out of depth, chewing his fat lower lip, perplexed. Lil cried, more quietly now, huddled against Mother. She stirred and straightened up guiltily as the lounge door creaked rustily open and some women and men came in. The place began slowly to fill up as the spidery hands of the clock perched high over the bar crept sneakily around. The people stood to shake snow from their neck and shoulders on the threshold before coming in and finding tables.

'I'm sorry,' said Lil, blowing her nose, dabbing at her eyes. 'I made a fool of myself.'

'Nothing like a good cry,' said Mother, satisfied, taking a sip of her own drink now that the storm had passed.

'She's been keeping it in too long,' said Joe, putting down his tumbler, turning to Mother. 'She hasn't slept since it happened. I've heard her walking around the room at night. Sometimes she'd pick up little Joe and nearly squeeze him to death, she'd be holding him that tight.'

'I don't think I'll have another baby,' Lil said suddenly in a hard, brittle voice. 'Not as long as we live in that dump.'

'Take your drink now,' Mother said soothingly.

'I mean it, Ma,' repeated Lil quietly. 'Why should I? Why should I go through pain bringing children into the world only for the worms to have them before I even get to know them?'

'Lil—'

'It was the filth and disease of that place that killed my babies!' said Lil, her voice cracking. Then she went on in a quieter tone. 'Do you expect me to go on having babies after this?'

'God's ways are not ours,' said Mother, looking thoughtfully into her glass.

'And neither are the Dublin Corporation's, Ma,' rejoined Lil. 'They treat people like pigs. This is no country at all for young people, for young married couples starting out like us. We were mad to come back from London. Ireland Mother Ireland is dead and gone, Ma. Only the carcass is left.'

They did not know how to answer her, having no answer. The table they sat at might well have been an island, so far away were each of them now from the others. Every now and then, as if by some secret signal, the porter would come across to their table with a fresh tray of drinks, although Lil kept her hand over her glass and did not take any more. A group of men in a corner were playing cards. Others still were throwing darts. Presently the lounge was fairly full and talk grew and became animated. More turf was piled on to the fire; tables were pushed further back as the warmth spread. Little pools of moisture formed on the wooden boards as the snow melted from the hob-nailed boots of dockers and labourers and soot-grimed coal hawkers.

Joe turned to Jem. 'Will you be okay back at Portobello, Jem?' he asked. 'It's getting late.'

'Don't worry,' Jem said, grinning cockily. 'Sure isn't the NCO's missus only mad about me? I can nip over into married quarters any time I like.'

'Sure mark,' said Mother, 'and you as raw as a rusty blade.'

Jem grinned wider, getting slightly drunk, folding his hands between his knees, sighing happily, the beer curdling cosily in his guts. His eyes as he looked about him were bright and expectant, yet softly clouded, as if he was ready to greet the people and even the furniture in the room as familiar, seldom-seen friends. He looked over at Lil, and his happy idyllic mood dissolved somewhat. He reached over and patted her hand timidly, as if he might hurt her. 'Cheer up, sis,' he said, squaring his shoulders. 'More to come, please God.' Then, as if gripped by a sudden inner storm of indignation and outrage, his usually mild blue eyes glittered and his fingers tightened round his glass. 'It's Stalin we bloody well want here, you know!' he said loudly. 'He'd soon put the skids under them big fat capitalist bastards up in Leinster House! Or better still – Lenin! Aye, bejasus – *that's* the boyo for them!'

'Lenin is dead,' said Joe mildly.

Jem's full-moon face grew redder. 'Who the hell cares?' he said angrily. 'A dead Lenin is worth ten living De Valeras! A modern Jesus Christ he was—'

'Don't be saying the holy name in vain,' said Mother.

'I don't know why I'm wearing this uniform!' Jem said, glaring down with incredible ferocity at his green tunic and trousers. 'A shower of bloody renegades, the lot of them!'

Heads were beginning to turn in their direction.

'Amn't I scourged?' said Mother. 'Not one of you is able to take a drink and hold his peace like any respectable man.'

'I was only saying, Ma, that if we had men like Joe Stalin or what's-his-name Lenin over here—'

'Remember where you are, and the time that's in it, if you can do nothing else,' said Mother, her own face very red now. 'Have you no feelings at all?'

Jem seemed abruptly contrite. 'I'm a bastard,' he said. He folded his arms and gazed with melancholy down into his pint. 'I should have gone into a monastery.'

Words buzzed from a cluster of elderly women in a corner, thick-laden with the treacle of maudlin sympathy and the after taste of whiskey gulped in cloistered intimacy.

'Isn't that the young wan that lost her twins?'

'Lives on the third landing.'

'Sure wasn't I there when she had them?'

'And she no more than a child herself.'

An old woman in a shawl sidled over, her yellowing face spread wide on an all-gum grin, proffering her hand.

'I'm sorry for your trouble, alannah,' the old crone said in a wheedling voice, darting out a paper-thin, thin-wristed, bone-hard hand and imprisoning Lil's in a rigid grasp before anyone could stir.

222

'Thank you, ma'am,' said Lil, wincing a little under the bony pressure.

'Sure don't you know me?' continued the woman, pulling over a nearby chair and sitting down unbidden, still holding Lil's hand. 'Sure everyone on the Quays knows Lettie Finucan. Always on hand at the time of birth and at the hour of death. That's me. That's Lettie Finucan so it is. The rest of the time I wouldn't trouble you for a match, but at the time of trouble I'm there before you can say Jack Robinson. Sure wasn't I there when your poor darling twins were delivered, the light of heaven shine on them this night?' The woman crossed herself, then hunched her shoulders forward, winking. 'I didn't like the looks of that oul midwife, alannah – the stink of whiskey off her would make Father Matthew turn in his grave.'

'She did very well, ma'am,' said Lil, knowing that the woman had never set foot inside her door ever since they went to live in the tenement. 'Very well indeed.'

The old woman grinned and wagged her shawled head knowingly. 'Ah, sure it's good of you to say so, alannah. It shows a real Christian spirit so it does. But we all know better, don't we now? Sure and bejasus the state that oul wan was in that night she'd be hard set to deliver the papers. Whatever happened the poor little angels at all?' She edged closer on her seat, her face creased and puckered, winking again. 'You can tell me, alannah. You can tell Lettie Finucan. May I be struck dumb if a word of it ever passes my lips.' She cackled to herself and squeezed Lil's hand tighter.

'There's nothing to tell, ma'am,' said Lil, furtively trying to extricate her captive fingers. 'It was gastro-enteritis.'

Old Mrs Finucan blessed herself quickly. 'What in the holy name of God might that be, alannah?'

'A type of bowel disorder, ma'am,' Lil said, looking desperately over at Joe.

'Er – will you have something to drink, ma'am?' Joe asked.

'Ah sure I won't be bothering you, son, thanks all the same,' said Mrs Finucan, fondling Lil's fingers vigorously. Without looking around, almost without pause, she went on. 'But on account of the sad time that's in it ... I'll chance a ball of malt.'

'Suffering Christ,' said Jem under his breath.

Only when her drink came up did the old woman release Lil's pinched fingers. She drank gustily, tipping her head back, resting the glass on the curling point of her wrinkled chin, in between times taking plentiful doses of snuff out of a black cloth purse pulled tight by two strings which was hidden in a pocket of her manifold skirts. She prattled moistly on, pausing only to swallow her whiskey in her peculiar fashion and sniff up each nostril the sickeningly sweet-smelling snuff, her movements so quick and birdlike that they seemed to flow into each other and were scarcely noticed after a while. She spoke in a high whine, pitched on the same monotonous key, so that even had what she was saying been interesting it would have sounded dull anyway. She fumbled once as she was stuffing the powder up her nostril, the purse jerked over and some of the snuff spilled out over on to Jem's lap, who immediately began to sneeze in such a violent, outrageous way that his knees shot convulsively up and banged the undersides of the table, overturning the remains of his own pint, which flowed down over his green-uniformed legs.

'Suffering *Christ*!' Jem yelled, jumping to his feet, the beer seeping down into his army boots. 'You bloody blind oul . . .' and went off into such a fit of sneezing that he turned purple and great mucous rivers ran from his nose. He belched enormously, eyes popping wide, and clutching one hand over his mouth and the other over his belly, he made a zig-zag dash between the tables out to the lavatory.

Old Mrs Finucan shook her head and clucked her empty gums. 'Ah, they can't drink like their fathers before them,' she said, complacently gathering up her snuff and picking up her glass. 'Now would you believe what it is I'm going to tell you? I remember, oh, years ago and donkey years ago at that, when a body could get a right dacent ball of malt for three ha'pence . . .'

At closing time they managed to dodge the old woman in the milling about as the lounge emptied, and were soon out once more in the brittle air. The Liffey stirred sluggishly under the time-smooth parapets, its darkness broken here and there by patches of crisp ice. Snow was still falling, but softly now, hardly felt. After the din and furore of the public house, a broad peace seemed to be abroad on the tart January night; everything seemed hushed, even the late-night drone of traffic scarcely intruded. The crowds streaming out from the cinemas moved quietly, in a subdued, pensive procession, standing patiently at bus stops, as if somehow the mood and mystery of the vast still whiteness had made a strange calm settle over everyone and everything.

'I wonder what happens to the swans in the winter time?' Jem said suddenly, pausing to lean over the parapet and look down at the black-scarred frozen river.

They came presently to the tall, gaunt tenement where Joe and Lil lived; a few lights still burned high up along its drab sullen front. Some cats were quarrelling shrilly among themselves in the black depths of the open hallway. A man walked past talking in a quick, argumentative way to himself. From somewhere high up in the house a piano could be heard tinkling out in ragged fitful rhythm 'The White Cliffs of Dover'.

'Will you come up for a cup of tea, Ma, now that you're here?' asked Lil, huddled in her coat against the sharp breeze blowing across the river.

'Not at this hour, Lil,' said Mother, stepping nearer and pulling up the fur lapels of Lil's coat. 'Get a good night's sleep now and I'll see you tomorrow.'

'I'll drop over—' Lil began.

'You'll do nothing of the kind,' Mother said. 'I'll cross over myself on the bus handy enough.'

'I hope the Da won't mind you being out this late,' said Joe.

'He knows where I am. He's probably in bed snoring his head off. Goodnight and God bless you both.'

She watched as they went up the blunt cracked steps; they waved on the top steps, then vanished into the dark of the hallway.

Mother stood still a few moments after they had gone, staring up at the black gap of the hallway, at the few garish lights that were still burning; she shivered slightly.

Jem noticed the movement. 'Cold, Ma?' he inquired. 'Here,' he went on, starting to open the fat brass buttons of his tunic, 'you take this—'

Mother stopped him with her hand. 'Not at all,' she said, turning up her own coat collar and starting to walk with him to the bus stop down the street. 'I'm not cold. I was just thinking things to myself.'

Jem pressed her arm under his. 'Lil will be all right, Ma,' he said. 'You'll see.'

He spoke quietly. Mother glanced up at him, wondering again at his sudden insights, his rare perceptions, the sensitive, alive young man so seldom seen behind the clown's mask. He had a way of grasping things that others might miss so that it was unwise to take him for granted, but soon the moment was gone as quick as sand on the wind and he was safe behind his laughter again. The funny ones were as hard to understand as the solemn ones, she thought.

They sat together on the bus taking the latecomers home. She was a little tired and closed her eyes; it was warm in the bus after the cold outside, the soothing throb of the engine reverberating under the boards lulling her into a short slumber. The bus jarred slightly as it rounded a corner, and she awoke instantly. It slowed to a halt at a bus stop and more people got aboard. A young couple, college students by the look of them, books under their arms, obviously, from the intense, remote expression on their faces, in the first glow of sweethearting, fingers interlocked, looking unerringly at each other, stumbling a little here and there to the annoyance of others. A short, stout woman with a round red turkey-cock face and small eyes like black berries sunk in

226

dough, clutched a straw bag from which protruded the decapitated torso of a dehydrated chicken. The woman glared balefully at the young lost couple and pushed her way up the narrow aisle of seats, her hips bumping ponderously all the way. A slight, stringy-throated sprightly little man in evening dress and bowtie, until then quiet and reserved, who began without preamble to sing 'Bonny Mary of Argyle' in a rather good tenor voice, sitting very straight on his seat, eyes shut, hands on his knees. 'If you must sing a song, do sing an Irish song!' someone shouted, parodying a traditional song programme on the radio.

Although all animals were disallowed, a big shaggy collie dog had somehow managed to smuggle on to the bus, and it soon began barking in perfect harmony with the tenor, stopping and starting at all the right places. Someone started to play 'Mexicali Rose' on a mouth organ at the top of the bus. A fat man clutching a briefcase with a cigar in his mouth looked disgusted and called over the conductor as if to complain, but the conductor merely smiled and shrugged his shoulders and went on collecting fares, giving out tickets and clinging his little bell.

'My Lord Bishops, ladies and gentlemen, fellow peasants,' declaimed a big boiler-suited cordial King Kong with a huge exaggerated bow in the direction of the cigar chewer, 'welcome to the Midnight Special!' A young man leaped up on the back of his seat, holding out a hand for silence. 'Hush, we are passing through Rathgar – hats off and ten Hail Marys!' The mouth organist began to play 'A Nation Once Again'. A bearded youth in a sports jacket with leather elbows started to recite in a loud voice that wavered with emotion 'My Dark Rosaleen'.

'He will never be dead, you know,' said a knobbly-skulled old man to his companion as old as himself. 'Who?' asked the companion. 'James Clarence Mangan.' 'Who?' asked the second old man again, cocking his head sideways, holding his hand to his ear. His friend repeated the poet's name, but still the old man couldn't catch it above the din. 'Who?' 'James Clarence bloody Mangan!' shouted the first old man ferociously, thumping his companion on the knee and sending him off into a paroxysm of coughing.

'Ireland unfree will never be Ireland at peace,' a pot-bellied man pronounced sonorously, holding his foot up and picking pieces of grit from the flap ends of his cement-stained trousers. 'Mark my words. The British they were marching the Irish for to fight, De Valera took his rifle and blew them out of sight.'

The turkey-faced woman, now all simpering smiles, had melted magically and, withdrawing a half-bottle of whiskey from her straw bag, was passing it around and lifting her hand from time to time as if in indulgent benediction. The mouth organist, now revealed as a motherly middle-aged woman with a large and rather dignified wart on her nose, got up and began dancing up and down the aisle, playing the instrument with one hand and flouncing up her skirts with the other as she jiggled in time to an old music hall number: 'Oh don't have any more, Mrs Noore, for if you do they'll be coming out the door.'

The briefcase man shrank back in his seat as the woman swept past him, his small piggy eyes screwed up in horror lest she might touch him. The woman grabbed hold of the conductor and began to dance with him, knocking his peaked cap off. 'All right, Nano,' the conductor said, grinning, as if he knew the woman very well, 'sit down and behave yourself like a good girl.'

'And Spanish wine shall give you hope, shall give you faith and health and hope, my dark Rosaleen ...' the bearded shoddy youth was still reciting loudly and tremulously to himself, eyes spilling tears that streamed copiously into his reddish beard. The slide window behind the driver's seat slid back and the driver shouted out: 'In the name of Christ, Larry, stop that bloody racket – there's a priest coming on!'

The bus slowed down and the priest duly stepped aboard, a fresh-faced country lad with a slow, hesitant smile who immediately fished forth his big black leather-bound breviary and began reading, his pale anaemic lips moving as he stood in the aisle, declining offers to take a seat. 'Are we in the presence of God or something?' the pot bellied man wanted to know, taking his share of the proffered whiskey with a loud luscious smacking of lips.

'Ssh!' a woman's voice hissed. 'Respect for the holy anointed now.'

'Ah, respect me bloody arse!' growled someone else reaching for the bottle.

The young priest glanced up from his prayer book, smiled nervously, and backed slowly out on to the platform of the bus, tripping over the collie dog on the way. They were now passing along the south circular road, the trees heavy with snow. The bus slewed to a halt once more, a few yards from the grim, Bastille-like edifice of the Portobello army barracks. A few soldiers from the upper deck got off, their heavy nailed boots clanging on the metal-rimmed stairway. Jem studiously studied his fag-end.

'Your stop now,' Mother reminded.

'I might as well see you home,' said Jem.

'Oh, no you don't,' said Mother quickly. 'You'll be after hours by the time you get back.'

'It's okay, Ma – I know the bloke on the gate tonight—'

'You can know the Chief of Staff himself for all I care,' Mother told him. 'You know what happened the last time the redcaps came looking for you. You almost frizzled up with the fright. Off with you now.'

'But honest, Ma—'

The bus was starting to move off. 'Get off before I push you off you coward!'

'Aw, Jasus,' mumbled Jem.

He got up gloomily, hesitated, squeezed Mother's elbow, then turned and went onto the platform, jumping from the moving bus to the pavement. He did not quite make it. Mother, looking back, saw a figure sprawling backsideways in the snow, struggling to get up. She knew it was Jem, and sighed.

She got off the bus, almost empty now, and walked the short distance to home. The streets were deserted, weirdly

229

silent, few lights showing in the winding rows of identical houses; she thought it must be quite late. A broken wire-mesh net swung from a lamp standard in the slight wind, making a faint metallic slap. She searched in the chaos of her handbag as she neared the house, finding the front-door key and letting herself in. She carefully lifted the weather board as she opened the door so that it would not scrape on the concrete step. The kitchen was in darkness; the curtains were not drawn, and the light from the lamp standard outside threw a fragile tracery on the faded wallpaper, and the large, rather lifeless picture of the Sacred Heart over the sideboard sprang strangely to life, the deep sad brown Jewish eyes seeming to look down at her so fiercely that for a moment she drew back, startled, giving a slight gasp. Then the curtains wavered in the draught from the open top window, the thin cobweb tracery on the wall broke like water rippling, and the strange moment passed. Mother took off her hat and coat, not turning on the light, intending to go quietly upstairs to bed. Then she heard a moan.

At first she thought it might just be the little mongrel dog whimpering, and she glanced around the kitchen, but saw nothing at all. A yellow slit of light showed under the scullery door. The strange sound was coming from inside the scullery, low, faint, like the whimpering of an animal in pain. She shivered, as if something cold had touched her, and stood motionless, heart pounding in a way that hurt her. A slow fear was working in her, a sick dread of what lay beyond the closed scullery door, and she wanted only to fly upstairs to the safety of the children and . . . who? She willed herself to move forward against the commotion and panic inside her, up to the pantry door; she tapped her knuckles upon it, lightly, feeling the pumping of her heart under her hand. She tapped again; nothing. Then the moan rose again, more clearly now because she stood right against the door, and she knew it was not the dog. Words were mixed up in the moan, half words that trickled off into mumbled incoherence and slow tortured gasps rising and sinking, ebbing into ragged breathing. A strange scuffling, as if fingers were feebly clawing at the door. Mother was warm now in a lather of sweat, she trembled all over, but she leaned her weight against the door and pushed; whatever it was behind it slid limply away, and she stepped through the opening.

After the dark kitchen the sudden gush of light blinded her for a time, then she looked down.

'Oh dear Jesus,' she breathed.

Father lay crumpled up on the stone floor of the pantry, face down, arms twisted at a curious angle, clad just in his vest and trousers, feet bare. Without knowing why, she knew instantly that it was not merely one of his drunken stupors, that it was something else, something she had never seen happen before. She dropped to her knees beside him and turned his face upwards, calling out his name. She shrank back in sudden horror, at first seeing only the blood that seeped from a gash on his forehead where he had struck the enamel bathtub as he fell; then slowly she became aware of the terrible change in the face itself, the half-open lifeless eyes, the crooked, hanging jaw, one side twisted grotesquely out of shape and sagging downwards, the mouth a mis-shapen Z.

Mother's terrified gasp seemed to reach the prostrate figure now cradled in her arms, for the eyes opened a little more and with what seemed enormous effort Father lifted his hand, the fingers twitching, and just touched her cheek.

'Bid – Bid—' he said, making a queer croaking noise.

Then his arm dropped and the eyelids slid shut.

27

HE HAD never before seen his father in pyjamas. Those he was wearing in hospital were a faded buff with vivid blue stripes across it, with a black prayer book the nuns had provided sticking up out of the breast pocket. The thinning grey hair had been trimmed and the long smoke-yellow fingernails had been pared, the almost day-by-day stubble of beard shaved, but the eyes were glazed, dulled, denuded of any light, the mouth crooked and slack and dribbling.

He sat in a straight-backed cane chair by the bedside, and looked not at that lean-jawed crumbling face propped up against the big snowy pillows, but out at the blackened chimney stacks and the gaunt uneven rooftops hump-backing away into the smoky distance. And when the ward window grew dark with the glimmering night and nothing beyond it was to be seen, he would gaze for a long oblivious time at the intricate lace embroidery on the overtop of the eiderdown, hearing the quiet nasal sounds of the men sleeping or sighing in the ward around him. And still he did not look at the face upon the pillows before him. Mother would sit quietly in her chair on the other side of the bed, peeling an orange and breaking it into thin slices to slip into the unresisting mouth to ease the almost perpetual thirst that plagued the dying man now. Now and then a nun would rustle by and stop to ask if anything was wanted, and after the first few weeks his brothers would come only at week-ends, for there was nothing to do but sit or stand idly around the bedside in desperate silence, staring at the floor or rising from creaking chairs to walk to the window and back, denying even to themselves that they were waiting for anything but a quick and complete recovery, and still not looking at the fading face upon the pillows, instead lighting innumerable cigarettes or trying unavailingly to chat with the other men in the ward only to be met soon by a blank stare or a snore.

'He is sleeping quietly now,' a fresh-faced country nun would stop to say in a hushed voice, coming up to the bed, arms folded and hidden under the black wings of her habit, carrying with her a faint musk scent. 'Such a good patient he is, too, never troubling us for anything.'

Mother, laying aside the orange peeling or the knitting she might have brought with her, asking in her direct way: 'What do you think, Sister – really?'

The nun, uncomfortable, hugging her arms tighter under the folds of her habit, blinking her long-lashed mild brown child eyes. 'Well, nothing is ever impossible to God, and he has been taking a little more food – intravenously, of course—' glancing up at the tangle of tubes and big glass jars hanging above the bed linked to a tape-covered vein on the upper arm. 'As a matter of fact . . .'

'Yes, Sister?'

'Well,' the shy nunnery smile breaking over the soft round face, 'we call him our saint around here, for he is always praying – well, not praying, but talking of our Blessed Lady every time he comes awake.' A look full of luminous reverence up at the rather shoddy little blue-robed statue standing on an altar over the ward door.

'He was always religious in his own way,' said Mother quietly, going back to peeling another orange.

Yet another day, full of brittle March sunshine.

'I saw Her today,' Father said, in one of his clear moods, looking around at them all, his eyes briefly alight with some of the past fire.

'You saw who, mister?' asked Mother gently, taking a handkerchief and wiping the sweat and saliva off the face and mouth.

'Her – *Her!*' said Father, pushing away the helping hand. He lifted a startlingly narrow arm and pointed crookedly at the statue over the doorway. 'Herself!' he said with a frightening return of vigorous anger, his long thin finely pared forefinger wavering like some wasted weed underwater.

His eyes spoke with an inner maniac triumph, yet with a childish perverse need to prove something. 'She spoke to me . . . smiling and beckoning me with Her hands . . . She spoke to me . . . said She was waiting for me . . . Herself!' And he nodded his head again and again with a desperate insistence to each of them in turn, the triumph and the vacuity struggling for possession in his face.

The first cousin, a broad-backed bull-necked charging dinosaur of a man with a ferocious unnerving squint in his left eye and large red hairy hands spread flat on his ponderous knees like the hands of a stultified drunken god, sniffed sorrowfully up one nostril and shook his great bullet-domed close-cropped head in grievous puzzlement. Everyone knew him as The Soldier.

'Ah, Jasus dear and merciful, it's awful,' said The Soldier, shaking and shaking his head, unfolding and folding his short stubby fingers upon his knees, curling and uncurling his fingers, neat and nattily dressed in his soft black grey-striped suit, the dragon-headed pin in his loud yellow tie glinting its red eye in the sunlight from the window. 'It's enough to draw tears from a statue to sit here and hear him raving like that and him one of the best buddies a man could wish for in a month of Sundays. Ah, Pat me sweet man, what's happened to you at all?'

Father glared at The Soldier fiercely. 'Who let that bloody communist in here?' he demanded with icy clarity. 'Don't you know he went to Moscow and drank vodka with Joe Stalin and goes to bed all wrapped up in the Red Flag?'

The Soldier leaned forward avidly, face lit up. 'Ah, me bould Pat,' he said, 'do you recognize me after all? Do you remember . . .'

But the face had settled back into its set immovable slightly owlish vacancy, and The Soldier gave a huge exasperated sigh and leaned back in his chair.

'Ah, Jasus wise and gracious,' said The Soldier, taking out a bottle that was half full of whiskey from the huge inside pocket of his overcoat hanging on the back of his chair. 'It's heartbreaking to sit on your arse and watch a good man sink into the arms of Brother Death right bang smack before your two bloodshot eyes.' The Soldier uncorked the bottle and moved it under his nose, sniffing it and closing his eyes as if in adoration before taking a big coarse gurgling gulp. 'It seems only yesterday,' said The Soldier, swallowing the whiskey after rolling it about between his bulging bulldog jaws, 'though the truth is it's many a yesterday ago, that himself and meself were up to our ankles in the gore of our fallen comrades-in-arms beyant in Boland's Mills and we down to our last round of ammunition and this chiner that was supposed to have water in his army flask had a quart of whiskey in it instead, and we all had a slug out of it while the bullets flew thick around us, and then we let out a bloody big roar out of us enough to wake the dead beyant in Glasnevin, and off we went lepping over the barricades and tearing into them bloody bastards of Black-'n-Tans like bejasus till they turned tail and ran like scarified geese in all directions and our revolvers spitting after them ... Ah, Pat, me sweet potato,' said The Soldier, rising like a colossal tadpole to his feet and standing gigantically over the bed, waving the bottle, 'for the love and honour of Jasus dear and sorrowful, take a swig out of this and throw them bloody sheets aside!'

The half-light came back into the clouded eyes looking up at the bottle that hung only inches away, as if struggling to identify and connect it with something.   -

'God, don't do that!' cried Mother, rising and stopping The Soldier's hovering hand. 'In the name of God—'

'Why not – why not?' said The Soldier excitedly. 'It'll cure him quicker 'n all the holy water in the Vatican!' insisted The Soldier, attempting to pour some of the liquor down the quiescent throat.

A nun on her rounds rushed over, black skirts flying voluminously, cherubic face flushed. 'Have you no fear in you, and the poor man almost ready to meet his Maker?' said the nun, grappling to confiscate the bottle.

'Well, if that is so itself, me reverend woman,' said The Soldier, calm now and easily resisting the soft futile fingers of the outraged Sister, 'what mortal or immortal harm can a drop do to him?' And lifted the bottle to his own beefy lips with a belly-deep gurgle.

The air in the deadhouse had been cold with a palpable dampness. The one window, a narrow oblong grille high up on one wall, let in a frail flicker of afternoon light that faded and ebbed less than halfway through, swallowed up in the gloom. Footsteps rang eerily on the concrete floor. Slabs jutted out from the walls, most of them filled with shrouded forms. A ghastly glimmer filled the place, like the ineffable sheen of marble in the dark. Now and then a muffled sob of a woman broke out; the least sound carried and echoed from floor to ceiling like waves breaking on some distant and immeasurable shore. The joints of the living could almost be heard creaking and cracking as people moved softly, a cough sounding suddenly loud, odd whispers coming and going, faces hovering queerly in space as if suspended and detached from the bodies. He stood before the slab and wished with all his soul he had not come. He wanted to be out again in the harsh but living air of the city streets, away from this mummified stillness broken only by the weak, baffled cries of the bereaved. A picture floated together in his mind; a moss-green stone overturning and underneath it, blinded and baited into panic by the sudden brutal blaze of light, a squirming mass of maggots milling about in a sightless frenzy. A hand reached out to lift back the brown cowl of the death shroud, and he looked.

The face seemed smaller than it had been in life, as if it had shrunken and shrivelled, yet it looked very much the same, the bushy brows rearing like cliffs over the sunken eyes, the sharp angular nose, the thin mouth with the lower lip still thrust forward truculently. A thin tracery of veins showed under the waxen skin like the shadow of a spider's leg. A few puffs of greyish hair showed under the hood of the habit. It was all so normal after all, after his reluctance and secret loathing, that he almost expected the eyes to open then and blaze up at him with their old fire and maybe a tired angry humour and a hint of hurt that his son should be there looking down on him laid out in the brown habit. He expected the voice to bellow forth from the thin hairy chest: 'What the hell are you doing standing there gawking at me?' Not the sick-puppy whine of the last weeks mumbling and bleating childishly in querulous gasps of deranged demand, but the full round frightening voice of old barking out its orders and commands, rolling over the lost sandcastle years of his childhood like a giant breaker flinging aside the delicate debris of his dreams. Nothing stirred inside him now save the need to be done, out of this chill and gloom and away from this silent gazing on flesh that was dead and would soon be rotten.

'Pop', murmured his brother beside him with grim gentleness, stretching out his big square-fingered hand and pressing the dead man's chin and jaw in a rough helpless caress. 'Ah, Pop, Pop . . .' the tall strong dark youth went on in the same sad, almost chiding tone, rubbing the cold flesh fondly with pugilistic fingers.

A faint trickle of bright berry-red blood seeped slowly down one of the nostrils and gathered on the slight bridge of the upper lip.

His brother jerked his hand away as if from flame and took a startled step back.

'My God – what have you done?' another brother whispered, terrified.

'Nothing – nothing,' said the first, shaken. 'Come on – finish your praying and we'll go.'

The hood was replaced over the face.

Outside at last in the green lawns of the hospital, the orange orb of the city sun slanting through the well-kept trees and the soft swish of nuns rustling on the air, he could still see the fleck of blood on the dead face burning like a geranium petal at sunset.

The black tie. It was almost his first tie. It lay coiled around his neck like a soft silk noose or a snake curling tighter with every impatient or impetuous movement he made. It lay like a burning black scapula round his throat, the knot just under his Adam's apple gently, caressingly throttling him as that grey gaunt ghost of a day had gone on, the heaped wreaths on the hearse in front of them wrapped in cellophane glistening with rain, their carriage swaying lightly from side to side as it rolled over the wet cobblestones and rounded the endless dingy corners of the early morning city. The black tie. Out of some forgotten cranny of the house it had come to be loped and gently tightened around his neck under the starched collar of his shirt, lighting in his heart a tiny voiceless dread that grew and grew as the day wore on, a fear he had not known even when he had been driven furiously through the rush-hour streets on the day they got the final news and had looked at last upon the dead face lying back upon the snowy pillows. All the avenues of his brain had been closed, shrouded in fog, only a few weak rays of common light filtered through. Like a mechanical toy wound up to go through the motions for a certain period of time, he had gone through that day with a stolid composure, not asking anything of anybody and at the end of it had gone to sleep all through the dreamless night hours, awaking next morning and once more going through all the motions the day demanded with the same brittle clarity, calm and uninvolved, as though everything were an elaborate and intricate ballet for lifeless animated dolls in which he was merely another figure set to go through certain steps and observing every movement of the other marionettes with bright mindless scrutiny. And for each day following until the morning of the funeral it was as if a mechanical spring inside him were wound up, tighter and tighter each time, set to slow down at a certain time each night when he would unwind and fold up in a nerveless lifeless mass of muscle and bone on his bed to sail dreamlessly through darkness and awake to the cold and weight of morning. Those days did not pass, but rather merged gradually into each other in a murky shapeless twilight in which he heard not voices but sounds, saw not faces or figures but forms, despite the glassy sharpness with which the antennae of his consciousness went forth and perceived things, as objects in a fog are seen with faultless clarity close

238

up but nothing whatever is seen beyond. Those things, shapes, objects that passed nearest to him were seen and discerned clearly and unambiguously, but beyond the periphery of this amputated vision he saw nothing save vague amorphous indefinite forms moving with slow disembodied gestures like shapes in an aquarium. And then they put the black tie on him as the funeral carriages stood waiting in a long black line in the street outside, and it was as if a light snapped on inside his head as he looked down at the tie, filling everything with a cruel implacable glare, making even the shadows burn balefully. The negative side of reality flared suddenly into relentless black-and-white planes blazing into his mind; ice crackled and a torrent of razor-keen images rushed and roared upon him, sending him staggering backward, blinded and groping in the swift murderous light. And now he saw the faces that had not been there before, filled with a surprising grief, a baffled awareness of life, an almost physical repugnance of death, dazed and defeated faces, faces cloaked with a private sorrow, anguished and alarmed faces unwilling to meet the reproach that lay deep in their own hearts, tired and tense faces wanting only peace now the long tumult of years had passed; and faces too young to hold sorrow or relief, wide questioning eyes looking on at all the muffled comings and goings of consoling neighbours and endless kettles of tea and bottles of wine and whiskey and brown porter and hastily baked soda bread, strange men arriving at all hours of the day and night with black diamonds already sewn on to their coat sleeves bringing their patent sorrow and surprise and recalling days of impossible bravado, the house being turned upside down and washed and polished and dusted and clean sheets put on the beds and new curtains put on the windows and the few good delft brought out for the meals that seemed to go on and on and on, and the priest arriving to give the blessing and hear about funeral arrangements, patting the heads of the younger children with a sad smile on his strong young bristly face; the alcoholic nostalgia and tears of the older boys recalling things that never happened

239

and someone they never knew, the older girls sitting by dry-eyed and pale, patching the cleaned clothes of the children, baking more bread, ironing clothes, polishing brass and metal, too tied down with all the bewildering trappings and topsy-turveydom of death to allow themselves the indulgence of tears or the delusion of quiet recollection.

Inside the carriage it had been warm and close, the windows drawn up against the drizzling rain that ran in broken zig-zag rivulets down the glass, though they could not hear any sound of it above the quiet purr of the engine. He sat between two brothers on the pull-out seat behind the glass partition between them and the driver, watching his mother's face from time to time under the dark lace veil, two of his sisters flanking her on each side. She was pale and intent, occasionally gazing over at him for long moments but not saying anything. She held a neat black and red covered prayerbook between her gloved hands, one of which she would lift to her eyes or her forehead from time to time and leave it there for a while. One of them asked her if she had a headache and would they ask the driver to stop to get her something for it, but she answered 'No, no' quickly and leaned back against the cushion and looked out of the rainy window. He looked out through the rear window of the car; as far as he could see the serpentine stream of carriages stretched unbroken, the tail end of it out of sight, moving by inches in the busy streets and gathering up a little speed along the broad and more open thoroughfares of the city, people pausing to stand on pavements and bless themselves, lips moving in prayer, men lifting their hats in quick respect for the dead as the funeral cortege wound its snail's-pace way past and the slow incessant rain pattered on the cellophane-wrapped wreaths heaped upon the roof of the long black sleek hearse. Variegated shop fronts and weather-coloured faces of buildings slid past in the rain; the slim dark spire of a church against the low sky, thin-armed trees along the wet sidewalks putting forth their first green glimmer of leaves, high windows of office blocks reflecting the scudding clouds. After a short time he realized they were not moving and

240

looked over at Mother to see why they had stopped, but she was looking out the window, leaning forward, a hand resting on her daughter's knee for support, and then he saw the tears shining behind her veil.

He looked out. All he saw at first was the front of a small grey public house with drawn dark green shutters and heavy mauve curtains drawn across the front upper windows. Then he saw set into the wall over the door a small gold plaque inscribed to the memory of a blind Irish poet who had been born in the same premises and whose melancholy verses later became famous and travelled the world. Over the front of the building in brown oak lettering he read: 'Brendan's Bar'. It was a building like any other in the street, stuck insignificantly between two others exactly the same; most of the time it squatted in the giant shadow of the ancient cathedral across the street, and the trees in the little park adjoining the grey edifice dripped and drooped with rain in the dull morning light. He wondered why they had stopped, there with no sign or stir of life about anywhere; a bony-ribbed cat of a dirty-grey colour slunk round the corner sniffing the glistening pavement in a perennial search for blackened scraps, eyed them malevolently for a second, back humped, and vanished down a grating close to the wall. Then suddenly the heavy beaded door of the public house creaked open and a tall man with receding hair and quick pale eyes stepped out, fixing a soft felt hat on his head, followed by a young woman as tall as himself dressed in heavy dark clothes, with a soft full face, brown hair, brown eyes, and a wide cherry mouth. Her kind of face seemed made only to smile, and even then a slight apologetic glow of bright affectionate humour hovered in those large nut-brown eyes as she stepped into the first carriage with them, followed by her husband, who clutched a brown-wrapped angular parcel under the heavy lambskin overcoat he was wearing. Room was quickly made for them and they settled in, the woman sitting next to Mother and the man taking a place next to where he and his brothers were seated. The cars started up again.

241

'Ah, Bid, Bid,' said the woman, crying easily and at once, clasping Mother's hand in both her own, tossing the long hair from her face with a toss of her head. 'It was so sudden after all!'

'It was, to be sure, and us up seeking him only the night before,' said the man, taking off his hat and resting it on his knee, running his hand over the smooth bald crown of his head, his skin as pale as a lampshade with a light shining behind it. 'Ah, many's the rare night meself and himself and all of us had in the oul shop up in the front parlour after closing time. We'll never see the likes again, surely.'

'He thought the world of yourself and Eli, Dick,' said Mother, her voice steady and clear, though she was still crying.

'God love him, he was the soul of the party,' said brown-eyed, brown-haired, soft-faced Eli, not bothering to check her tears flowing copiously down her cheeks. 'We never know the time or the place, but wherever he is now you can be sure he's in there regaling them with a few bars!'

'He thought more of Eli than her own father,' said Dick.

'Oh, he was a lovely man!' said Eli, shaking her head, her hair tumbling down and half veiling her face. 'A real father to me!'

He sat upright against the hard partition of the seat, looking at the young woman crying, bronze glints stirring in her brown waterfall of hair, her soft blossomy knees visible under the skirt where her coat draped apart. She exuded warmth and a strange pleasant smell of foamy cork and mellow dregs and in the gloom of the carriage her small pink pointed shoes were a vivid red, berry-blooming as was her mouth now tremulous with deep luxurious sobbing, her fingers long and white against her hair as she brushed it back from her face. He stared at her.

'Meaning no disrespect,' said Dick carefully, withdrawing the parcel from under his overcoat, 'but it's a bitter morning to be going on such a sad errand, and to warm us all up a bit and in a way pay a last respect to his memory, I thought a drop of this might do us a wee bit of good.'

242

Dick unwrapped the brown paper and took out a big fat-bellied slim-necked green bottle that had on it a label with a dour-faced dark-jowled foreign-looking man wearing a queer three-cornered red hat with one hand stuck into the satiny breast of his army tunic. Across the neck of the bottle he saw the silver lettering, 'Cognac' and wondered what it could mean. Out of the perfumed depths of her handbag Eli brought two tiny dandy glasses out of which Mother and herself drank as Dick poured; the girls declined, but his brothers eagerly put the bottle to their lips and drank deeply, and when the bottle at last came to him he too opened his throat and let the stuff flow down. It burned and blistered his tonsils and glowed down in the depths of his belly like hot coals. He gasped and twisted his head away and the liquid ran down his neck under the collar of his shirt, spattering his black tie, anointing his flesh with a fiery touch.

'Is he all right?' asked Dick anxiously, leaning forward to look up at him from the other end of the seat.

'He's fine,' said Mother smiling. 'Just too greedy!'

He got his breath back and sat up and looked again at Eli, and her face now seemed surrounded by a sort of incandescence and her eyes were some dark exotic flowers floating in a radiant sea and her fingers lying on the dark down of her coat were slim white stalks and he felt a slowly rising warmth and awareness that thrilled and terrified him and he pressed himself back desperately against the hard wooden partition and closed his eyes, feeling the fire in his belly and the dark wings beating in his mind hiding him in shadow. He lay back, feeling his shoulders relax, and half listened to the voices around him and the cat purr of the engine and the soft slushy slewing of the tyres as they slithered around corners on their processional way through the bus-rumbling bell-pealing feet-teeming rain-dim city.

'Passing the Brian Boru already, bedad,' said Dick.

'Cross-Guns Bridge coming up,' said one of his brothers.

He opened his eyes and, looking out and through the

243

easing rain, saw the broad imposing front of an ornate public house with many-coloured mosaics of heroic Celtic figures set into the silvery stonework. Soon they were passing over a wide bridge and through the railings he saw the murky weedy waters of a mean little river choked with rusty debris and rotten planks and gnarled iron bedsteads. A few hungry black crows swooped and cawed over the sparse decaying trees.

He twisted his head around and glanced through the glass wall; the driver wore a peaked black cap and had a fat-jowled pig-pink face and stared straight ahead, pudgy pork-thick hands on the steering wheel, the windscreen wiper swish-swishing back and forward across the teeming window. He observed with absurd oblivious interest several scab-encrusted boils and weak watery pimples on the back of the driver's neck above the black collar of his uniform; tiny hairy holes pitted the man's roughened skin and through the overhead mirror he watched his eyes, the colour of smoked ham, the lashes and brows almost invisible, scarred red blotches on the puffed cheeks. The man's ear was curled up in a kind of question mark and grey wisps of hair sprouted out of its hole.

Ahead he saw the silver knob on the coffin gleaming dully through the rain and the shaken petals of the funeral flowers drooping under the assault of the weather. And the bells kept pealing and knots of people were thronging the streets in their Easter finery on their way to church, blessing themselves as the funeral went by in its long snake-like tedious procession through the bell-loud face-swarming iron-clanging worshipping rain-swept city.

They were going down a wide sweeping avenue with cleaner trees on either side and through the back window he could see the other cars stretching far behind in an endless straight line now reflected in the glistening surface of the road, pale indistinguishable faces staring out of the car windows like forlorn prisoners in tight glass cells, and he thought a while about those people who had come down to stare at their grief, people he would never see again who had

244

come in dark veils and wearing black armbands and bearing flowers and who had kissed and pressed and patted him with ready tears in their eyes and claimed his flesh as their own and left him feeling desolate and desperate and hungry to be away from those strangers. And then the fiery bottle had come his way once more and he had widened his throat to admit the golden water and again it had burned and bruised his tongue and set up a fire in his dark belly depths and a turmoil of soft-edged music in his mind and the face of the woman on the seat in front of him grew soft and full as a flower swollen with pollen and her eyes were deep brown pods oozing dew and the feline purr of the engine lulled the drowsy terrors in his brain and the gentle see-saw rocking-chair swaying of the car rounding innumerable corners lulled the tension in his limbs and he leaned back more peacefully now against the hard wood behind him and shut his eyes and lay in a rare lassitude half listening to the velvet voices around him and the soft mushy slewing of tyres pitter-pattering under the small quiet rain through the steel-ringing smoke-rising prayer-lifting garrulous cloud-touching city.

And at last through the huge iron gates of the cemetery, passing under the cold shadow of that gracious stone obelisk pointing like a giant finger skyward under which reposed the broken bones of the man who had set this land of green fields and squalid cities breakneck to bitter freedom under the lash of his silver tongue. Slowly the cars ground to a halt and disgorged their passengers, swarming in their black-barbed grief and importance over the glistening pavements and standing in gabbling clusters waiting for the incense-swinging priest to come out from his snug little white-walled house next to the ivy-covered chapel to lead the wind-raw way to the grave, gaping like a jagged wound under the wailing sky.

28

THE FIRST volley of shots rang out in the dull-lidded morning, booming against the ear drum, fluttering leaves from the nearby trees and startling some late-sleeping birds into the air. He braced himself for the next rattle of rifle fire, holding grimly to the arms of his two brothers on each side of him, standing rigidly like someone facing the firing squad; when the second volley came his nerves jangled like high-tension wires screaming silently. While the others prayed or cried or looked on with graven faces, he cursed inwardly at his own involuntary response and this final folly of rain-sodden pomp. In his mind each crescendo of shots sounded like a maniac screech in the wind.

He felt the sweat on his forehead trickling down, stinging his eyes; he ached all over with the effort to stand straight and look boldly, stonily ahead. The women cried quietly into their handkerchiefs, all of them wearing dark veils over their faces. The men stood unmoved and only occasionally shuffled their feet. Something white hovered towards him out of the corner of his eye; he grunted and shook his head doggedly as his brother tried to wipe some of the sweat from his face. He drew his sagging knees up, lifted his head higher. His new patent-leather shoes were spattered with mud, the turn-ups of his good suit wet and stained with yellow flecks of clay; he had refused to remain in the warm-cushioned comfort of the funeral car or even to be driven nearer to where the new grave lay. He had walked with the others along the endless paths and avenues of the cemetery, supported by two elder brothers, feeling from time to time chill drops of overnight rain drip down onto his bare head and nape from branches drooping along the way.

He had felt good at the start, walking it out with the rest, peacock proud, even lengthening his jerking stride when his brothers slowed their paces to suit him. As the cortege wound slowly and moved deeper into the desolate acres of Glasnevin his brief triumph ebbed and with each step his muscles and nerves throbbed painfully. A haze swam before his eyes, obscuring the shapes around him. The sweat seeped into his mouth tart and salty. He thrust his head and shoulders forward, a slightly mad dog straining on a tight leash, propelling himself through the cutting wind, shutting his mind to everything save the task of going forward, driving himself on almost past the pitch of feeling pain. He felt every eye focused on him, watching his laboured progress, waiting for him to sink to his knees in the mud; yet the people were walking on obliviously, in hushed groups, heads turned sideways against the wind, the men holding on to their hats, the women clutching their blown skirts and coats. Still, he felt their expectant scrutiny, and bile rose bitter in his mouth.

'We'd better lift him,' said one brother to the other. 'You take one arm, and I—'

'You better not, damn you!' he hissed between ragged raging breaths, twisting his face around ferociously.

His brothers, defeated by this driven perversity, shrugged and went on, holding him at the elbows.

He caught sight of Mother walking slowly at the head of the procession between two daughters. She was looking anxiously over at him, but knew enough not to say any word of protest however mild. He wanted to sink down on the ground, the mud and the hard frosty grass and shut his eyes and never open them. The thought of the plush warmth of the car was excruciating, waiting back there at the cemetery gates.

People passing on the way back from other new graves looked curiously at them, stepping aside onto the grass margin to let them pass. Some of the people looked disapproving, as though thinking he should not have been allowed to come at all. He saw the pity, disapproval, mingled emotions in the faces of these strangers, and he gritted his teeth and growled at them and felt a marvellous exultancy

247

when they drew hastily back as if encountering some sort of tethered beast.

A pale syrupy trickle of sun slithered out from behind the massed turgid clouds, throwing a weird unreal semi-light over everything, and the bells of Easter morning tolled out over the risen city and across the windy wastes of Glasnevin with a dry-throated perfunctory joy, telling blithely of life everlasting in the muddy midst of death.

At last he stood by the graveside, seeing the damp tricolour of green, white and gold draped over the coffin resting on a trestle of ropes to be lowered down into the black gaping sore of earth. He raised his wind-smartened eyes to where a firing-party of old veterans of the War of Independence knelt on the far side of the grave, kneeling forward on one knee, some a bit unsteady, their hats wobbling slightly on their greying heads, rifle butts sunk in crook of shoulders, trigger fingers poised, lifting their sights above the uneasy treetops. For a moment that seemed unending they were etched against the swollen sky like figures in an old mildewed painting lit by the garish streak of light. Suddenly he jack-knifed upright and his nerves snapped like taut strings pulled viciously, sending widening ripples of shock and disorder through his mind and body, slapping him back hard against the strong arms that supported him. The firing was over.

He opened his eyes, the relief of no more shooting soothing the slowly ebbing panic in his blood. What sounded like the wail of a bereaved banshee rose upon the air then, a brassy, uncertain keen, wavering in the bleak morning as some unseen trumpeter began to sound the Last Post. It limped across the grave in a broken and somehow baleful cacophony of farewell, dropping coldly on his spirit. He jerked his head upwards, vainly trying to escape the bronzed moan; a huge blue-black cloud was rolling sluggishly across the sky like some grotesque undersea monster, its edges rimmed and shining with the sun that lay behind it, the stark limbs of a nearby tree etched vividly against it. He stared until blinded by the burning bulk of cloud. When he shut his eyes at last he could see the cruel corona of light flaming behind the dark and shuttered lids of his eyes. When he looked again the figures clustered round the grave were blurred, with white blobs where their faces should have been. The harsh peremptory tones of the priest were raised and saying something about dust and ashes. The long narrow black box had been stripped of the sodden tricolour and lowered into the grave. As if at an invisible signal, the grave-diggers had sprung instantly to life and stepped sprightly forward, bending proudly to their task and were soon shovelling clay sturdily, with precise powerful strokes landing with a dull moist thud upon the entombed box below. He saw their faces, live, purposeful, absorbed, eyes riveted to the earth to the exclusion of everything else, as if what they were doing was the sole and supreme justification and their very existence, the one thing on earth for which they were created. Then he heard a sob and looked up and saw Mother being led gently away by a group of women, her heels sinking in the mud.

It was over. He turned away between his brothers and began the long walk back to the plush warmth and lush comfort waiting for him at the iron gates. This time he felt nothing; neither the tiredness and pain in his limbs nor the dull defeated ache in his mind as once again they passed under the cold shadow of the obelisk, not feeling the ground under his feet nor the cutting wind in his face, hearing again the dull plop of clay upon wood and seeing again the quick live oblivious faces of the gravediggers going about their task, sealing the dead from the living; he wondered vaguely if they were through yet.

The mourners, uncertain now which way to go, milling about on the wet pavements outside the cemetery, uncertain which car was theirs, hands in pockets, shoulders hunched and faces turned against the wind and rain. Words lifted from them like steam vanishing quickly in the air: 'A lovely funeral, a grand turn-out ... never saw a better corpse in all me born days ... which way are you going, Jack? ... and leaving all them children behind ... Can't go home

249

without a jar be hook or be crook . . . she's looking well
herself, considering . . . never saw him looking better than
he did beyant in the deadhouse . . . ah sure that's a road we
all must take sooner or later . . . Will you wait for me,
Nano? . . .'

Back through the noonday city, rain-washed and clean,
a cold sharp sun in the blue-patched sky and people with
glad relieved faces blinking as they streamed down the steps
of cathedrals and churches, yellow splashes of commemora-
tive Easter lilies in their hats and lapels; children playing
hopscotch and piggy-beds over chalk squares on the pavements in a precarious game of balance as they clutched their
gaily wrapped chocolate Easter eggs. Along the thronging
quays, big towering foreign ships with blue and red and
black and orange and silver hulls tied up at the quayside
unloading their manifold cargoes; scent of exotic fruit and
spices from dark burning faraway countries, the pungent
tarry whiff of coal and slack from Wales, the sharp clean
aroma of yellow timber bound for the great pulp factories
around the country; little terrier barges linked to the giant
tankers, bobbing gently on the imperceptibly moving waves;
harsh cheerful obscenities of brawny-armed dockers in shirtsleeves reaching upwards to the swaying cranes overhead,
swinging crates and containers and boxes and barrels and
thick-twine-wrapped parcels from the swarming decks of the
ships, metallic screech of wheels over cobblestones as trolleys
laden with pyramids of goods were trundled away to waiting
trucks and vans and freight cars; and overhead the forlorn
screech of gulls with fiercely flapping wings swooping low
above the foam-flecked water, scavenging for food; and still
the bells rang out as if gone berserk, carolling lyric-tongued
out over the black swell of the immemorial river.

Back to cold ham sandwiches splashed with mustard,
steaming mugs and jugs of tea, creamy thick-handled
tankards of clear red ale and glinting tumblers full of amber
brandy and dark dreaming burgundy wine in the brown-
floored buff-walled front upstairs parlour of the pub where
once a blind juggler of words and images had been born.

The sun spilled in through the partly opened curtains and fell like a sliver of buttermilk across the clean red-checkered tablecloth on the long narrow last-supper table in the middle of the room; the ancient bow-legged hump-backed green-baize grand piano in the shadowy corner with mellowing sheets of music still clipped together in the music stand, the dulled white keys splotched with brown beer droppings, a black-stemmed long-cold pipe lying on its side in a big diamond-edged glass ashtray on top of the mahogany board. Eli now once more the woman of the house, perfect hostess and publican's wife, a neat little apron tied around her snug waist, heaping plates with sandwiches and hunks of cold meat, refilling mugs and jugs and tankards and decanters almost as soon as they were drained from two huge swan-necked silver urns standing on the floor by the table. Dick leaning forward in his spotless shirtsleeves at the head of the table, picking his teeth with a matchstick, his pale delft-blue eyes following the agile movements of his wife as he recalled haphazard hair-raising days and nights he had shared with the man now beyond in Glasnevin. 'Ah, he could bring a party of ghosts alive,' the soft unhurried lilting northern voice said fondly, eyes contemplating now the chewed tip of the matchstick. 'Ah, the life that was in him with a few half ones, jazzing up and down enough to make Jolson himself look a second-rate bum . . .'

'You're not lonesome now, are you?' said a woman's voice kindly, and he looked up to find Eli smiling down at him, stooping towards him slightly, the foamy scent of her tumbling hair alarming him, the creamy tops of her burgeoning breasts just peeping over the rim of her tight dress.

Speechless, he shook his head, his mind slipping and sliding on burning ice, tumultuous wings beating, beating darkly about him in a blind flurry of disarray.

Eli smiled warmly into his transfixed eyes, her lovely even teeth glistening behind her moist lips. 'I'll sing a wee song for you,' she said, resting her hands on her knees, snowy crest of her bosom deepening. 'Just between the two of us.'

251

And she sang in a soft sibilant voice that did not carry above the chatter and platter at the table:

> 'Where Lagan stream sings lullabyes
> there grows a lil fair
> the twilight gleam is in her eyes
> the night is on her hair.
> and like a lovesick glenshee
> she hath my heart in thrall
> no life I owe nor liberty
> for love is lord of all . . .'

Twilight, and lights glimmering through the trees in the park across the street, the dome and needle spire of the cathedral in sombre silhouette against the pale evening sky spread like a mantle of fine silk over the city streaked with tawny tendrils of downy cloud. A horse-and-cart rumbled by in the street below, wooden wheels rattling over cobblestones. He sat in a deep chair by the partly opened window, feeling the coolness brush his cheeks, his brain a still dark pool upon which his lulled thoughts swayed and floated . . .

A pair of mud-splashed cement-caked working boots, blunt-snouted and black-eyeletted behind the coalhouse door. A dulled silver trowel pointing up like a miniature monstrance out of a dust-grey broad-strapped army-kit tool-bag bulging with lump hammer, claw hammer, chisel, plumb line and spirit level honed to a fine-fettle edge by the toil and turnabouts of time. A hard-prodding foot and a gravel-vowelled voice alarming them awake in dark December depths and simmering bread-and-milk Summer mornings: 'Up and about you lazy shower of buggers!', the sparse silhouette tremendous against the lightening pre-dawn window, tobacco-brown thumbs taut behind striped suspenders against the curiously pale skin. Saturday nights. The long palpitating wait between the revolving non-praying hands of the clock, Mother by the fire or by the lightsome window sewing ageless socks over a bottle in a spotless blouse and sugar-smelling skirt, crooning softly to them endless sad verses of long-ago songs and tales of past tyranny and past romance; when the sewing was through, teaching the girls the steps of the reel and the jig and the hornpipe to no other music but her own light voice. Growing tense and subdued as the hands of the clock implacably crept around to the unheard bellow that was then echoing all over the rowdy rumbustious rollicking Saturday-night city: 'Time, gentlemen, please!' Listening past the furious thumping and pumping of her breast for the uneven unsteady footsteps on the path outside, the sudden lurching up against the bushes, the unsure unquiet fumbling of the key in the front-door lock amid the already free flow of querulous curses and spittle-thick maledictions. The brown trilby hat cocked at a rakish cocksure angle on the greying head, the bright brittle bemused belligerent blue eyes riveting each of them in turn, the polished shoes twirling puckishly into a feet-tangling music-hall dance routine. 'I wanna go to dear old Idaho to make that brown girl mine . . .'

The brief bewildering half-snarling play-acting, roughly pulling reluctant young feet and faces forward, pinching ears and cheeks, cuffing necks, bawling unanswerable questions; the leather belt swinging and swishing in the air and the tongue-thick maddened tones lifted suddenly in apocryphal wrath: 'Honour thy father and thy mother!' That terrifying day when, goaded into brief reckless rebellion by the insensate badgering of the household, he had faced with echoing venom that strident wild-eyed figure and had shouted back his own helpless bitterness, clutching the table, leaning on shaking legs while the stark blue eyes stared back into his own in vast comical surprise. Like a weak angry breeze rushing into the livid jaws of a hurricane, he had soon fallen back into his chair exhausted, trembling and torn in body and mind, and the figure had stood still for several breathless moments carved in incredulity and shock, then had jerked back and tottered blindly upstairs. And the radio had gone on blaring its inane insane delivered-from-war music, and the dazed faces around him looked at him with buttered mouths agape, and he had lain in his chair spent and

253

cross-footed, hearing the hum of his anger fizzing faintly away inside him, slowly feeling the familiar dull patina of dusty weariness settle once more over his sealed spirit, and once more the heart-wrenching time-barbed landscape of stone and concrete met his defeated eyes as the street lights flickered on and new boys sat in brief camaraderie playing cards under the false glow.

He heard now faltering familiar footsteps sounding down a long chill corridor, saw a fierce eye beckoning and a crooked finger raised in fierce challenge, daring him to rise up and follow, and fiercely he strained in his deep seat by the partly opened cool swaying curtains and strove to rise and follow that defeated ghost in brash intemperance and defiance, but lay back, held down by invisible chains and not even now could he narrow or bridge that implacable distance that hung like the dark sky itself between him and that sparse titanic tyrannic tormented shape throwing its ubiquitous shadow over his life beyond these buff-coloured walls and the creaking stiff-jointed piano, the voices of fumbling nostalgia and those other quieter voices of sad inescapable release, faces flushed, shadowed, driven, drained, looming in yellow light over brimming jugs and mugs and tankards, slack wrists and hands lolling over backs of chairs and table ledges, slack jaws and gauzed eyes fixed impenetrably on nothing. The spire of the brooding night-shrouded cathedral rising into the burning blandished in-turned bowl of the night sky over the fist-flinging lip-snarling boot-thudding tree-sighing heart-loud city.

Through a crack in the curtain and a rent in his mind he saw the broken half of a hopeful misty young moon hang like a suspended sliced sixpence behind the sentinel spire.

He awoke out of nowhere in the sunken chair by the cool window to Eli's lilting voice as if he had never moved out of the room and the day still burned green outside:

> 'And often when the beetles' drone
> hath lulled the eve to sleep
> I steal on down to her sheeling-lorn

and through the half-door creep.
There on the crickets' singing stone
she stirs the bogweed fire
and croons in soft sad undertone
the song of heart's desire.'

Midnight, twilight, dusklight, dawnlight swayed and stirred
and sensuously sauntered through his awakening mind. He
raised himself and bent over a tankard by his side and looked
down into the flickering amber depths at his own face, thin
as a hawk's and the eyes already voyaging, rising to meet
the world.

Sean O'Casey
Frank O'Connor

SEAN O'CASEY wrote his first evocative and richly entertaining autobiography in six volumes over more than two decades, re-creating in Vol I the days of his Dublin childhood. The second volume tells of his coming to manhood and includes episodes later used in his play RED ROSES FOR ME. Each volume is essential reading for a proper appreciation of this major Irish dramatist.

FRANK O'CONNOR 'A Master' – *The Listener* 'Perfect' – *The Spectator*

Also in PAN is the enthralling and entrancing story of O'Connor's life from schoolboy to revolutionary to librarian and his association with the Abbey Theatre.